I0637640

Kitty and Cadaver

CLAN
DESTINE
PRESS

First published by Clan Destine Press in 2019

PO Box 121, Bittern
Victoria 3918 Australia

Copyright © Narrelle M Harris 2019

All rights reserved. No part of this book may be reproduced or transmitted in any form or by any means, including internet search engines and retailers, electronic or mechanical, photocopying (except under the provisions of the Australian Copyright Act 1968), recording or by any information storage and retrieval system, without prior permission in writing from the publisher.

National Library of Australia Cataloguing-In-Publication data:

Harris, Narrelle M.

KITTY AND CADAVER

ISBN: 978-0-6485567-1-8

Cover Design © Willsin Rowe
Design & Typesetting: Clan Destine Press

Clan Destine Press

www.clandestinepress.com.au

KITTY AND CADAVER

BY

NARRELLE M. HARRIS

CLAN
DESTINE
PRESS

Lyrics of *Banishing the Bones*
by Narrelle M. Harris and Jess Harris
All other song lyrics by Narrelle M. Harris
Extracts of poems The Munias' Nest and Brahmin Girls
by Joseph Furtado (1872-1947)

CHAPTER ONE

MELBOURNE, AUSTRALIA, 2014

'This is it?' Mr Malone's gaze took in the four people in front of him. 'This is the band? I thought you were a six piece?' The band room manager's Australian drawl was just this side of rude.

'A five piece, normally,' said Laszlo Kantor. 'I don't play.'

'So you are in fact a three piece?'

'Yes.'

'Where are the other two?'

'Dead,' said Yuka, the drummer, prosaic and defiant.

'Don't worry about it. It's all under control.'

It was totally not under control.

BUDAPEST, HUNGARY: ONE WEEK AGO

If anything was more ludicrous than five people walking through a city crossroads at 2am, singing and playing instruments, it was their pretension that the bizarre activity was an excuse for vampire hunting.

Laszlo Kantor didn't tell the patrolling musicians they were preposterous. He'd learned long ago to keep these opinions to himself, especially from preposterous people.

The oddest at the moment was the Swede, Kurt, who had a tablet computer in one hand, open on an app that displayed a keyboard. He played it as he sang into the quiet buildings of this area of light industry.

Water, fire, air and earth
Let no evil cross this line
Weave a web, protect this path
And to their den, evil confine

Six times already they'd sung this song at crossroads all around Budapest's District 22, including the memorial park of old communist statues where the gigantic, over-earnest figures were ripe for ridicule. Alex had laughed at the derisive nicknames, but they inspired only contempt in Laszlo. He'd known the regime too well to find humour in its graveyard.

'What are you doing?' he'd asked Alex at the fourth rendition of the strange song.

'Hunting,' laughed Alex, who laughed a lot. 'Isn't that right, *cicci*?'

'Well, *sötnos*,' Kurt replied – full of little endearments, those two, even in the midst of this absurdity – 'It's more like herding.'

'Herding cats.' said Steve the Texan, the oldest of them.

'Herding vampires,' Sal countered.

Kurt sang as he walked the western arm of the crossroad, his voice and the tablet keyboard weaving into the harmonies made by other voices and instruments at the points of the compass. Those at east, north and south sang with their guitars. At the centre of the crossroads, Yuka knelt and beat a tattoo on the street. Laszlo liked the way she played – economical in her movements, beating her sticks like the whole world was her drum.

Kurt and his bandmates converged on Yuka's spot and the song came to an end.

'Clear in the west.' Kurt smiled at Alex, the leader of these talented fools.

'Clear in the east, *cicci*,' Alex said. 'Sal?'

'Clear in the north.'

'Ain't a whisper in the south, either,' Steve finished.

Yuka rose to her feet, twirling the sticks in her hands. 'Clear for blocks around. The earth says they're hemmed in.' A twirling stick froze and pointed like a compass in the direction of a derelict factory in Erdődülő, by the statue park.

'Let's see to this vampire nest,' Alex said. He shifted his guitar and took Kurt's hand. 'You all right with the app or do you want the keytar?'

'I hate the keytar.'

'You're not fond of the app.'

'I should learn the flute,' Kurt said. 'Much more portable.'

'So you don't like my idea of putting rollers on a baby grand?' Steve teased.

'You people,' Laszlo said in disgust, forgetting his rule about not expressing his opinions. This cavalier stupidity was, Alex claimed, an investigation into the unsolved murders and disappearances of a dozen people in the last month.

'What's your beef?'

'People have vanished, Steve, and all you do is talk nonsense. Vampires and wheels on pianos.'

'Only one of those things is nonsense,' Alex said.

'Wheels on a piano,' Kurt scoffed. 'It would roll away every time I played *prestissimo*.'

'You are not funny.' The disappearances reminded Laszlo too much of the humourless secret police in the Bad Old Days for him to find even black humour in the situation.

Yuka laid a hand on his arm. 'It isn't funny. What we do is not funny. We only pretend it's a game. Do you understand?'

He understood very well. At the blackest times, ridiculousness was a lifeline, but twenty years later, he was still too heartsore to find relief in banter. 'People who disappear in Hungary don't think it's a game. Does this talk of vampires keep your heart light?'

'No,' she said with grim sincerity. 'Vampires are only darkness.'

'You don't need to come with us for the next bit,' Alex said. 'We'll get what we need from the van and meet you later.'

Kurt took out his phone and made a call as they walked to the parked van. 'Harper? How is she? What? But why? All right, all right.' A moment later Kurt spoke in a tiny sing-song voice. 'Gretel! Little Gretchen! Why do you cry for Harper? Can't you sleep, bubba?'

'What's she doing awake?' Alex demanded, nipping across to walk with Kurt.

'Pappa and Dadda are coming home soon!' Kurt held the phone out to Alex, who made kissy noises through the speaker. 'Pappa loves you! And Dadda loves you! Oh, Harper, hello again. We have one more song tonight and we're done. Sing Gretchen her lullaby; that always works.'

Laszlo ambled along behind the group, alert to the chill of the night, the scent of loam from the nearby garden centre and the faint odour of ammonia given off by the water treatment plant on the edge of the Chamber Forest. A flurry of alarmed squawking rose up from the forest to the north and fell suddenly silent.

Even the birds weren't happy with these strange activities.

Sal was reading from the notebook he carried everywhere, its pages well worn and cover marked with water stains and smudges of ink. His lips moved and he muttered to himself a line Laszlo recognised as Marcus Aurelius. *A man when he has done a good act, does not call out for others to come and see, but he goes on to another act, as a vine goes on to produce again the grapes in season.*

'I want my djembe,' Yuka said, ignoring the young fathers chatting with their infant. Laszlo had the impression Yuka was agitated by the call. In fact, everyone seemed uncomfortable while Alex and Kurt talked to their babysitter.

Sal shoved the book back in his pocket. 'Not the den-den? You can use the handle as a stake.'

'Better sound from the djembe,' Yuka said as they closed in on the van. 'Better not to get close enough for staking.'

'Sleepytimes now, *älskling*,' Kurt was cooing into the phone. 'There's our good gi- *aaah*!'

Kurt shrieked and disappeared up, up so fast, up. Alex, almost as fast, leapt to wrap his arms around Kurt's legs.

'No!'

Sal leapt to hang on to Alex's legs and all three were lifted high into the air, while the thing above them made an unholy screech and beat its giant wings, wafting down a musky animal stink.

Steve, instead of joining the kite-tail of people, whipped his guitar into position and began to play. Yuka took a more direct approach: she leapt and clambered up the ladder of bodies to the beast, to stab the stick into one of the great taloned feet that gripped Kurt's shoulders. She drew blood and the flying creature screeched in rage.

Laszlo stared in shock and wonder at the thing he could barely comprehend. A *griffmadár*, its shaggy body and hindquarters that of a lion, the forequarters and head of the royal *turul*, the mythological falcon. Its giant wings beat, its talons dug deeper into Kurt's shoulders. Kurt screamed and twisted, trying to free himself. Blood from the talons in his flesh, and from Yuka's drum stick in the beast's foot, dripped onto Alex's face below.

'*Cicci*!' Alex shouted, desperately hanging on.

Steve was crying out for everyone to let go. The *griffmadár* was rising so high that a fall would be damaging, and soon fatal. Besides, the weight of all of them on Kurt's body was making the claws tear deep furrows into his flesh.

The beast screamed again, rolled in the air and shook Sal off easily. Yuka clung so tight, with her drum stick buried in the thing's leg, that it took longer but she was thrown free soon after. Alex hung on tight for three turns before he was thrown clear.

The monster's triumphant screams mingled with Kurt's yells of pain as the *griffmadár* flew away into the night, in the direction of Erdődülő. Those it had shaken free lunged towards the van.

Alex shoved Laszlo out of his way and opened the back of the van to rummage among the contents.

Laszlo was struck with awe and horror. 'What was that?'

Nobody answered.

'How the hell did that get past the wards?' Sal snarled.

Yuka, muttering curses in her native Japanese, climbed past Alex into the van to find her djembe.

Steve had retrieved Kurt's phone, which had smashed against the road. 'We warded against evil, not griffins,' he said.

'Aren't... aren't *griffmadár* evil?' Laszlo stammered.

'Depends on the griffin. Seems this one's made a deal with Prince Vladimir.' Steve held his own phone to his ear and turned away from Laszlo to speak urgently into it. 'Harper, it's gone to hell. Get Gretel out of there. Not in the morning. *Now*. Go to London, then home if you don't hear from me again.'

Before Laszlo could ask any more questions he didn't really want answered, Alex shoved a violin into his hands.

'Can you play?' Alex's eyes were feverish bright with fury and fear. 'I saw you eyeing this off when we played at Dürer-kert.'

Laszlo twitched. The pub show he'd organised on Tuesday seemed suddenly of an alien world. 'I used to.'

'Good enough.' Alex thrust the venerable instrument into his hands.

'I don't know your songs.'

'The violin does.'

Laszlo's confusion doubled and doubled again. Sal was in the driver's seat; Steve and Yuka were in the rear. Alex impatiently dragged Laszlo by the arm to the front door, and Laszlo resisted. Alex was paying him to organise gigs, be a local guide and interpreter, and tolerate the crazy. He suspected he wasn't being paid enough.

'What are we doing?'

'We're getting my Kurt back and putting down that nest of leeches for good.'

'We are going to fight a griffin?'

'We're fighting vampires,' Alex corrected, his grin savage. 'Are you in or out?'

Laszlo held the violin and his heart pounded harder than ever.

Vampires, in his city. And a violin, a reminder of his sins. Rising out of his panic and terror was, strangely enough, a surge of hope.

'In. What do I have to do?'

'Draw the bow across the strings. The violin will do the rest. Come on.'

'You go right to their front door?' Laszlo was horrified.

'We hemmed them in with the wards,' Alex explained. 'They know they can't escape.'

'It is why they sent the griffin,' Yuka said, as though that were obvious. 'There is no escape. Only revenge.'

'But surely we should... sneak up?' Laszlo said.

'Bit late for stealth anyway. They know we're coming,' Steve said.

'Just because they lure you, you don't have to follow.'

'They've got Kurt,' Alex said. And that was that.

The band known as Rome's Burning piled out of the van in front of the factory where the vampires had been trapped by the series of spells in crossroads all around the district. They took up their instruments. Laszlo tucked the violin under his chin and listened to the music building up around him, wondering when he should play, and what he would play when the time came, and whether he really believed what was happening.

The melody that wove around the five of them as they spread out along the street softened their footfalls and made the trees rustle as they passed.

They were greeted by Vladimir, Prince of Vampires, at the threshold of the abandoned factory he had made into a home. He held Kurt by a fistful of bloodied shirt. The metallic smell of too much blood loss was noticeable.

'You don't give up, do you, Torni?'

'No,' Alex said in almost his old, flippant voice. 'Not when you go around eating people and recruiting the occasional unwilling survivor into your pack.'

'Not a pack. My *House*. And I warned you what would happen if you interfered.'

'Interfering's what we do. Still, let Kurt go and we'll parlay.'

Vladimir's answer was to tear Kurt's shirt to better reveal the ugly bite in Kurt's throat. Human blood mingled with a darker substance oozed from it. Laszlo heard the moment when Alex's breath stopped.

'Your beloved Kurt belongs to my House now.' Vladimir laughed, the blood between his teeth, as Kurt convulsed at his feet. 'Burn my House,' he said, 'and you burn your beloved.'

'Let him go.'

'And we shall parlay?'

'And I won't burn you all to cinders.'

'You will never take us all.'

Kurt shuddered one last time. Then he rose smoothly to his feet and even Laszlo, who hardly knew the man, knew that this was no longer Kurt.

'Alex. *Sötnos*,' said the monster with Kurt's face. 'You look good enough to eat.'

Alex's face drained of colour. His mouth made the shape,

Kurt, but he had no voice. He grit his teeth and raised his arm as a signal.

'No quarter,' he snarled, and plucked the strings of his guitar for the opening notes. The destruction began.

Come to me sun
I beg of thee a whisper of your breath
Come to me sun
I beg of thee a tongue of flame
To ignite the world where I name

Laszlo drew his bow across the strings and played the tune without knowing how he knew it.

Rome's Burning advanced on the factory and lived up to their name. The door frame ignited. Vladimir fled, leaving Kurt to his own devices. Kurt swiftly disappeared inside the building.

The band sang an inferno and the front wall burned so brightly Laszlo thought their instruments would ignite from the heat. Instead, the wall caved in.

Shrieking, the griffin rose from the fire and flew into the night, a great egg in its talons. Later, the survivors would conclude the griffin had abducted Kurt in return for its offspring. At this point, however, the griffin wasn't important.

Wooden features and plaster burst into flames all around them. Even bricks burned.

Vampires began to flee the burning building, like cockroaches when the light flicks on, but they didn't get far. Sal was singing something counter to the main melody (*green and growing things, defend the earth*) and trees responded to his call.

From every thick-trunked tree to every sapling, roots and branches curled and whipped and became spears, staking the mostly newly made vampires who couldn't avoid the writhing mass of weapons. Stabbed with wood through the heart, they dissolved into ash.

Alex stormed through the front of the building and his band followed without hesitation, Laszlo with them.

Within, glass shattered; floorboards cracked. Monsters, trapped between flame and wood, screamed as they died. The air burned with no fuel but the song that made it.

Even water burns
Even the sky
Let the flames scorch the earth and purify
Where I guide.

Alex choked short and Laszlo saw Kurt loom out of the smoke, snatch Alex by the throat and disappear. He cried out a warning and the others drew closer together, still singing. In turns, they took cloves of garlic from pockets and strewed them about the room.

'Don't stop playing!' Steve shouted.

Laszlo didn't; he couldn't. It felt much more like the violin was playing him – drawing on his long-abandoned skills and guiding his fingers through music he'd never known.

In that Erdõdülõ vampire nest, Laszlo's bow slid across the strings, eliciting notes sweet and pure and relentless, which scorched the air. The firestorm never touched him or his fellow musicians. Flames licked the walls, ate the ceiling, melted the glass. Transformed the vampires into pillars of blue fire.

Prince Vladimir was cornered in the factory's former workroom, stripped of its equipment, leaving only the pitted concrete floor and windows that had cracked in the heat. One or two feathers and a gaping hole in the ceiling showed that this was where the griffin's egg had been held and liberated.

Vladimir laughed. 'I took your House from you. Kurt Stefan is mine. Alex Torni is mine. Kill me if you like. I still win.'

Rome's Burning sang. The dozens of branches and roots of a single tree burst through the shattered panes and speared Vladimir's body through. He laughed even as he choked; even as his heart was pierced, even as he burned.

The band turned from the vampire prince as he was reduced to ash, and moved through the factory to finish the job. The stench of old blood, of burned metal and brick, of flesh, was everywhere.

When nothing else moved in the ember-filled darkness, Rome's Burning sang the fire into submission.

Come to me, firestorm
Come to me, burning brook
Come to me, stones on fire
Come to me, burning air
Come to me, flames
Come to me, molten earth
I beg thee return to heart and sun
I beg thee be quenched, now my work is done.

Naturally, they searched for Alex. They found him huddled and bleeding under tin from the fallen roof, his throat torn. Sal cradled the dying man in his arms.

'Kurt.' Alex was sobbing. 'They killed my Kurt.' He turned blazing eyes on them. 'You killed my darling. He's dead. You burned him.'

'He wasn't Kurt any more,' Steve said, as gently as he could.

Alex, on the cusp of human and monster, sobbed again. 'I'm not Alex any more. Soon. Oh my god, oh my god. Steve. Steve?'

Steve's hands trembled. 'Okay. Shh, Alex. I'll do it.'

Not-Alex glared at him again. 'Yes. You're good at it. Watching the people you love die.'

'Don't,' Steve begged.

'Sorry, sorry, sorry,' muttered the human part of their friend.

Sal stroked Alex's hair. 'It's all right, Steve. I'll do it.'

Steve tried to protest, but he gave in when Sal insisted. Anyone could see that Steve didn't have the heart to insist.

'You don't have to stay,' Sal said.

'Oh go on,' Not-Alex jeered. 'Watch. It'll be educational.' Then he looked horrified and cried tears of blood.

Steve gave Sal all the garlic remaining in his pockets. Yuka, too. Laszlo didn't have any garlic – he'd thought the whole thing nonsense.

'Laszlo,' Alex rasped.

'I'll take care of them,' Lazlo found himself promising.

Alex laughed. 'Good. They need a roadie.'

Sal took out a bowie knife and held it to Alex's throat. 'Wait outside.'

'Save me,' Alex whispered to Sal as the others left them among the ashes.

'Of course. You saved me, didn't you?'

When Sal joined the others outside, he looked like his soul had gone with Alex's into the beyond.

CHAPTER TWO

The smell of funeral flowers was cloying. Two weeks ago, Kitty Carrasco had finally convinced Grandpa to let her hang all the arrangements from Grandma's funeral in the laundry to dry, but now the living room was full of lilies, carnations and roses again.

Orphaned twice in her 21 years, it felt like the grieving would never be over. She didn't recall her parents at all, and her grandparents had raised her with a stern, puritanical kind of love. The silence of their house had been a lifelong, songless lamentation.

Kitty breathed through her open mouth to avoid being overwhelmed by the scent of mourning. Far from making her want to cry, the smell made her want to scream. She wanted nothing more than to build a bonfire and to replace the stench of sweet, decaying things in this musty old house with clean air.

The pressure of the silence on her ears was painful, but lacking a record player or even a radio, her options were limited. She couldn't bear the thought of the television and all those yakkety voices.

In her restlessness, Kitty threw open the kitchen window to listen for traffic on Lygon Street. A few crows in the cemetery over the road cawed melancholy notes over the bass hum of the cars.

Music had been forbidden all her life, but she heard it everywhere.

Grandma and Grandpa had forbidden outings where she might even hear music; they'd discouraged friendships that might take her from their orbit, so her unintentional school status as a lonely weirdo had been guaranteed. They'd found her work experience and later a job at the business where Grandpa was an accountant and Grandma arranged garlands and wreaths, the best in the business. The ones for her funeral, and for Grandpa's, had been done by someone else and were disappointing by being perfectly adequate.

In a sudden fit, Kitty gathered all the flowers in her arms and dumped them in the bathtub. She stormed to her room next and threw the cloth cover off her little work table, revealing crudely painted white and black keys. This she dragged to the centre of the living room, placed her fingers on the painted keys and banged away at it.

She heard the notes in her head, memorised from the times she'd snuck into the music room at school. The living room heard only a dull thud. She stopped abruptly.

Kitty glowered at a photograph: her smiling grandparents, and her squashed between them, smiling too. Her skin was paler than their olive tones, thanks to her Scottish mother's heritage, but her hazel eyes were the same as Grandma's, the same as her father's eyes, Grandpa always said, when he spoke of her father at all.

'I know you loved me, but I'm tired of living in a cage,' she told that photograph. 'This week I'm buying a radio; and that proper keyboard I want that I knew you'd never let me have.'

Agitated and filled with the need to move, Kitty swooped to the telephone and called her boss.

'Schumacher Funerals. How may I help?'

'Marcus. Hi, it's Kitty.'

'Oh, Kitty. How are you doing? Do you need anything, dear?'

'No. I just. It's too quiet at home.'

'It must seem very strange.'

Not as strange as it should be, Kitty Carrasco wanted to tell him. This house is always oppressively quiet. Losing Grandma and Grandpa a month apart had only emphasised the solitude of it.

'It is odd,' she said.

'Let me just say again how very sorry Trudy and I am,' Marcus said with his usual compassionate warmth. 'We valued your grandparents' contributions here enormously, and of course they introduced you to us.'

'Thanks Marcus. Speaking of that. I was wondering if I could come back to work today after all.'

She counted the beats before Marcus replied. He never replied to anything in a hurry.

'I'm concerned that you need more time, Kitty.'

'I don't.'

Another few beats and then, 'Why don't you pop in for the afternoon, if you like. You don't need to stay if it's too much.'

'The Driscolls are coming today, aren't they?'

'Yes.'

'I know you're really busy. You have two funerals this afternoon. I can help.'

'This is not the time for you to worry about us.'

'I know. But honestly. I'd rather be working and doing some good, Marcus.'

'Your presence would be very welcome, Kitty, but truly, if you find it too much, please don't feel you need to stay.'

'I'll get changed and be right there.'

Two trams later, Kitty was in Richmond and breathing much more easily.

'Good morning, Kitty,' Marcus Schumacher said as Kitty arrived. Marcus, in his fifties, had a kind face. He was buttoned-down, respectable, and exuded an air of peace and respectful acceptance. Clients liked him because he made them feel safe. Kitty liked him because he was never condescending.

'Good morning, Marcus. Thanks for letting me come in.'

'You're welcome, but I mean it. Leave again if you need to.'

'Thanks. Do you want me to sit with you when the Driscolls come in?'

'I've just left Maddie's parents and her brother to gather themselves in the sitting room. Bring in some tea and I'll introduce you.'

In the kitchenette, Kitty brewed a pot of fresh tea. Along with the fine tea set, she prepared a dish of lemon slices along with the honey and sugar. She added an array of thin, light biscuits. People's grief settled in their stomachs sometimes and they couldn't eat, and others ate blindly through the process. Some were like her, ambivalent in their mourning. Plenty of others didn't mourn at all, and didn't even bother to pretend.

Kitty carried the tray into the faintly formal yet cosy sitting room. The couch in it was comfortable but not squishy. It held people up when sometimes people couldn't hold themselves up.

Marcus introduced her to the Driscolls in his wonderfully comforting baritone. 'This is Catalina Carrasco. She'll be looking after Maddie's make-up and clothing for you.'

Maddie's family, like most clients, were surprised at her youth. Kitty didn't let it bother her. She simply went about, calmly and kindly, greeting them by name, pouring tea, sitting in the slightly less comfortable seat opposite them.

'I'm so sorry for your loss,' she said, genuinely sympathetic. 'Maddie seems to have been a lovely young woman.'

Mrs Driscoll nodded, tears welling up already. 'Yes, she was. My Maddie, she was…' And she couldn't go on. Mr Driscoll patted his wife's hand, and it was left to Jayden Driscoll, Maddie's older brother, to speak for the family.

'We've brought some of her clothes. And I made up a disk of her favourite music. Like Mr Schumacher asked.' Jayden clumsily shoved an overnight bag towards her. 'Oh. And. These.' A folder full of photos, mostly printed out from the internet. They showed a bright teenager with a mischievous smile, as though she was planning a prank to pull on the photographer.

'Thank you,' Kitty said. 'Anything I don't use, I can give back to you, if you like, or we can manage it here. There's no need to decide right away.'

Jayden nodded miserably.

Kitty placed her fingers gently over one particularly lovely photograph of Maddie in a vibrant summer dress, vivid blue flowers splashed over a pale yellow background. Mrs Driscoll caught the movement.

'We've put. That one. In the bag. She loved that. That dress. She was. She.'

'It suited her. Would you like me to make her up like she is in this one?'

Mrs Driscoll nodded mutely.

'She looks very happy here,' Kitty said, not expecting anything but leaving space for whatever might happen.

'She was,' Mr Driscoll replied. 'That was her eighteenth birthday. She'd just been accepted to Monash. That's her best friend, Nicole, there.' He gestured. 'And that's her boyfriend, Mathias. He's a good boy.' He blinked rapidly. 'He made her laugh. So much. With those. What do they call them? The game with the birds and the pigs.'

Jayden's laugh was sudden and brittle, but genuine. 'He got her those silly slippers, remember, the big red birds with those eyebrows.'

'And Jasper attacked them,' Mrs Driscoll said with a similar bad-but-good laugh. She gave Kitty a watery smile. 'Maddie's cat. Had him since he was a kitten. He's so lost without her. Breaks my heart.'

'Would you like to put something of Jasper's with her? We can include something from Mathias, if you and he would like that.'

In the end, the family decided to bring Jasper's collar for Maddie's wrist and tokens from Matthias – a necklace and a mobile phone charm of a cross red bird. The bird had made her giggle, especially when Mathias impersonated its enraged little cartoon face. Beloved things and memories to keep her body company, although her spirit was gone.

Marcus saw the grieving family out, soothing them with his air of gentle authority. After they'd gone, Kitty cleared away the undrunk tea and untouched biscuits, and took the bag downstairs.

Maddie Driscoll was on the metal table. Trudy Schumacher, Marcus's sister, hadn't needed to do much reconstructive work. The blow from the fall off the brick wall had crushed the back of Maddie's head, but left the nineteen year old's face unmarred.

Calmness settled over Kitty as she put the bag of clothes aside. She'd first come to the Schumachers for work experience in high school, doing office work and helping Grandma with the flowers. By the time she graduated, she'd already started helping Trudy with make-up. It hadn't helped her reputation for lonely weirdo-ness but she was used to that. She'd given up trying to make people understand that what she did had a sacredness to it, and that it was a service for those left behind. For people like her and her grandparents, who didn't even have a grave to visit.

'Hello Maddie,' Kitty said as softly and as kindly as she had spoken to Maddie's family. 'I met your parents and your brother today. They're lovely people. Jayden is watching out for your parents, and for Mathias too. I'll look after you, now. I'll help them say goodbye to you.'

Kitty knew that Maddie didn't live in that house of bone and skin any more, but that was hardly important. The dead didn't scare her, and she liked talking to them. The dead didn't judge, and they were good listeners.

CHAPTER THREE

'Six days.' Sal's accent – English undercut faintly with an older accent from Goa – thickened with anger. The fact that he couldn't seem to get his teeth unclenched wasn't helping. '*Six days* to be ready to perform, without a lead singer, a lead guitarist or a keyboard player. Without half our *band*.' The way he said it, it sounded like he was being asked to play without half his heart, which was much closer to the truth.

'We'll work it out,' Laszlo assured him. 'I've seen you do much more with much less.'

Sal's brown eyes blazed. 'Not with much less of the fucking *band*, you haven't. Alex and Kurt are *dead*. How much *less* do you think we can be and still function?' He loomed over the older man, his dark skin flushing with emotion. 'We can only perform so many miracles. Raising the dead isn't one of them. That is the actual opposite of our job.'

'What do you want me to do?' Laszlo demanded. 'You said we needed to be very far away. This is very far away. I'm sorry Alex and Kurt are dead, but I'm not the one who killed them.'

'*You sure as hell didn't save them,*' Sal snarled.

Yuka pushed her slender body between the two men. Neither of them made the mistake of thinking that because she was small she wasn't strong. She could probably have broken at least one of them in thirteen places with only her left hand and a well-aimed drum stick.

Laszlo, in fact, had seen her perform a similar feat against the undead in that factory in Budapest, so when she glared at the two much taller men, Laszlo did the sensible thing. He took a step away, dropping his gaze to his feet. 'Sorry, Yuka.'

Sal had backed off fractionally, his expression mutinous, his eyes glittering bright. He transferred his glare to Yuka.

She glared right back, her accent clipped and firm. 'Laszlo is not the enemy.'

A shudder ran through him. Sal closed his eyes and the glittering brightness in his eyes escaped in wet tracks.

'I know. Sorry, Laszlo.'

'And I, Sal.' Laszlo managed to tilt an awkward smile at Sal. He felt bad that it had spiralled out of hand so quickly. They were new to each other, Laszlo and the others. One week acquainted, when Alex, Kurt, Sal, Yuka and Steve had been a team for years. When three of them were still mourning their murdered friends.

Laszlo is not the enemy, Yuka had said. It made him… he didn't know. Sad. Determined. Afraid.

I am not the enemy, he told himself firmly, *I never was.*

That felt like a lie.

I never will be again.

There. That felt more like a true thing.

The sound of Steve clearing his throat garnered everyone's instant attention. If their bass guitarist – the eldest of their group at nearly sixty and the most experienced in both battle and loss – had something to say, everyone was going to listen.

'You know,' Steve said in his slow drawl. 'We can do it as a three piece if we have to. You can sing lead and play lead guitar, Sal, you've done it before.'

'I…'

'Ain't no disrespect to them that's gone. It's wrong Alex and Kurt ain't here, but that ain't no-one's fault but the fang-faced bastards what killed 'em. We got guitars and drums. We got singers. We can do this.'

'It's not enough.'

'It'll have to be. Hey, Laszlo,' Steve nodded at the Hungarian. 'You played a mean fiddle when we needed you. You told Alex you used to play.'

Laszlo's left hand twitched involuntarily. 'A long time ago.'

'Reckon you can learn some songs in a week?'

Laszlo shrugged, the gesture disguising the thrum of excitement that travelled from his heart to his fingertips. 'Yes. If you need.'

'We need, and it'll be a lot easier to pick up the melodies when you're not trying to slay vampires at the same time, I promise you.'

Laszlo snorted a wry laugh. 'Oh, but it's so motivational.'

'I can give you motivation,' Yuka said. Laszlo couldn't tell if she was joking. She grinned, somewhat savagely, which was not enlightening.

Steve's mouth twitched smile-ward and he settled back into his previous taciturn calm, hip hitched on the corner of the small table in their dorm room. They were short on funds – nothing new there – so the four of them were sharing a room at a backpackers' joint at the north end of Melbourne. Beds were covered in duffel bags and instruments. A small, battered metal chest was shoved between two of the bunks.

'You teach Laszlo the songs,' Yuka told the band. 'I will get food.'

With that, Yuka patted her belt, checking that her drum sticks were held in place, and left them to it.

She checked her reflection in the hostel's foyer window, satisfying herself that she was neat enough to venture into public. 'Foyer' was putting it grandly. The shabby sofas, chairs and tables were filled with a scattering of equally shabby travellers, and the battered reception desk, jammed to overflowing with brochures and notices, boasted a perky and chaotic receptionist festooned with piercings and bold tattoos.

Yuka wasn't tattooed – she'd left the inking to Kurt all these years. Only her earlobes were pierced, and they remained unadorned at present. She had the slightly misshapen once-torn ear to prove that wearing too much embedded jewellery while battling an armed and armoured mermaid, for example, could be a very bad idea.

What Yuka did have were her wrist cuffs and the necklace; her mementos of the dead. Her leather wrist cuffs were decorated with the parts of smashed drums, keyboards and guitars she had retrieved over a decade ago – all that was left of her first band.

She fingered the chunky necklace, made of the strings of Alex's guitar and keys from Kurt's keyboard. The weight of it around her neck was like the weight of them in her heart. Yuka's grief was heavy but her anger held her up. Her rage had been helping her to carry grief for 15 long years.

Enough. Food now. Rehearsal later. They would take their respite while they could by simply playing music that was music and not a weapon, and decide how next to move. They were no longer Rome's Burning. Alex had forged that band when he'd become its leader a decade ago. Alex was gone and they needed a new leader, and with that leader would come a new name. That had been the system for hundreds of years.

The drummer's short, fast stride took her away from the hostel and to the dying activity of the Queen Victoria Markets, in the final phases of closing up for the day. Her plan had never been to do any actual shopping. For that sort of thing, she needed actual money. They had some, of course, but everyone became adept over the years at not spending it unless absolutely necessary.

Yuka walked through the undercover section of the markets that traditionally housed the fruit and vegetable stalls, redolent with the scent of overripe bananas, citrus and cabbage. Abandoned boxes not yet collected for disposal held discarded produce, more or less edible but not strictly saleable. Yuka found some plastic bags and, keeping her movements swift but unobtrusive, filled them with salvageable refuse. The overripe, split tomatoes would make a good base. A couple of broken carrots; a chunk of cauliflower; a bruised eggplant: a beggar's feast right there. A half-smashed watermelon would pass for dessert.

Down the road apace was a supermarket. She'd be able to find rice there, oil, spices. There'd be enough for dinner, at least. Yuka was just wondering if she might splurge on a few fillets of chicken when she felt it. The movement, under her feet.

Like pins and needles, but on a string, wound around her feet and wriggling. The pins and needles were tugging her to the east.

Yuka's toes curled inside her shoes, but the sensation didn't go away. Her toes tingled. Her arches, too. Everything still felt like it was pulling to one side. Even the weight of her necklace seemed to have a magnetic drag to the east.

Not good.

She spotted a grey granite marker on the opposite corner of the street. East. She followed the tug in her aching feet to investigate.

A plaque in the footpath told her that these markets and adjoining car park had been built on top of an old 19th century cemetery, and that only 914 of the interred had been exhumed and reinterred elsewhere by 1922. Many, many more dead must have been buried here in the eighty years of the cemetery's use.

The tingle-pull in her feet was strong here, though not malevolent. Nevertheless, Yuka could tell that the dead underneath the car park were *restless*.

Yuka's sigh was in part long-suffering resignation, in part annoyance, and another part determination. She crossed the mostly empty street to the even emptier car park and began to walk it, the intensifying tingle in her feet like thin ropes moving along and over her arches, heels, the balls of her feet.

These dead are long decayed, Yuka reminded herself. *They are not going to burst out of the earth in a zombie parade. There will not be enough tissue to hold the bones together. There are no minds under the tar, only bones remembering they used to be alive. They have probably been rolling over in their sleep for a hundred years and no-one's ever noticed before.*

Yuka was reluctant to put the scavenged meal on the ground – the restless dead had been known to rot food through proximity before – so she tied the plastic bags together and draped them around her neck. Watermelon to the left; vegetables to the right. *A balanced diet. Ha.* The strong odour of overripe plant life rose around her face.

Hers, Yuka reflected, was not a dignified life.

She crouched and put one hand on the asphalt, letting the ropey tingle move over her fingertips and palm. There was no malice in the sensation. The dead weren't angry, though she sensed a *frisson* of longing. That might be the component parts of the dead remembering what it was to be whole and alive.

Yuka crouched and patted the ground. Patpat. Patpat. Patpat. A little hushing rhythm. The restless tingle hesitated then resumed.

Yuka pulled the drum sticks from her belt. The asphalt was not going to do the sticks one bit of good. Well, that's why she had lots of drum sticks, she reminded herself, and why she went to the effort of singing every new set strong: for emergencies like this. Besides, although she was on her own, Yuka didn't think the whole band was needed. Her drum sticks and her voice should be enough. Bartos, of revered memory, had achieved more in one cruel hour on the River Somme with merely a rusty horseshoe, a tent peg and his own baritone.

Balanced on the balls of her feet, Yuka began to drum a tattoo on the ground. Taptap, taptap. Taptap, taptap. The rhythm of a heartbeat. It wasn't an ancient piece, but it had been over fifty years in the band's repertoire – the song was 20 years older than Yuka – so it had a proven record. And these bones under her feet were old and not really a threat. All she had to do was send them back to sleep.

Asleep
The dust
And all
Your bones
Lay down

She knew the words in Japanese as well, but sometimes the magic was stronger when sung in the composer's original words.

There's no
Place here
For you
To go
Lay down

The heartbeat rhythm had the attention of the dust and bones. The taptap, taptap brought all that restlessness into focus. Yuka could feel it, almost like the dust had eyes, and all of them only for her.

Almost imperceptibly at first, Yuka slowed the heartbeat. Taptap, taptap. Tap-tap. Tap-tap.

You're old
The world
Won't know

You now
Lay down
Lay down
Lay down

The things under her feet grew sluggish. She could feel them remembering not only the heartbeat, but how the heartbeat fades. Yuka could feel the dust and bones calming, settling. Tap-tap. Tap-tap. Tap tap. Tap tap.

Be dust
Be bones

They were going back to sleep, forgetting they had ever once been alive.

Tap. Tap.
Tap.
Tap.

Be gone
Be gone
Lay.
Down.

Yuka held the silence after the last note, breathing as silent as a tree, and listened with her ears and heart and feet and hands.

There. Quiet in the graveyard. Much better.

The spike when it came was so quick that Yuka didn't feel it until it hit – a sharp jab, like an electric shock, jolting out from the earth. This burst of rage wasn't something from the restless dead. It came from something deeper; something she hadn't sensed as she sang. It burned up from the ground, across her feet, into the tips of her drum sticks on the asphalt.

But Yuka was an old hand at this, and though surprised, she was not unprepared. Her sticks had been sung to might and potency. Her voice was in the wood, but so was Steve's, so was Sal's, so were Alex and Kurt's, binding that wood and making it powerful, even if not impervious.

As the burn of that unanticipated wrath arched between the

ground and her skin, Yuka felt it, raised her sticks and punched them down, tips first, not beating but stabbing into the shell of tar and, through it to the soil below. The jolt of power pierced the sticks, but with the magic in her body and in her tools, she met it, blocked it, threw it back.

A force like two concussion waves meeting and rebounding threw Yuka onto her back. She lay there, gasping for air, feeling the ground with her whole body. She pressed her skull, shoulders, spine, thighs, calves, heels, to the asphalt. With her palms flat to the asphalt, the bags of groceries over her chest and sagging against her throat, she listened with every cell. She looked like a bag lady committing some sort of extreme yoga.

The whole, quiet ground. Whatever had attacked her was gone.

Yuka got to her knees, her joints creaking. The bags of dinner-in-waiting draped over her shoulders were slightly less intact than before. She half crawled to where her sticks were buried in the tarmac and, with effort, she pulled them free. The tips and necks were shredded, the shafts split. Damn. She'd lost her strongest set of sticks in Budapest, and now these were ruined. They'd just have to spare the cash for new ones.

Yuka adjusted the bags across her aching neck with her numb fingers and proceeded with the shopping. She decided to buy the chicken anyway. The restless dead happened all the time. Actual meat protein for dinner was much less common.

CHAPTER FOUR

NAGOYA, JAPAN, 1999

Yasuko Hidaka discovered drumming as a child, pounding on the Taiko drums with a grin as wide as the sky. Long before she was Yuka, way back in high school, she discovered the driving howl of heavy metal and gleefully became a trial to her family's neighbours, and her family, as a member of Fierce Stagecoach Bandits with four high school friends.

'You chose that *gaijin* name from that American book,' Yasuko had accused the band's lead singer, Akemi. 'Jesse James and his gang.'

Akemi laughed behind her black bangs and dark eyeliner. 'It's funny, though.'

'Are we funny?'

'Chibi Heavy Metal is,' Akemi insisted.

'Is that even a thing?' asked the band's token white guy, Todd, whose English father worked with a car manufacture in Nagoya.

'It is now.'

Akemi's indulgent and wealthy father was the one who negotiated for his daughter's band of 16-year-olds to use Shibo Joto High School's old sports equipment shed for rehearsals, now that the shiny new one had been built. 'He just doesn't want us to keep practising at home,' Akemi said, wrinkling her nose.

Akemi had brought something special for their first rehearsal in the shed. She refused to tell them what it was until everyone was set up. Yasuko finalised the placement of her drum kit while Naoki checked that his keyboards were properly connected to the amp. Natsuko and Todd played guitar flurries to check their volumes before Akemi strolled up to do the same for her own guitar.

'Hey, Nat! Pass me a pick!' Todd called out, knowing that Natsuko hated the diminutive. He liked to tease her, not having worked out yet how best to say he would like to kiss her, if she was interested. Teasing at least kept her noticing him.

Natsuko was predictably annoyed. 'I've told you, it's Natsuko. Na-Tsu-Ko.'

'Fine. Na, pass me a pick.' The request came with a cheeky grin, to show he was joking.

Natsuko passed him a pick and a scowl, wishing she knew how best to tell Todd that if he wanted to kiss her, he should just say so, because until he did, she wasn't sure if that was the point of all his charming idiocy.

Akemi was planning to tell them both to damn well kiss and get it over with to save them all the awkward, oblivious flirting. Tomorrow, maybe. Today she was excited about their new song. Super metal. The best. Yesterday's lyrics had been awful, but she'd found the answer.

Todd strummed the melody of the song they'd been working on all week and regarded Akemi with a quizzical frown. 'You said you were going to rewrite this one.'

'I've written new lyrics!' Akemi announced, brandishing a sheet of paper. Naoki, Natsuko and Todd peered over her shoulders to see.

'These lyrics are weird,' Natsuko said.

Naoki was impressed. 'They're awesome!'

'You think everything's awesome,' Todd said absently while peering at the Japanese characters on the page. 'What does it even mean?'

'Ha, Britboy, are these words too hard for you to understand?' Akemi teased. Todd's Japanese was good for everyday, but he stumbled through a lot of the nuances.

"I get the gist of it fine,' Todd protested. 'It says "Hey, Demon of the Earth, we call you. Take this... ah... gift"...'

Yasuko joined them in studying the new lyric. 'Sacrifice.'

'What?'

Natsuko and Naoki were both troubled, but Akemi was amused.

'The lyric means "take your sacrifice",' Yasuko explained. 'Akemi, where did you find this?'

'You know my dad, always buying old books at auction. The older and rarer, the better, and this book was very old, with all these notes written by hand in the margins. It must be three hundred years old at least.'

'Very old and very weird,' Naoki said. 'This is freaky.'

'Freaky and very metal, that stuff about sacrifice,' Todd said.

'And there are those lines about blood,' Natsuko added.

'I know!' Akemi said excitedly. 'So I worked it up to scan with the new song. Want to give it a run?'

Keen and intrigued, they took their positions. Yasuko counted them in on the snare and Natsuko's bass built on the beat. Naoki brought his keyboard in as Todd's rhythm guitar threaded through, and Akemi's lead guitar whined over the top of it before she began to sing her new lyric.

Aiooo, Demon of the Earth,
We summon you, we give you birth.

There is a Japanese proverb – *asa no kougan, yuube no hakkou* – which means "a rosy face in the morning, white bones in the evening". It means that life is fragile and death comes for us all, young or old. Especially if we call it to us.

Let our instruments and voice bring you life
So you may bring this world blood and strife

None of the Fierce Stagecoach Bandits noticed how Akemi's guitar or the tips of Yasuko's sticks began to glow.

But to bind you to our will, we pay the price
Demon of the Earth – choose your sacrifice

Nobody noticed how the floor began to crack like crazed glass, it was so fast then, just as Naoki heard the concrete split, the floor erupted with rocks, dirt and sulphurous steam. The five of them were tossed up with the eruption, then to the smashed floor, where they gaped at the thing that stood in the epicentre of destruction.

A red-skinned monster loomed there, with black horns and yellow teeth and a laugh like mountains falling.

'Thank you, little humans, for the summoning,' the oni rumbled, turning each belly to water, each heart to terror. A leathery red tentacle unfurled from its body, wrapped itself around Todd's throat and squeezed. 'I have chosen my sacrifice.'

The brimstone-stinking claws of its left hand struck Naoki, sank into his body. The claws of its right slashed at Natsuko, and blood arced behind her as she fell.

Akemi, speechless with terror, tried to run. The monster sprang at her and another tentacle unfurled around her ankles and lifted till she dangled, inverted and screaming, above the rubble that had been the floor.

'Stop it! Stop hurting them!' Yasuko screamed, the only one the oni had not yet attacked.

'Gladly,' it said with a horrible courtesy, and dashed Akemi head first into the floor.

Yasuko heard the snap of Todd's neck, the shrieks as it disembowelled Naoki and Natsuko.

Yasuko should be been screaming too, but the speed with which the oni had arrived and destroyed everything, everyone, hadn't caught up with her yet. Spotted with her friends' blood, her fury smothered the blank terror of it all. 'How will you kill me, then, you bastard?'

'Oh, little one, you do not die today. That is how I thank you.'

Her fury tripped on those words. 'Thank... me?'

'The words this little morsel found were powerful, but her song magic was weak. Without your magic to give strength to hers, I would not be free.'

'M-my magic?'

'Funny little one. The music magic was in you both, but yours is stronger. You have powerful earth magic in your voice and your hands.'

The demon laughed, rocks tumbling down a ravine, at Yasuko's horror and dismay. It leaned close to her. 'You are responsible for the success of my summoning.'

The oni laughed and laughed and laughed at Yasuko, standing blood specked and numb amongst the wreckage of erupted floor, shattered instruments, her fragile, dead friends.

She tried to speak and only sobbed. Her harrowed eyes asked the question: *What next?*

'You cannot stop me, little minstrel.' And wasn't it pleased with itself. Didn't it find this all deliciously, cruelly funny. 'You are not strong enough.'

It taunted, but Yasuko wasn't listening. Her heart pounded, guilt burned, but rage surged and she tried to think. *The stories say that demons lie with the truth.*

And she thought: *We were strong enough to raise it. And this bastard says I have strong earth magic, whatever that means.*

The demon wasn't likely to explain, but Yasuko could feel the power underneath her skin. She reached for it, just as she had always reached inside for the rhythm of her music. Her heart thudded with this awakened power. Her fingers itched with the pulse of it.

She reached for the spare drum sticks she always kept in her belt when playing.

I have power. I can feel it.

Her fists closed around the drum sticks, gripping so hard her knuckles stood out pale against her skin.

I can use it to stop this demon. Even if I die trying.

The bastard demon was still laughing at her and its arrogance fuelled her fury as well as her courage.

'What will it take to send you back to hell?' she demanded, but she already knew the answer.

'More than you have,' the demon replied, in a voice to curdle blood.

'I don't believe you.' Because the demon had told her she had magic in her voice and hands. She hadn't been singing when it was summoned, only drumming. If she combined the two, perhaps she stood a chance.

'Believe what you like,' the demon said. 'I will devour your world all the same.'

Yasuko raised her drum sticks like weapons, then crouched as though ready to pounce.

The demon regarded her, amused, as she opened her mouth to let free a pure vengeful note.

And Yasuko Hidaka beat her drumsticks on the floor while she sang instinctively.

Aiooooooooooooooooo, Demon of the Earth
I curse you, I abort your birth!

She launched herself at the oni and the demon, shocked by her audacity, did not defend itself as she crashed into it and began to beat its head and body with her glowing drum sticks.

The demon recoiled, wincing at the pain of the blows and her song.

With my drumming and my voice, you I banish
And you will go now from this world, you I punish.
We paid your price and bound you to my will

The demon collapsed to its knees as Yasuko beat it down. She stood atop its bent back and shaking shoulders, singing and drumming with savage intent.

Demon of the Earth, **become forever still!**

The notes rang out, the rhythm of her sticks upon its skin filled the air. Beat upon beat, the demon changed. Froze and transformed into grey, grey stone.

And then, with a final blow, the stone broke into a million pieces, into dirt and dust and gravel beneath the feet of the girl who had defeated it.

Yasuko, covered in blood and grime, bruised and bleak, stood as the floor began to shake. The rubble of the demon vibrated all around her. The ground opened like an earthquake and swallowed down its remains.

Only when the shaking stopped did Yasuko move.

She fell to her knees, her fists gripping the drum sticks. Her knuckles and fingers were raw, bleeding, from where she had scraped them against the demon without knowing.

She was kneeling, numb, in the rubble when the firemen arrived, when the police and the paramedics came.

Behind her, someone said: 'It was a…a gas explosion? Yeah. That must be what it was.'

'She's lucky to be alive,' an unknown person said.

'Being behind her drum kit must have saved her.'

'What happened? An earthquake?'

'Hardly. A gas explosion we think.'

Yasuko had never felt so alone, hearing and understanding that these people would never understand what had happened. Even if they believed her, what would they do? What could she do? It was partly her fault, even if she hadn't known what her voice and hands could do. Akemi's fault too, but Yasuko could hardly tell Akemi's father that his ancient book had summoned a demon to slaughter his child.

Everyone thought Yasuko's mind had been damaged by the tragedy. She hardly spoke, except to beg for pieces of the instruments that had been smashed in the disaster.

Silently, she sewed the fragments of drum and guitars and keyboard onto leather braces for her wrists. Nobody asked her to explain why, which was a relief. She wouldn't have known what to tell them.

Her soul had become heavy with an ancient secret that nobody wanted her to share. The only thing she knew was that she had to leave.

The oni had said both she and Akemi had music magic. Where two had it, surely more carried it too. They must, or her life would be too lonely and dangerous to bear.

More than that, she knew she had to learn how to stop anything else like the oni from ever threatening the world again. She would avenge her friends and redeem herself. She swore it on the blood of her friends, on the memory of them she carried in her wristbands.

A month after, Yasuko packed her bags and slipped away in the dark of a winter night.

An elderly woman named Shiniqua was the first teacher Yasuko found. Shiniqua had lost her legs to the blades of the *kama itachi.*

'The sickle weasels didn't beat me, though,' Shiniqua insisted. 'I'll teach you the song I beat them with if you like, girl.'

Yasuko bowed and thanked her, but didn't otherwise speak.

'You have a name, girl?'

'No, Shiniqua-san.' Yasuko Hidaka had been left behind in a smashed shed. She didn't know what to call herself any more.

'Before I teach you, Yuka, fetch water for me.'

The girl raised her eyebrows.

'I have to call you something,' the old woman said.

Yuka obeyed her music-magic sensei in every way, and learned everything she could. When Shiniqua said she had nothing more to teach, she gave Yuka the name of a *hichiriki* player in Fukuoka who shared their gifts.

From Fukuoka, Yuka sought a teacher in Sri Lanka, then in Somalia, then Croatia.

By the time Yuka met Steve Borman, nobody knew Yuka had ever had another name. Then Alex Torni invited her to become part of Rome's Burning, and it was like she had never had another home.

CHAPTER FIVE

Despite its desperately humble origins, the evening meal Yuka assembled was well received. With Yuka's history of sourcing meals in the cheapest way possible, this was considered a terrific success. Laszlo even went so far as to compliment her sincerely, an event which left Yuka speechless with embarrassed pleasure and Laszlo gruffly carrying dishes to the sink to hide his face.

As further distraction from the awkwardness of the exchange, Yuka laid her damaged sticks on the table. 'I need new ones.'

Sal brushed a curious finger over the pulverised tips.

Yuka shrugged. 'The dead under the market woke. I put them back to sleep.'

'And you're only telling us now?' Sal wasn't amused.

'If it was serious, I would have fetched you. They and the energy that woke them sleep again. Now I need more sticks.'

Before Sal could argue the point, Steve, leaning back in a chair with his hands behind his head, drawled, 'You know what those old burial places are like, Sal. Folks shift a few bones, build a car park or a shopping centre right over the rest and think that's it. They don't hear the dead spinning in their graves.'

'It's not funny,' Sal said.

'Naw, ain't funny,' Steve agreed. 'Ain't nothing too serious either. Some bones are just bones remembering flesh for a space. No evil in it. Hush 'em down, like Yuka said, and it's fine. You know it, Sal. You're just on edge. Let it be.'

'I can't be the only one on edge, Steve. How can you-?' His throat closed up before he could finish the accusation.

Steve leaned forward, dropping his hand over Sal's fingers splayed on the tabletop. 'I've been with this band since before Alex and Kurt. I've seen people I love die. I've seen 'em be eaten by the dark, and by monsters, and you know I'm not being merely poetical when I say that. But I keep going because if I give up, I watched people I love die for nothing.'

Sal's chest rose and fell in a shuddering sigh. 'I know,' he said. 'I'm trying.'

'I know you are. Try to breathe. The world's full of restless things, but it don't mean they're all trying to eat us. Let's get our heads around the new gig, sort out our rehearsal schedule. Tomorrow, we'll get Yuka's sticks and we'll scout for new talent.'

Not *replacement* talent. Never *replacements*. Whoever they found to join them – if anyone – they would change the band and make it something new. It's how the band had worked for seven hundred years, since the first piper and drummer joined forces to protect their city. Band members came and went; the name of the troupe changed with the changing leaders, but the band endured under the Grandfather's Axe principle. The component parts had changed over and over again, yet the troupe maintained an historical continuity.

That's how each generation had explained it to the next, at any rate, and every Minstrel who ever joined embraced the philosophical paradox, because who would remember every single person who had ever been part of it, who were recorded into the oral history and carefully stored journals, if not them? They had to be the recorders of their own history, since the rest of the world generally had no idea who they were or what they did. They worked for nobody but the balance, they answered to no-one but each other. They did what must be done and moved on, generation after generation, with nobody but themselves to know that the singer who had closed a ghoul in a tomb in Zagreb in 2002 had any connection to the medieval piper and drummer who had sealed a guilt-ridden god in a stone jar in the Thames.

Yuka had recovered from Laszlo's praise enough to help him dry and stack away the dishes he'd washed. While they took care of the domestic chores, Sal and Steve drafted a potential set list and a rehearsal schedule.

As Steve, Sal and Yuka worked through the set selection in more detail, Laszlo, who knew none of the songs, cradled the violin Steve had earlier handed to him. He'd spent hours polishing and tuning the instrument, and played some of his old repertoire on it, wondering what he'd done to be worthy.

The 'fiddle' that Steve had retrieved from the trunk was the same he played that terrible day in Erdődülő. It was very old, the back elaborately carved with birds and vines. Whoever had made it – and it wasn't a Micheli or Amati or any of the other early known luthiers – had been a genius with both wood and music. The violin was beautifully balanced and modulated. Laszlo had been lucky enough to hold and play a Stradivarius in his time, an exquisite instrument. This faded, battered, beautiful thing was ten times the instrument that Stradivarius had been.

Well, for a start, it was unlikely the Stradivarius had ever been used to sing trees into weapons to stake vampires or ignite the air itself.

Laszlo ran his finger gently over the fretboard, and wondered if the old violin knew it had been used to help kill two men who had cherished this instrument as part of their heritage: who had loved each other and their little daughter as fiercely as they had loved their not-famous yet somehow infamous band.

As the last members of that infamous band reached the end of a song, Laszlo asked into the hush: 'What did that man Malone mean about "what they say about you"?'

'We got a reputation in the business,' Steve said. 'Musos like to have us as their support act. It's a word of mouth thing.'

'But why?'

'Word spreads about a band like ours,' Sal said, like it was a lecture he'd heard before but never given. 'There's magic in our music, even when we're not singing spells. If you sing enough magic into the instrument, it will seep out no matter what you're doing.' He nodded at the violin. 'That one has almost four hundred years of music and spellwork in it.'

'No offence to your playing, Laszlo,' interrupted Steve, 'but a six year old could've played that day and it would've helped.'

Laszlo believed it. He remembered too well the power of the song swelling out of the violin, and how he had merely to follow its lead.

'When a Minstrel band plays support, it's a golden ticket for the main act,' Sal said. 'No matter how good or bad the headline act is, we play and the audiences love them.

'The gigs are always the best. Merchandise sells faster,' Yuka added.

'That's why we only play shows when we need the money, even though we always need the money,' Sal added the old joke with a faint smile. 'Great power must be used wisely.' Then sadness enveloped him again, because the person who used to tell that tired joke was dead.

Laszlo wondered if he should say something comforting, or change the topic – but Sal scrubbed at his face again.

'You know we have to send half of what we make for Gretel.'

Steve shifted his bass from his knee to the floor. 'You don't need to worry about Gretel. We're going to take care of her.'

'How? Where's she going to end up? Your niece can't babysit her forever; nobody knows where her birth mother went after she handed Gretel to Alex and Kurt. *We* can't look after her. We couldn't keep either of her fathers alive, we certainly can't keep a child safe on the road.'

'I *said*,' Steve said with sharp emphasis, 'she's gonna be fine. I got it under control.' He met Yuka's glare. 'And don't you start with me, Yuka. We heard all you and Sal had to say about the irresponsibility of Kurt and Alex wanting kids way back then. It's done. A hundred told-you-sos won't change the situation.'

Yuka's challenging glare didn't falter. 'Being right does not make me happy, Steve. But I don't see why Harper can't-'

'It ain't on Harper to be a mom to that girl just 'cause she's babysittin'. Harper's just a kid herself.'

'Is Gretel safe?'

'She's takin' good care of Gretel for the time being. Quit frettin'.' Steve angrily pulled the bass back onto his knee. 'So given that

Gretel's *fine*, and given that we have six days to pull a show together, I suggest we get on with rehearsing these songs. Laszlo, have you heard enough to start working out harmonies yet? Sheet music's right there on the table. Sal, you get to forgettin' the rhythm part and get to rememberin' the lead, that'll be a whole lot more help here.'

A brittle silence followed, then Sal swallowed and started picking out the notes of the first song. He stopped again.

'I didn't think they should have had Gretel. That doesn't mean I don't love her. It doesn't mean I'm not going to do what's best for her.'

Steve released a hissing breath. 'I know that, Sal. I know Yuka loves her too, even though she don't say so.'

Yuka narrowed her eyes at him, but didn't deny it.

Sal plucked out a simple melody on the strings. 'She's going to need protection.'

'She'll have it.'

'From us, I mean.'

Yuka scowled at Laszlo's startled expression. 'From those who would use her to get to us.'

The melody Sal was playing remained gentle but strong. Steve began to play a bass line through it.

'She'll be protected,' Steve said.

'Will this have any effect from this far away?' Yuka asked, beginning a quiet beat anyway, her hands against the skin of her smallest drum, marking a sweet-sounding rhythm.

'It's her song. It'll find her,' Steve said.

Laszlo listened to them, and to the words that the three of them began to sing.

Heave a sigh, baby girl
Don't you cry, baby girl
Your daddies are guarding the door

He lifted the violin to his chin and raised the bow. The melody was simple, and this old instrument was full of magic. It couldn't hurt; and he was one of them now.

Laugh out loud, baby girl
Be strong and proud, baby girl
Keeping you safe is what your daddies are for

Laszlo drew the bow across the strings, harmonising. The song was sweet and uncomplicated, as lullabies should be. It reminded him of his own long estranged children, and he poured his heart into the next two stanzas. He didn't know if he had any music magic of his own, but the violin had enough for both of them.

Sleep after rehearsals proved a challenge in their crowded hostel room. Sal kept them awake again with muttering, reading aloud from the poems and epitaphs written in his notebook; then later, with his nightmares. He'd had them almost nightly since they'd lost Alex and Kurt. Since he'd had to behead Alex, to keep his best friend dead. Cut out his dead heart. Stuff his mouth and heart cavity with garlic. Burn the body. To be sure.

It took four days before Sal had been able to sleep at all. The nightmares were only better than the insomnia-induced hallucinations in that Sal could at least wake up from nightmares. That tiny speck of comfort was hardly enough, when Sal whimpered and cried out in his sleep and everyone woke fractious and unrested. By unspoken agreement, nobody ever talked about it. Nobody knew how to make Sal feel better. They hardly knew how to make themselves feel better.

Breakfast – toast and butter cadged from the 'take this leftover food' shelf in the hostel's communal kitchen – led to rehearsals. Laszlo was getting the hang of the set list and finding his place in the music.

Sal was more confident with Alex's old part in the lead too, but often as he was hitting his stride, he'd falter, stumble and end in a jarring mess of notes.

Steve called time out seconds before Sal began to smash his guitar to splinters.

'I'm gonna get some air. You might want to go get your sticks, Yuka. Then we better check out the venue, see what we might need. Then we'll try rehearsing here again,' and Steve stalked outside.

CHAPTER SIX

Trudy Schumacher was in the embalming room when Kitty went down to the basement workroom to make the final preparations before the Driscoll funeral. She waved hello through the glass partition separating it from the area where the departed were made-up and dressed in their eternity-best for their funerals.

Kitty waved back. Trudy was beginning the embalming process for a middle aged man. Another table held Mrs Entwhistle, an elderly woman in the final embalming stages before she would be laid to rest in a family crypt. A third table bore a journalist, Meredith Lawler: a recent arrival whose face and throat were in the process of reconstruction.

Trudy peeled off her gloves and scrubbed her hands. 'Maddie Driscoll is ready for you.'

Maddie's body was laid out in her coffin, clad in the pretty summer dress her family had chosen for her. The dress had been cut up the back so it could be arranged properly without having to jostle her body too much. Pads in her mouth gave the girl's face the illusion of fullness, though Maddie's white skin had none of the glow of life about it.

'I have to go out,' Trudy said. 'Will you be all right on your own?'

'Of course,' Kitty assured her.

'By the way, have you heard from the institute yet?'

'I should hear this month.' Kitty set up her work station with brushes, photographs and palettes of colour. She had, on Trudy and Marcus's urging, applied to become a fully qualified mortuary worker, so that she could conduct embalming and reconstruction work as well. With their letters of recommendation, submitted with the application, Kitty was almost certain to be accepted despite her twenty-one years.

'I'll be an hour or so.' Trudy left to change out of her work clothes and run errands.

Kitty compared the dead girl in the casket with the photographs propped on an easel for reference, assessing the differences so she could compensate for them with her palette.

Kitty's tools and materials were laid out on the bench – the brushes and sponges, the special make-up designed for use on skin that had no warmth or blush of blood beneath it; skin that perished more every passing moment, despite the best preparation. It was a body's business, after all, to return to the component parts from which it came, like it was the soul's business to go wherever souls go.

Using a sponge, Kitty first restored colour to Maddie's exposed arms and hands.

When the make-up had dried and was ready to be touched again, Kitty wound Jasper's collar around Maddie's wrist, the royal blue of it matching the pattern of blue flowers scattered over the dress. She arranged Maddie's hand to be cupped open and placed the phone charm of the outraged red bird into the hollow. Matthias's necklace was in a box on the workbench, ready to place around Maddie's neck after her face was made up.

As Kitty worked, she hummed a wandering melody, inventing words to go with it as she sang.

Once outside, Steve pulled his phone from his pocket and checked his messages. One had arrived from his nephew, Angus.

Of course we will. Nothing could make us happier. We'll sort out tickets and meet you and Harper soon.

Well, that was something. Gretel would be cared for the way Alex and Kurt would have liked. And if Steve hadn't told the rest of the band yet, well, it was partly that he didn't want to say anything until everything was confirmed.

Truth was, he was reluctant to involve Yuka and Sal in the

arrangements. They'd been right about Kurt and Alex's lack of wisdom in becoming parents, and they loved Gretel, but their early opposition still rankled. That little girl was the closest Steve would ever get to grandkids. He was going to do right by her, no matter what it cost him.

It was high time he retired, anyway. Sometimes Steve couldn't believe he'd made it this far without being killed or losing a limb. The band had operated under three names – AnnaTomic, Dragonsbane and Rome's Burning – since he'd joined them at fifteen years old. When Anna died, he'd accepted his probable fate. The idea that he might make it out alive had never occurred to him before Budapest.

Now, though. *Now.* He was starting to see the appeal in it. Sitting on a porch in a rocking chair, singing to Gretel as she grew up. Dying twenty or thirty years hence in his own bed, of some nice old people's condition, not bitten in half by a dragon or poisoned by an enraged witch or murdered by vampires, or any of the ways he'd lost other friends in the last forty-odd years.

Steve stabbed at the text pad on his phone, squinting at the letters, until he finally sent: *Good. See you then.*

He jammed the phone into his pocket, hooked his thumbs in his belt, and ambled towards the centre of Melbourne to see what was going down. All these decades travelling and he'd never made it to Australia before. It had to have more going for it than simply being a long way away from Hungary.

The stretch of road along which he walked wasn't giving him much to go on. Perhaps Melbourne's charms were more of the hidden type. Some cities were like that – garden variety on the surface and all buried treasure once you started poking around underneath. Of course, where treasure was buried was mostly where the monsters were found, too. At least it wasn't boring, he supposed.

Today, Steve Borman was not in the mood for surprises. Garden variety was fine by him, if the universe would be so obliging for once.

His feet led him finally past an elegant, colonnaded Victorian-era building sheltering a café and filled with the enticing scent of coffee beans and toasted sandwiches. The building ended where a traffic-free plaza began, split in two by tram tracks down its middle.

Steve regarded the collection of tall posts at the top of the plaza, which bore narrow flags advertising a recent art exhibition. At their feet was what looked like a giant, pink, narrow, naked backside. A few steps took him to the front of the thing, which showed it to actually be a giant marble coin purse.

Well, okay Melbourne, thought Steve, *I kinda like your big pink ass-purse. What else you got for me?*

That's when he heard the music, playing from halfway down the length of the plaza. Even half a city block away, Steve sensed that special something humming through the notes, and promptly went to investigate which one of the band was not garden variety.

The four-piece was set up in front of a department store, a folded square of cardboard declaring them to be Firedog Brigade followed by a list of their social media sites. The sound was unpolished and threatened constantly to slip out of rhythm. The lead singer strained slightly at the high notes. On the surface of it, they made up a perfectly fine busking indie band. The thrumming core of power in them came from only one of them. The bass player.

Turn to face the sun
Blazing bright
Everything warm and light
But there's something colder
At your shoulder
Behind you, you know
There is a shadow

A young man bent over his bass guitar, fingers flying over the strings, his feet braced wide and steady. From the throbbing low notes to the counter-melody that wove through the higher register, that boy was the one knitting the players into a whole, keeping the drumbeat in line, keeping the lead guitar from wavering off into blurry fingering, tugging the singer back into key and rhythm. His was the power bringing out the inherent threat of the lyric yet also keeping it at bay: a careful balance.

Keep your eyes on the light
Keep your back to the shadow,
Dark as night
And maybe you won't see it
And maybe
It won't see into you

Steve folded his arms and watched the bass player. The kid was in his mid-twenties, dark-skinned and dark-eyed, with strong and graceful hands, his focus entirely on his instrument. He seemed unaware that he was guiding the others to be better than they would have been alone.

That shadow
Eclipses your better self
There's strength in that darkness
When you need it
You'd better, you'd better
Hope to god you won't need it

Steve had been playing guitar since he was nine. He'd been manifesting the Minstrel Tongue since he hit puberty. He could see power with his naked eye. And this boy? This boy had power, both musical and magical.

And it does not forget
And it will not forgive
Fight it, fight it
For as long as you live

Steve waited until their set was done and, while a flurry of onlookers went to buy a CD from the drummer, he sidled up to the bass player. The kid stood apart from the others, plucking at a string and listening to its vibration.

'Sounds in tune to me,' Steve said.

'Hmmm.'

'Pitch perfect, in fact.'

'That so?'

'That is indeed a fact,' Steve said, smiling at the other's dryness. 'Though I guess that string gives you trouble, sometimes. Mine used to. Turned out to be the peg.' Steve forbore to mention that this was because the offending peg had been a last minute fix whittled out of a finger bone found in a Dresden graveyard. It was much too early for that kind of detail.

'Thanks for the tip.'

'Any time, kid.'

'I appreciate the advice and everything,' the kid said, 'but I'm sort of busy.'

'I can see you're plenty busy. You carry this band.'

That made the boy's eyes flash. So: he knew it.

'Is there something you're after?' asked the kid.

'Do you have a passport?'

'Yeah, but you'll never pass for me, so I'm not selling.'

Steve liked this boy. A lot. 'No, seriously. I got a feeling you'll be going places soon.'

'That's a terrible pick-up line and dude, you're deadly, okay, but you're not my type.'

Steve grinned at the boy, pleased at being thought deadly, even while suspecting it meant more like... *wicked cool* rather than actually *deadly*. He was certainly the latter when he had to be.

'It ain't like that at all, kid. This ain't a proposition. Well,' he laughed, 'it is, but not the one you think it is. I'm what you might call a talent scout. No, not like that.' Annoyance at the boy's cynical expression crept into his tone.

Steve's irritation prompted a sudden laugh from the kid. 'Hey, all right, calm down, mate. You're not queer, fine.'

'Never said I wasn't queer. I said I wasn't propositioning you in that manner.'

'So you *are* queer then?'

'You are missing the point of this conversation.'

The kid, with that infectious grin on his face, folded his arms across the top of his guitar. 'Which is?'

Steve closed the gap between them, hazel eyes fixed on brown.

'Have you ever made things change with your music?' Steve said, low and earnest.

The boy's grin faltered.

Steve continued, too soft for anyone else to hear. 'Have you ever played to the dry ground and made it rain? Sung a baby to sleep and the whole house went quiet? Played so angry you broke every glass in your house, or cracked a paving stone outside? You ever made a fire with your fingers on those strings, kid?'

The boy's jaw clenched shut. His eyes were wide. 'What do you know about that?' His whisper was forced out like a confession over vocal cords tight with fear.

'I know all there is to know about it, including what it's for.'

The boy swallowed so hard the sound of it swelled in the air between them.

'Come with me when you're done here,' Steve said. 'I'll tell you a story.'

The kid hesitated, but Steve had been in his place before – full of questions and suspicions, and then full of hope when someone at last offered an explanation – and with it a way out of poverty, misery and fear. Well, Steve guessed he still had a lot of those, but his new bedrock of certainty made it bearable in a way it never used to be.

'Fine,' the boy said suddenly. 'I'll go with you and you can tell me a story. But that's it. No promises from me.'

'I haven't asked you for any yet.'

'The name's Aaron. Aaron Maclean,' said the kid.

Chapter Seven

'So,' said young Aaron Maclean, sitting opposite the older man. 'Music is a conduit for magic, it's the natural defence against demons, ghosts and other creepy things if you're born with the gift to use it, and you play bass in the rock band equivalent of Merlin the Magician, fighting dragons in C Major. Does that cover the basics?'

Steve nodded coolly. 'Maybe more Buffy than Merlin most of the time, and C Major has some more specific uses against things that live in water, but yeah.'

'You are full of shit.'

'Could be,' conceded Steve, 'and it could be that you imagined those times when you played guitar and set fire to the carpet.'

Aaron frowned uncertainly.

'Or sang to keep yourself from being afraid of the dark, and had a little light glow on your fingertips, from nowhere.'

'Used to light up the end of my nose,' confessed Aaron before he thought to deny the charge. 'Tickled.' Then he pressed his mouth shut.

'I used to glow from my palms to my elbows,' Steve said matter-of-factly. 'I was living on the streets at the time, so you can imagine the inconvenience.'

Aaron arched an eyebrow despite himself.

'It weren't so bad. There were a lot of hippies and dope heads in California. That's a lot of people with a funny way of looking at the world. Half the time folks saw me, they thought I was an angel.' Steve grinned. 'I wasn't. In case you're wondering.'

Aaron dropped his gaze to the cooling cup of coffee in front of him. He'd sat here, listening to this mad story of music and vampires, songs affecting the elements and stealing the cries of banshees and who knew what else besides. It was, if not actually insane, then a ludicrous yarn spun by this softly spoken Yank to pull his leg.

Except for his gran.

Aaron sighed. 'My gran always reckoned when I sang to birds they listened.' He cleared his throat gruffly and gave Steve a steely glare. 'Mind you, towards the end she also said her own grandmother had power over the weather so, you know, not quite sure what to believe.'

'Maybe she did have power over the weather,' Steve said. 'I know a pretty good rain song myself.'

'You're off your nut.'

Steve shrugged. 'It sure seemed like it in the early days. I tell you kid, there's never a time you wish more that you were hallucinating than when you're hip-deep in a spring thaw river, freezing your ass off and trying to work out how to decapitate a hydra.'

Aaron stared. 'What's a hydra?'

'Thing like a snake with *way* too many heads,' Steve sounded disgruntled at the memory. 'Plus it transpires cutting 'em off is a stupid idea. Little bastard grows heads back and then some. Pays to read your classic mythology before stepping into *that* river.'

'What did you do?'

'Oh, Anna sang down some fire on that slithery sum'bitch. I used a scythe we'd found on the farm the river ran through, sang it sharp enough to cut silk, and while I mowed, she scorched the stumps with a sweet tune in good ol' E Major.'

Steve grinned at Aaron's rapt attention. 'I could sing you a little rain, if you need more convincing. Not here, though.'

'Down by the Yarra?' said Aaron, lifting his chin in the general southerly direction.

'Alrighty.' Leaving Aaron to pay for the coffee, Steve rose and headed towards the wide river he'd sensed before he saw.

'Cheap bastard,' complained Aaron as he caught up, his guitar case heavy in one hand.

'Ain't a lot of cash in saving the world.'

'You're doing a shit job of selling this gig.'

'I can't get you into it by lying about riches you won't make.'

'No, really, shut up. I'm losing interest.'

They came to the bridge spanning the river then followed the steps down to the riverbank.

'I'll keep it low,' Steve said. 'No sense bringing on a whole storm, and I haven't got my guitar. Unless I can use yours?'

Aaron made a show of considering it, then handed over his beloved Fender Kingman acoustic. He'd brought it along after the rest of the gear had been loaded in the van because it had felt like the right thing to do. He hadn't questioned the odd impulse. 'Should I go back for the amp?'

'Hell, no. Like I said, we don't want a big sound. That'd bring a torrent down.'

'You're certain this'll work.'

'So're you,' grinned Steve. 'Hoping, anyhow.'

'How do you figure that?'

'You're still here, ain't ya? Now sit and hush.' Steve sat cross-legged on the bank and arranged the guitar on his thigh. He began to pluck out the melody, senses reaching into the instrument. There. A trace of that raw magic talent embedded in the frame, the strings and the hollows of it. Softly, coaxing a gentle rise of power from the instrument, Steve began to sing.

Listen to the ocean
Surrender water to the sky
Listen to the streams
Soak the clay and earth nearby

Watching, listening, thinking that it was such a simple tune for something that was meant to be magic, Aaron suddenly fancied that he could – that he really could – *hear* something. Water. Moving. Small and slick. Not the slap of the Yarra on the banks: something *other*.

The lullabies of lakes
Evaporating droplets with a sigh
All these drips and beads and mists
Spinning invisibly by

The drops were not quite invisible. Aaron could see, though he couldn't understand how, a haze in front of his eyes, in which he could see individual droplets. Reverse teardrops, heading... *up*.

Rain come down

Then, in the clear, blue, cloudless sky, he felt but did not see the mist of droplets coalesce, combine, condense...

Rain come down

And there, in their own little patch of dirt by the Yarra, it rained: proper rain on two square metres of land; a fine shower but heavy enough to leave spatters on his shirt. Water gathered in his hair and trickled down his face.

Steve repeated the refrain *'rain come down'* in ever-decreasing volume, until he reached the final stanza.

Then go back to your seas
And river beds and banks and quays
Waiting for the cycle to repeat
Flow and ripple and fall again.

Their little burst of rainfall pattered into silence.

'I skipped some stuff, but you gotta do the last verse, or it keeps on raining for hours,' Steve said quietly. 'Days, sometimes. Found that out the hard way.' He seemed amused by the memory.

Aaron's rain-damp face was tilted up to the bright sun in that clear sky.

'That was amazing.'

'Want to meet the rest of the band?'

'Hell, yes.'

CHAPTER EIGHT

A brief panic followed the realisation that four-year-old Aaron had wandered away from where his father and uncles were fishing.

Ern ran along the river bank, threading through the stands of skinny eucalypts that marched down the flat ground and into the tributary running off the Murray River, calling for his son. The opposite side of the river, the New South Wales side, was too high for an adult to climb, let alone a small child. His little fellah must be on this side somewhere.

'Aaron! Aaron, call out to Daddy!'

Ahead he caught a glimpse of his mother-in-law's white hair and a bright red shirt. 'Mum! Have you seen Aaron? He wandered off!'

Susanna raised her hand and calmly waved. Reassured, Ern's startled heart slowed along with his feet. She put her finger to her lips as he approached, and pointed. Aaron squatted on his haunches by the river, giggling and rocking rhythmically from side to side. He was singing to himself.

Hello sky, hello cloud
Hello land, hello water
Hello fly, hello bird
Hello snake, hello fish
Hello tree, hello flower

As he sang, the tiny boy dabbled his fingers in the muddy brown water, leaving in it shiny trails of light from his fingertips.

'Have you ever seen the like,' Susanna said, more in wonder than fear. An Irish lilt clung to her accent, despite nearly forty years in this parched country far from the green land of her youth.

Ern stared at the boy and didn't answer.

'The birds are coming to him,' Susanna went on, whispering in sweet amazement. 'Those are dragonflies circling his head. And... oh my god!' She gasped in sudden horror as she realised what creature had swum up close to the boy, writhing black body fluid as a brush full of ink squiggled across the water. Only its wicked head, raised above the current, seemed solid. 'Aar-!' she began to cry out in alarm.

'Hush,' urged Ern, seizing her wrist. 'Don't scare it.'

'Don't scare *it*?'

'See what it's doing?'

Heart in her mouth, Susanna watched as the snake rippled up to Aaron's hand in the water and swam in a circle.

Aaron giggled and sang. 'Hello snake, hello Gane!'

The black snake swam another circle and raised its head, flickering its tongue along the boy's arm, wrist to elbow. Aaron giggled 'That tickles, Gane!'

'What's Gane?' Susanna asked in a terrified whisper.

'The rainbow serpent. That's not Gane. It's a red belly black snake.'

Susanna stuffed her fist in her mouth so she wouldn't scream and startle the venomous thing.

But the snake lowered itself back into the river and after swimming another circle, writhed away across the surface of the river towards the reeds of its nest, while Aaron sang 'Goodbye Gane, goodbye snake!'

Ern and Susanna strode down to the riverbank as soon as they could, Ern scooping up his son and giving him a fierce hug.

'Don't go wandering off, boy!' he said, kissing the child's black hair. 'The river doesn't always want to be sung to, and sometimes it's hungry.'

'*I'm* hungry,' declared Aaron.

'Then you run off up to Mum and ask her for a cheese and vegemite sandwich. Quick sticks!'

Aaron wriggled out of his father's arms and as soon as his feet hit the ground, he ran back through the trees to the caravan where his mum and aunties were making lunch.

Susanna and Ern watched him run.

'Has he done that before?' asked Susanna, surprisingly unfazed by this sign of otherworldliness in her grandson.

'No.'

'We should ask Debbie. She might have seen things.' Debbie was her daughter, who laughed about being a 'Shamrock Aboriginal', proud of both her father Albert Haley's ancestry and her mother's Irish heritage.

Susanna Veronica Haley had come out to Australia in the fifties as a nurse, but she was born and raised in Ireland and was as mixed in heritage as her children.

'My grandmother was from Norway, you know,' she said quietly. 'Mormor's kulning was famous in our village.'

'Kulning?'

'Calling the cows with a kind of song. She'd call home the lost cattle not only on our farm, but for our neighbours too.'

'Aaron wasn't kulning, was he?'

'No, but I saw Mormor kulning the cows back from pasture one day, and there was a light in her voice. All the animals came. Eagles and doves together. Rabbits and foxes. It was the strangest thing I ever saw. She told me to keep it secret, even from Grandpa. Said it scared people, and she only ever sang to the animals. Mormor thought that might be how Saint Patrick banished the snakes, by singing them into the sea. One summer, when we were parched for rain, she took me to the fields and we danced, and it finally rained. Of course, Ern,' she said, 'maybe he gets this from your and Albert's people.'

'Maybe,' Ern said. 'Grandma used to say we had a medicine man in her family, but she was stolen from her mob when she was only six. She didn't remember much about them or her culture.' Too late to ask her now, just as it was too late to ask Albert, both having passed too young.

Ern regarded the river solemnly, then the camp. 'I'll tell Debs, but we'll keep it secret. This country got a history of taking away Koori kids. I'm not giving them any excuse.'

'We'll teach him to keep it quiet,' agreed Susanna. 'Things didn't end well for my Grandma, when the next village found out.'

They shook hands on it, and walked back up to the campsite.

CHAPTER NINE

The band members reunited in Richmond to assess The Corner Hotel's small stage with practiced, sceptical eyes. Laszlo stalked around the stage itself, mentally noting the best positions for this new iteration of the band. Riser there for Yuka, yes, Steve and Sal's guitars fine downstage here and here, and a spot discreetly stage left for him and the violin. Laszlo knew he was fussing but it felt important for his first time on a stage since he'd quit the orchestra.

'Not a lot of room for you to move,' Sal pointed out.

'I am playing a violin, not performing interpretive dance,' replied Laszlo impatiently. 'How much room do I need?'

'As long as nobody loses an eye to your bowing.' Sal's half-smile signalled it as a joke, but the humour bypassed Laszlo.

'There is nothing wrong with my bowing,' he said through clenched teeth.

'No, of course there isn't. It's just... robust.'

Sal's attempt to salvage the banter rammed into a brick wall.

'My bowing technique is beyond reproach,' Laszlo said with great formality. 'The great Tibor Vargas himself commended my playing at his 1987 masterclass in Sion. I-' He fell suddenly silent, as though he had blurted out some terrible *faux pas*.

'I will stand here,' he said stiffly, 'and restrain my bowing.'

Steve cleared his throat as he arrived. The three others happily seized on the distraction.

'Hey, all y'all. I met someone. Meet Aaron Maclean. He plays bass.'

All eyes went the newcomer, and Aaron did his best not to shrink back. 'Uh. Hello.'

Yuka's piercing gaze moved from the young bass player to the older. 'Why do you bring us a bass player?'

'Oh, you know, one of us for weekdays, one for Sunday best.'

Aaron arched an eyebrow at Steve.

'You're not going anywhere, are you Steve?' Sal managed to sound both anxious and aggrieved.

'Well, I had half a mind to retire soon,' he said blithely. 'So happens I heard Aaron here play today and thought he might audition for my spot.'

'Retire?' Yuka snapped.

'You can't go!' Sal wailed.

'You want to leave the band?' Laszlo strode to the edge of the stage, disbelieving.

'Does he have,' Yuka darted a sideways glance at him, 'the Minstrel Tongue?'

'Would I bring him if he didn't?' said Steve, crankiness finally colouring his tone. 'I haven't seen him set fire to anything yet, but I know magic when I hear it.'

'Guys,' protested Aaron. 'Can we slow down a minute? Steve spun me a yarn and made it rain on a patch of grass on the Yarra. I'm just here to find out what the hell it is you mob do.'

'Don't listen to him,' countered Steve. 'He's here to confirm that *we* do what *he* can do.'

'He doesn't even know what that is,' protested Sal.

'Oh yes he does.' Steve grinned entirely too knowingly at Aaron. 'He's here to see if we can make fire and talk flowers into growing. The usual stuff we all start with.' Steve caught Yuka's glowering eye. 'Well, okay, not all of us start small.'

Aaron knew he was missing something – the number of somethings he was missing in this conversation amounted to nearly everything – but he hadn't expected the hostility.

'This was a bad idea.'

'Timing's bad, is all. Ironic for a bunch of musos, but the world don't always play fair. I haven't had time to talk to 'em yet.'

'Did you tell him about Alex and Kurt?' Sal wanted to know.

'No. Like I said. Timing.'

'Who are Alex and Kurt?' Aaron peered around, wondering if more angry band members were going to stride out of the shadows to make him unwelcome.

'They're dead,' Yuka said tightly.

'Ah... okay.'

'It's really not,' she glowered.

Aaron's hand tightened around his guitar case. He would have left right then and there except that this tiny, domineering woman squinted at him and suddenly plucked a pristine pair of drum sticks from her belt and pointed them at him.

'Let's start with my new sticks, then,' she said. 'At worst I'll have to buy more.'

'Ah...'

'Good thinking, Yuka,' Steve said approvingly, impervious to the glare she cast his way. 'Got a patch of dirt in mind?'

The next thing Aaron knew, he and his guitar case were being marched out of the Corner Hotel, surrounded by this band of strange, strange people. They passed the concrete barrier decorated with street art that stretched between the train station hub and the light industrial offices to the immediate north. They emerged ten metres later at a bare public space made up of triangles of brown gravel dotted with spindly gum trees and blue geometric blocks that served as seating.

Again, Aaron wondered why he didn't walk away. Again, he stayed.

Here were answers to questions he'd been encouraged not to ask and to never, ever discuss for almost his whole life.

Choosing the smallest of the plain patches of gravel, the band members arranged themselves cross-legged at three of the compass points of the straggly park. Sal gestured for Aaron to sit at the fourth point, while Lazlo sat between Yuka and Sal.

'Should I be here?' asked the roadie.

Yuka nodded sharply. 'You are one of us, yes? You've seen us do this. We will take your voice in with ours. Follow my lead.'

Laszlo seemed to have no more idea of what that meant than Aaron, though he quietly preened that Yuka had said it.

Yuka reached out with the drum sticks grasped together in one hand. Her other hand was poised on her hip. She placed the two sticks exactly parallel, the tips pointed at her own crossed ankles with a care and precision that was clearly owed to ritual.

'What are we doing, exactly?' Aaron asked.

'Singing strength into my new sticks,' Yuka said.

Aaron's expression indicated that this was not helpful.

'We've all got the Minstrel Tongue,' explained Steve with an encouraging grin. 'We can sing that magic into our instruments. Yuka likes to make her sticks stronger by singing magic into 'em, and we all help. Seems having different singers weaves something stronger. It's handy in a fight, I'll give it that. Your guitar there,' Steve tapped a nail against the Fender's case, 'had raw power humming away inside when I played the rain in for you. You got a natural talent, kid.'

'The Minstrel Tongue,' repeated Aaron thoughtfully.

'Maybe.' Sal tempered the comment. 'We don't know how strong you are, yet.'

'We'll find out,' Yuka said with a meaningful glare, 'if you ever stop talking.'

Steve laughed. 'Yuka's got virtues, but patience ain't one of 'em. You won't need your guitar for this. Just listen.' He tapped the centre of Aaron's forehead, then beside his ear, then over his heart. 'Here. Here. Here. Join in when you're ready. You'll either get this – or you won't.'

A test then. One that Aaron suddenly, desperately wanted to pass. *I want this. I want it to mean something. I want to know how to use it.* Although his next thought was: *This is crazy. They're all crazy. I'm crazy.*

The other three had started to clap. Twice on the thighs and a hand clap, then a silent beat. A familiar rhythm from a familiar old song. *Well, who doesn't love Freddie Mercury?* Aaron didn't know the point of it all, but he joined in the clapping.

Yuka started the singing, but by the second line the others had joined her, harmonising in a way the original song had never done. By the time the chorus came along, Aaron had found a harmony line and his hands felt warm; much warmer than could be accounted for by the clapping.

As the song continued, the other band members threw in a hand gesture during the silent beat after the clap: flicking their palms outwards as though shaking off water onto the precisely placed drum sticks at the centre of their circle. Even Laszlo made the motion, echoing Yuka's.

More singing, more clapping, with that little flick. *We will rock you.*

Aaron joined in the flick. It felt strange – yet completely natural. All the while, his hands grew warmer. His fingers tingled. When he did that little outward flick of the hand, if felt like tiny, hot particles were flying off his skin onto the sticks.

Aaron risked a glance around the ring, and damn, he could, if he squinted, see those same particles flying off the fingers and palms of the others. The effect was fainter on Laszlo, but everyone's hands were rosy-tinted, warmth radiating from them as the fizz of white-gold speckles arced gracefully from those flicking hands, dropping like an energy spritzer onto the drum sticks.

And those sticks seemed to be sucking that energy into their carved wood, which began to glow, almost to pulse – like the wood was still alive and trying to grow.

The last clap reverberated and Aaron knew instinctively to stop. He, like the others, placed his warm, fizzing hands on his thighs and waited. His heart hammered and he was covered in perspiration, filled with exhilaration. It felt like playing a brilliant set; like writing the perfect song; like *belonging*.

Yuka stretched a hand out over the sticks and nodded approvingly.

'Good. They feel very… *ah-tss! zuki!*' she cried out. Yuka snatched her fingers into her mouth to suck on them.

'There is a problem,' she said. 'Worse than the market.'

Before Yuka could elaborate, the ground began to vibrate, like the thrumming skin of a drum. The brown gravel was jostling and jumping.

'Is that supposed to happen?' Aaron asked, post-magic bliss fracturing.

The rest of the band was regarding the moving earth with alarmed – and alarming – expressions.

'Not exactly,' admitted Steve.

'He means "no, not at all",' muttered Sal.

Next came a rumble, the baritone of a train passing close by.

None of the trains passing through Richmond Station behind its soundproofing concrete barrier had been so loud. The increasingly loud sound clearly wasn't coming from the station – it was emanating from the ground directly beneath their crossed legs.

Almost as one, the musicians stood. Yuka scooped up her newly song-strengthened sticks and held one in each fist.

The rumble of an impossible train was augmented by the unexpected hiss of steam and a piercing whistle that belonged to no train currently operating on the Richmond line. The rumble became a rattle, the steam whistle shrieked more loudly, and both sounds suddenly fused with the scream of metal scraping on metal, the squeal of a locomotive braking fiercely.

The unearthly metallic din rose inexorably up out of the earth.

Around them, the offices and houses remained closed; no-one rushed out to the street. It seemed possible that the five of them on this patch of land were the only ones hearing the screech and roar of stressed metal, cracking sleepers, human voices raised in panic and then the cacophony, the unholy roar of twisting metal and blasting steam and the screaming, oh god, the *screaming...*

Aaron pressed his hands over his ears, but it didn't help.

Yuka had dropped to one knee and was drumming against the earth, a simple heartbeat rhythm. Aaron could see her mouth moving but the song was merely a series of shapes on her lips, the sound drowned by the clamour of the phantom train crash.

Oh, thought Aaron.

'Train crash!' he shouted. Nobody heard. He grabbed Steve by the arm and pressed his lips close to the Texan's ear. '*It sounds like a train crash!*'

'Yup,' agreed Steve curtly, dropping to his knees and leaning close to the earth to sing to it. Sal was already down beside Yuka, singing, although their song could hardly be heard over the din. Laszlo watched, frightened and helpless.

Aaron dropped down beside Steve. 'What does it mean?'

Steve left off singing. 'Don't know yet. Something's pounding on the door between the dead and the living. Ever been a train wreck here?'

The ground jumped under them, and the shriek of metal reached a crescendo.

'About a hundred years ago,' Aaron shouted into Steve's ear, and found he was shouting into a shocking silence.

Steve winced and shook his head, jamming a finger in his ear canal as though to dislodge Aaron's shouted words. He stomped a foot on the ground, testing it, but all that was left was the ringing in everyone's ears.

'Train wreck, huh?' Sal dropped to his knees again and patted the ground. There are no bodies under here, but… yes. Old blood and trauma.'

'This is bad,' Yuka said. 'Something has stirred the dead.'

Sal stood and dusted his hands off against his jeans. 'I hope it isn't zombies again. I hate zombies.'

'Worse than vampires? Really?' Laszlo's hands were curled into fists, trying to keep the trembling at bay. 'Because the vampires were very bad.'

Yuka had lowered herself to both knees and dug the tip of one drum stick into the gravel. Her necklace of cobbled together guitar strings and keyboard keys swayed, listed to the east in defiance of gravity.

'That way.' She jerked her head towards the streets eastward, one of her hands raised to wrap around the necklace. 'Someone's singing.'

No sounds reached them, but Sal and Steve nodded sagely and wriggled their feet against the ground.

'Someone strong,' commented Sal. He pressed fingers to his ears, against the point under his earlobes as though that would alter the pressure on them.

Steve held out a hand to help Yuka up. 'Guess we better go see who it is.'

CHAPTER TEN

Kitty sang to herself as she made Maddie Driscoll in her silk-lined casket perfect for the funeral service. She smoothed out Maddie's dress, carefully adjusted the girl's blonde fringe and corrected a smudge of uneven colour on her arms. She made sure the pendant sat neatly in the hollow of Maddie's throat. A dab of adhesive would keep it from moving when her casket was taken out to the chapel for her family to say goodbye.

Kitty was hit with a sudden surge of sorrow for this empty house where a girl used to live. Maddie was like a wax sculpture of someone sleeping, in her summer dress, the little mementoes of her cat and her boyfriend and her family placed carefully at her wrist, in her palm, at her throat.

The sorrow wasn't only for Maddie. Not everyone got a long life, and lives that were long weren't necessarily happy. Nevertheless, Kitty couldn't help wondering what her life would have been like if her parents hadn't died. Her grandparents' lives might have been happier, too.

(Kitty harboured small, nagging doubts about that story of the car accident. Grandma had once, resentful-drunk, muttered about *evil* and *monsters taking my son*. Grandpa, discovering Kitty listening, had been furious with both her and Grandma.)

'You would have been so many things,' Kitty whispered to the late Maddie Driscoll. 'Anything you wanted, and some things you didn't. Maybe you'd have learned to like them, or learned how to change again.'

But Maddie wouldn't know everything she could have been. Her family wouldn't know, and they'd change in other ways because Maddie wasn't there.

'I'm still here,' Kitty told Maddie firmly, 'so I'm going to be more things, even if my family will never know. If I don't like the life I have, I can change it, starting with music. This payday, I'm buying a real and proper keyboard that plays actual out-loud notes.'

There. She'd verbalised the promise she'd made to herself. Her grandparents' disapproval; Maddie's approval; both were non-existent and neither mattered, because she made her own choices now.

Kitty curled her fingernails into her palms to bring her back to the task at hand. Neither Maddie nor her family had use for her personal pain. The Driscolls first; Kitty would address her own issues later.

The crash of metal made Kitty jump. Kitty twisted to see what could have fallen and entirely missed the metal bowl on the floor of the embalming room because Mrs Entwhistle was sitting up on her table.

Sitting up.

On her table.

Mrs Entwhistle, 88 years old, most definitely dead. Embalmed and everything.

Well. That's not usual, thought Kitty, battening down a haze of panic with determined practicality.

On the table behind the embalmed Mrs Entwhistle, the middle-aged man in the first stages of embalming was also sitting up. She couldn't remember his name. George Carmin. Cummings. Carmichael. George, anyway.

George Carmin-Cummings-Carmichael swivelled his head in her direction. His eyes were blank, milky. A tube ran from his body, though nothing flowed through it now.

Definitely not usual.

Over to the right, the journalist – *Meredith Lawler*, Kitty thought – sat up too.

And right behind her, Kitty heard the rustling of the dress and the slight sound, a snick, of the charm sliding out of Maddie's hand

and against the side of the coffin. Kitty heard a faint moan, and it certainly didn't come out of her own mouth.

Slowly, slowly, slowly, Kitty turned until she was face-to-face with Maddie Driscoll. The girl was blank-eyed, and not all that menacing, except for the fact that *she should not have been sitting up.*

Kitty knew for a fact Maddie, Meredith, George and Mrs Entwhistle were all one hundred per cent dead. She'd been there for the embalming. She'd watched Trudy perform the reconstructions. Realistically, the only way any of these people could be more dead would be if they were cremated.

And yet.

Up they sat.

Kitty's heart was pounding but her mind was strangely clear.

They can't hurt me. They don't even seem to want to. They're not evil. They're just empty houses and I see them all the time. I talk to them all the time.

Out of nowhere came one simple idea.

I need to tell them to go back to sleep.

Kitty drew a breath and the words began in her head.

Whoever you were, how good or how bad.

She thought the line again, and with it came a melody, and more words.

Whoever you were, how good or how bad
It's over, what made you happy or sad.

Behind her, Mrs Entwhistle and George C and Meredith Lawler were moving. She thought they were trying to work out how to stand. In front of her, Maddie Driscoll placed her stiff hands against the sides of the coffin.

'Maddie. No. Lie down.'

Maddie sightless eyes gazed past Kitty's shoulder. She continued to push herself up from her coffin.

Kitty tried singing the stuff in her head.

Whoever you were, how good or how bad
It's over, what made you happy or sad

Maddie stilled and regarded the space next to Kitty's left ear with interest.

The lines and scars of the life you lived
The love that you had is the gift that you give

The words flowed, sure and even kind. Kitty wasn't afraid. They were only bodies, and she perceived no malice in them. If anything, the dead seemed as bemused she was.

Kitty angled herself so that she could see Maddie as well as the others in the embalming room. She sang again, from the beginning.

Whoever you were, how good or how bad
It's over, what made you happy or sad
The lines and scars of the life you lived
The love that you had is the gift that you give

All of the bodies paused, their heads tilting to listen to her. New words and an extension of the melody flowed easily into her head, and she let them flow easily out of her mouth.

Return to earth, return to sky
Like stars, your atoms learn to fly
Your bones and flesh, no longer you,
Rejoin the world, make something new.

Maddie's stiff hands rested against the sides of her coffin. She was no longer trying to climb out. The dress drooped away from her shoulders, and Kitty was half aware that when this was over, she'd have to reset Maddie's dress and hair; the necklace and the bird charm.

It never occurred to Kitty that there would not be a 'later'.

Kitty lifted her chin, determined to be heard.

Leave your body with a sigh
Those you've loved to say goodbye
This precious frame, beloved skin
Is just the house that you lived in

Without planning to, Kitty raised her arms, opening them, as though to embrace them all.

Return to earth, return to sky
Like stars, your atoms learn to fly
Your bones and flesh, no longer you,
Rejoin the world, make something new

Mrs Entwhistle seemed to sigh and deflate back onto the table. She listed to one side, but she was quiet. Likewise, George C, without so much as a groan, drooped onto his table again. Meredith Lawler lay down.

Maddie alone still listened. Kitty sang for her.

This body is the dress you wore,
Faded, broken, torn
This flesh and bone the loving home to your
Heart and soul
Return to earth, return to sky
Like stars, your atoms learn to fly
Your bones and flesh, no longer you,
Rejoin the world, make something new

As the final note left Kitty's throat and Maddie Driscoll wilted easily back into her coffin, the door opened and five strangers jostled for space in the entrance to the workroom.

Kitty's heart, so steady while she sang, began to race. The dead sitting up was one thing. Living intruders in her workplace were something else entirely.

'You're not allowed in here.'

The eldest of the group grinned at her, his eyes sparkling with an unsettling yet appealing glee. 'Two in one day,' he crowed in a southern American drawl. 'Maybe our luck's back in. Don't suppose you got a passport, kid?'

The young Indigenous man to his left, clutching a guitar, was agitated. 'Seriously, Steve. You need a new pick-up line.'

Kitty narrowed her eyes at them: at the way the small Japanese woman was peering in grim satisfaction at out-of-kilter bodies; at the Indian man unconsciously tapping the rhythm of the song she'd been singing against his own chest with his fingertips. Behind them, a grey-haired, middle-aged man stared wide-eyed around the room, nervously scouring for signs of life where none should be.

She realised that they had seen, if not everything, then how everything had finished. And jittery one or two of them may have been, but you'd have to be pretty damned thick not to notice how *interested* they all were.

Kitty firmly ignored the question, the comment and all the *interest*.

'You are going to tell me who you are,' she declared, 'and you are going to *explain* this to me.'

CHAPTER ELEVEN

Steve of the terrible pick-up line replied. 'Steve Borman,' he said, sticking out his hand for her to shake. 'This is...' He paused to consider his words. 'The band,' was what he decided on.

Kitty tentatively shook the offered hand. 'Band?'

'It's kind of a long story.'

Kitty pursed her lips at him. 'Make it shorter.'

Her terse response made Steve Borman laugh. The short Japanese woman gave her an approving nod.

'I'm almost certain he doesn't mean to be a dick, but I'm not sure he can help himself,' the Indigenous man said. 'Look, it's all new to me too; I only met this mob today, but it's been a bloody strange afternoon.'

He winced at the disarrayed Maddie. 'My name's Aaron Maclean. What Steve means is he thinks you and I've got what these people call The Minstrel Tongue.'

Kitty resisted the urge to stick her tongue out to stare at the tip of it. Instead, she introduced herself. 'I'm Catalina Carrasco. Kitty.' Steve Borman, she noticed, managed at last to appear surprised. 'What do you mean by the Minstrel Tongue?'

Aaron Maclean elaborated. 'You've just done magic with your singing. So can I. Steve here made it rain in a two metre radius by the Yarra today, with a song and my guitar.' A grin finally tugged at his mouth. 'It was deadly.'

Kitty stared from face to face, and all of them merely smiled encouragingly, *yes, magic; he is not mad; nor are you* – even the ferocious Japanese woman.

'You make magic?' Kitty said. 'With music?'

'There's more to it than that,' chimed in the Indian man with an apologetic tone. 'Hi. I'm Sal. This is Yuka; and Laszlo.'

'The band.' Kitty's tone was flat; unmoved.

'More... *the* band, you know?' said Steve, his expression a little knowing and a little uncertain, like he was sharing an in-joke with her that he only half expected she'd get.

'You say that like it *means* something when I have *no idea* what you're talking about,' Kitty said, annoyed.

'Yes you do,' Steve countered, the confidence of his words undermined by the tremor of an underlying doubt. 'You know what we mean. About music. About the things you can do when you play. When you sing.'

'I'm not allowed to play.' Kitty didn't know who her anger was directed at. She'd start with Steve and work through a list later. She was pretty sure her grandparents were at the top of it.

Steve stared at her. 'You mean, you ain't never done anything like this before?'

'Never.'

His expression changed, reflecting confusion. 'But I thought... You said your name's Carrasco, right? You look a lot like someone I once met. I'd have sworn you... You really ain't never done anything like this before? Never sang and made it rain? Never hit out a drum beat and broke a chair clean in two?'

'I told you. *No.*'

'You ain't actually any relation to Pablo Carrasco, are you? Or Bridget McNair?' Steve was frustrated and puzzled in equal measure.

Of everything that had occurred in the last fifteen minutes, this disappointed pronouncement was what derailed Kitty's composure at last.

'What do you know about my parents?' she snapped. 'What happened to them? They didn't die in a car accident, did they? What Grandma said, I *knew*, I just *knew* it. Why did she lie? What-?' Kitty inhaled sharply in on the torrent of questions.

Steve regarded her with round, shocked eyes. 'Oh hell. Oh my lord. It really is you. We all thought you were dead. Nobody could find you, after. Rodrigo swore none of the blood was yours, but we couldn't find you, and then we had to get the hell out of Chile. Jeez, kid, I'm sorry, I'm so sorry. We-'

Kitty, eyes scrunched shut, face tilted away from the flood of nonsensical words, held her hands in front her face. 'Stop, stop, *stop*!' She took a deep, shuddering breath, and a second, which she held, before exhaling slowly. She opened her eyes again to see Steve and all the others, staring.

'I n-need… I. I need you to slow down.' Her eyes darted to Maddie, to the other bodies. 'I need to fix these people before Trudy gets back. And then I need you to tell me *everything*. But *slowly*.'

'Who's Trudy?' asked Laszlo.

'One of my bosses. She'll-. I don't know what she'll think. I don't know what to tell her.'

Steve became all business. He jerked his head at Yuka and Sal, and they immediately marched off together to the disarrayed bodies in the embalming area. Kitty made to protest, but she saw how the two strangers were with poor George: gentle and respectful as they straightened his limbs on the table. She turned to Maddie.

'She's my responsibility. Her family's coming this afternoon.'

'Can we help?'

'No. No. It's all right.' Kitty plucked at the edge of Maddie's summer frock, tried to tuck it under her. She'd need to lift Maddie to rearrange the dress. 'On the other hand, yes.'

With the gentlest care, Steve put his hands under the dead girl's shoulders and raised her, so that Kitty could tuck the ends of the dress away, then lowered her again. Steve brushed a strand of limp hair from Maddie's forehead. 'Poor kid.'

Yuka and Sal returned. Kitty could see that the other bodies had been set to rights.

'I'll fix Maddie, then meet you at the Richmond Club Hotel on Swan Street,' she said.

Kitty finally felt in control again. It settled her and, being settled, she could see that Steve, Yuka and Sal were shocked and sad, hopeful and afraid, all at once.

Laszlo and Aaron were mainly confused and distressed to unequal degrees, clearly as ignorant about some things as she was. Calm descended on her. She knew how to deal with distress.

'It'll all be fine,' she told them, even believing it herself as she placed a gentle hand first on Laszlo's shoulder, then Aaron's wrist. 'They'll tell us what's going on. Won't you?'

Steve nodded. 'Yes. We will. I promise.'

Almost an hour later, Kitty Carrasco walked into the Richmond Club Hotel and found her strange new friends – she felt quite sure they meant to be friends – huddled around a table at the furthest point from the door. Kitty bought a glass of cider before joining them.

She slid into the booth next to Steve and fiddled with a spare coaster before laying it flat on the table and lifting her glass for a sip.

'Everything okay?' Steve asked.

'Maddie's ready for her family to say goodbye,' Kitty said evenly. 'I've told Trudy that I need more time off after all. I don't think she noticed anything strange.'

'Most people pretend not to see, if they can,' asserted Yuka darkly.

Kitty could tell that history was there, but she wasn't here for other people's stories. She was here for her own.

'Tell me about my parents,' she said.

'What do you already know?'

'Dad was born in Chile. He and my grandparents escaped Pinochet and migrated here. He met mum at an art school in Spain. She was Scottish. They came back here and had me.'

'Your mother is descended in a direct line from The Piper,' Steve said.

'You're still talking like I already know the story,' Kitty said.

'Sorry. But how far back do I go? If I want to explain Pablo and Bridget and the Piper, I gotta tell you about the band first, what we are and what we do.'

'Start there, then,' Kitty took another sip of cider. 'What's the Minstrel Tongue?'

'It's a kind of gift,' Steve said. 'Of the gift-and-curse variety. Ms Carrasco, there are dark things in the world. Things that humans and the universe make between 'em. Dark thoughts and dark deeds made manifest, as it were. It ain't always clear where they come from, let alone where they go. But they exist. That's a stone cold fact. So it seems nature or god or whatever you want to name things, it doesn't like imbalance. If there are energies to make things to hurt the world, then the balance says there's gotta be things to heal it too. You know how it is. Some plants that are poison grow right near the antidotes.'

'I read that once.'

'Well, that's us. The band here, and Aaron, and you and me, we're the antidote the universe grows so that the poison won't spread. We're what stops the brambles taking over. We're the energy that's meant to make it right when the things that are ugly in their soul try to hurt the world. It's not war or nothin', and there isn't any winning. Not in a once-and-for-all way.'

'More like gardeners?' suggested Kitty.

'Yeah, that's good. We're the world's gardeners, and even the ugly plants have their place, see, but sometimes they get out of hand. Sometimes they try to choke out all the good plants too, and we have to weed. We have to keep the balance. So the universe gave us a way to talk to the dark stuff grown wild. It gave us music, and songs to help us shape a way to talk to the elements. It didn't make many of us with that elemental magic inside, but enough. The magic gets out through music and we keep the balance with that.'

'And that's the Minstrel Tongue?'

'That's what we call it. Different parts of the world have different names for the people who do this. Our band ain't the only one, though it ain't like there's hundreds either. I know of two groups in the Americas, one in all of Africa. A few more around Asia and some Island folk in the Pacific. There used to be a band in Russia, till Stalin, I hear. Some people, they have the Minstrel Tongue but for one reason or another, they ain't with a group. They maybe help us out from time to time. It's not a life for everyone, what we do.'

'Was it the life for my parents?'

'It wasn't meant to be. I met Bridget once, before she lit out for Spain. Nobody here was in the band at the time. After Anna...' He cleared his throat before going on. 'When Anna died in '88, Rodrigo Lopez became the leader, called us Dragonsbane. We sheltered for a time with your uncle Finlay, The Piper, just as Bridget was quittin' for a new life.'

'Was he a- a Minstrel too?'

'He still is.'

'And my Dad?'

'Not as far as we know. Maybe he carried it from generations back. The Minstrel Tongue has a way of going dormant, sometimes for generations, unless darkness is spreading. It gets woken when it's needed. We think that's what happened to him, when the time came to save you from the Coco.'

'I know about the Coco,' Kitty said with a shudder. 'Grandma and Grandad used to tell me all the time. "Be good or the Coco will eat you".'

The whole table leaned closer to hear. All of them except Steve were too young to have been there, Kitty realised.

'Tell me,' Kitty said impatiently. 'From the start.'

CHAPTER TWELVE

'You're leaving.' Finlay's tone was flat and disapproving.

'I'm going to Spain, nae the moon,' replied his sister Bridget patiently. 'I'll write.'

'I need ye here. The band needs you.'

'You dinnae need me, Fin. You have minstrels enough in your wee army.'

'They're not all my minstrels.'

'No, some of them are strays, like that poor huddle of musicians that just left.'

'Are you saying I shouldnae let them heal their hurts here?'

'Some of those hurts won't ever heal, Fin. D'ye think Borman's ever going to be healed, wi' what that dragon took frae him? That's not the life I want.'

'So you're abandoning us for Art School.' Said like it rhymed with turd.

'Aye, and ye can quit your girning about it, Finlay Douglas McNair. I'm nae the Piper; you are. You're the one wants to make Granda proud with song magic. I want other things.'

'Music magic's in yer blood, Brid. The McNairs have been Pipers for centuries.'

'The magic is thinner in my blood than yours, brother, and I'll not be made a prisoner to it. I want to see more than this town. I want to do more with my life. Whatever magic I have, it's mine to do with as I will.'

Finlay scowled at her. 'I may be your little brother, but I'm the head of the family.'

'Joy to ye then, ye wee scunner,' she said, brutally lacking in due respect for the patriarch. 'Be the grand auld man, like Granda, wi' yer piping and yer Minstrel Tongue. He broke Nan's heart with all he gave to it, but that life's nae for me nor ever will be.'

'Awa' wi' you then,' scowled Finlay.

'Oh, I will be.'

Finlay couldn't resist the last word, though, shouting after Bridget as she left, 'What's for ye'll no go past ye.'

Later, when Fate had its way, Bridget never had time to ponder whether that was a prediction or a curse.

CHILE 1992

Bridget McNair of Inverness met Pablo Carrasco of Melbourne in a fine arts class at Madrid's *Universidad Complutense*. Within a week they were inseparable. Within a year they were married. Within two they had a daughter. In their third year together, Australian-born Pablo took Bridget and the baby to visit his extended family at their farm in a village outside Valdivia, in the north of Chile.

When the little family drove into the village, Bridget was preoccupied with singing her fractious infant peaceable again, so it took her a while to notice the oddness outside the car doors.

'Strange,' murmured Pablo.

'What?' She attempted to tickle little Catalina with a squishy toy wombat. Little Kitty sneezed and glared, affronted, at the toy.

'No kids anywhere. When Mum and Dad brought me here as a boy, there were always kids around. Not a peep today.'

'Maybe they're all at school?'

'It's half past three in the afternoon. They should be home by now.'

Bridget dragged her eyes away from Kitty to see what Pablo saw – a ball here, a bicycle there, a doll huddled by the roadside, an abandoned blue and glittery shoe – but not a single child.

The few adults in the village, however, walked with dragging feet and bowed shoulders. Those adults raised their heads and glared dully at the car.

Pablo wound down the window, and foul air roiled into the air-conditioned interior. It smelled of rotted meat; it tasted dark and oily, like slime in the throat.

'Hola,' Pablo greeted them. 'I'm looking for the Carrasco farm. This way, isn't it?' When the reply was dumb silence, he tried again in the stilted Chilean Spanish he'd only poorly learned from his parents.

The man Pablo had asked pointed the way, then scowled as he saw the baby in her bassinet strapped into the back of the car. 'You should leave while you can,' the man said in his own tongue. 'Before the Coco comes for her.'

'Right. Ah. Gracias.'

The man glowered at him. 'None are left for the Coco, except for this one. You should leave.'

'After I've seen Vicente,' Pablo said easily, not willing to engage in conversation with someone so surly, and when the atmosphere felt so tainted. 'Chao!'

Finlay McNair tried to rise from his bed when he got Bridget's urgent, frightened message, but the thigh fractured by the Loch Linnhe kelpie wouldn't let him stand, let alone sustain him as far as Valdivia. He called Rodrigo Lopez of Dragonsbane instead.

Steve Borman took the call. 'We got business in Texas. We can git goin' tomorrow.'

'Soon as ye can,' Finlay said. 'Somethin' rank's afoot wi' their bairn, and with this leg I cannae get there tae help.'

'They got a kid? We'll leave today.'

Rodrigo, Steve, Marta and Letitia found Pablo, Bridget and Catalina in a hut on the edge of the abandoned Carrasco farm.

'It's the Coco,' Pablo told them, grey with exhaustion when he finally believed who they were and let them in. 'I thought it was only a story my parents told me to frighten me into good behaviour. But it's real. Oh my god, it's real.'

'A lot of things are real,' Rodrigo said calmly. 'But we're real too, and we'll take this Coco down. Tell me what you know.'

Pablo and Bridget between them unravelled the story that had begun a week before their ill-timed arrival in Chile.

A farm worker's son was teasing the dogs when the Coco came. Felipe wasn't a nice little boy – always bullying and thieving, fighting and arguing, even with his elders. A rascally charm and his affection for his auntie suggested he might not be irredeemable, but his potential would never be realised.

Someone had summoned the Coco to punish a naughty child.

That Coco ate little Felipe, quick as a flash, a bite and a gulp, in front of his screaming playmates. Parents come running and then they screamed, because the Coco, excited at being called for the first time in a century, was hungry. With a bite and a gulp, snap, snap, two more naughty-ish children disappeared into its maw.

The papas drove it back with shotguns and fire. The mamas gathered their babies to them and Old Lady Matilde piled them into her apple truck and drove them all the way to Valdivia and safety, until the village could learn how to banish the Coco.

The Coco didn't want to go. Its taste for children had been reawakened and it was reluctant to leave without one more bite.

And here were the Carrasco family on a surprise visit, with their sweet, chubby baby girl. What a morsel! Naturally, the hell-damned thing tried to eat her.

'I fought it,' Bridget told the members of Dragonsbane, not so much proud as amazed. 'I sang us free of it while Pablo brought the car around. We drove away while I sang and sang and sang at it. The Coco bit rear lights off the car and I kept on singing. Another bite and it would have smashed us completely.'

If Pablo was grey with exhaustion, then Bridget was almost translucent with it. Her flesh seemed shrunken on her bones, her skin loose. Catalina, their wee Kitty, was crying. Bridget struggled to find the strength to lift her for feeding.

'We only escaped because of Pablo,' Bridget said. She smiled proudly at her husband. 'He saved us. He sang.'

Pablo was shell-shocked with his sudden and timely manifestation of the Minstrel Tongue. 'They say my great grandfather had a way with a quena flute, that he could make it rain,' he said in wonder. 'I thought it was just a story.'

Pablo had sung up a dust storm to envelope the Coco and they'd fled, only to have the car run out of gas. Bridget was able to get one message to Finlay on the farm phone, but they could feel the Coco coming. They hid in the storage hut behind the fruit crates.

Pablo and Bridget sang soft hiding songs, but for long and sleepless hours, they could hear the Coco snuffling around the orchards and fields, hunting them.

The arrival of the band was a help, but also a danger. The Coco had heard them. The Coco was coming.

'Take our car,' urged Rodrigo, pushing the keys into Pablo's hand.

'Won't it attack you?'

'We can handle a Coco.'

'Like you handled the dragon?' Bridget didn't mean to be cruel, but she was terrified.

'We're called Dragonsbane now,' Steve said darkly. 'The dragon paid. So get outta here so we can protect y'all instead of avenging you.'

Bridget meant to apologise to him, but Pablo hustled her and their daughter out to the band's car before she could.

Letitia had her fiddle, Rodrigo, a drummer, plucked the castanets from his pocket. Steve and Marta had taken their guitars from the car.

Marta, who always liked the direct approach, chose to sling her guitar on her back and use only her voice. She picked up a pitchfork and marched out to meet the monster, which was strong on the blood of children. It changed its shape as they watched, from a hulking fanged ape-monster to an armadillo with spines down its back, forming scales and a forked tongue.

Dragonsbane began with the old Chilean lullaby, an everyday magic that kept El Coco at bay.

Leave Coca. Leave Coca
Go to the top of the roof
Let the child have
A quiet sleep

The Coco ceased to lumber after the departing car and opened its foul mouth, ready to bite and gulp at the musicians who stood between it and the fleeing morsel.

Dragonsbane was startled to find a fifth voice join with theirs. The newcomer changed the song.

Great Coca, El Coca
Leave the children alone
I am the one who called you
To teach that brat a lesson

The Coco was not the least bit affected by his song.

'Who the hell are you?' demanded Rodrigo as the old man stumbled among them, face stained with tears.

'Luis Garrido,' trembled the old man. 'I'm so sorry, so sorry! I didn't know what I was doing when I called the Coco. I thought it was a myth. I was only trying to frighten the boy.'

Another voice then joined those still singing – tremulous with age yet powerful.

'My wife, Carla,' choked out Luis. 'She is Pablo's great aunt. She promises we can save the baby.'

Senora Garrido clearly had the Minstrel Tongue and she had it rare.

The Minstrel Tongue usually manifested with affinity for one or more of six of the elements: Fire, Water, Air, Wood, Metal, and Stone. The rare seventh element, known erroneously as Aether or Spirit, was the magic that worked on living flesh and bone.

Senora Carla Garrido commanded flesh magic. She'd kept her gift deeply secret all her life. Her neighbours were more frightened of her power than were helped by it.

'How did you summon the Coco?' she demanded of her husband.

'When you pricked your thumb pruning the trees,' said the crying old man. 'I used a drop of your blood. I only wanted a day's peace and quiet from Felipe's nonsense.'

'We'll have to make amends,' Senora Garrido said gruffly.

'Yes,' her husband replied, head bowed. 'Do what you must.'

'I'll sing a song to undo El Coco,' Senora Garrido said to Dragonsbane. 'You take care of my great nephew and his family.'

She began to sing even before they could regroup and retreat. Senora Garrido took her husband's offered hands and she sang a spell into his wrinkled old body until that old flesh looked ripe and full and young. She sang his bones to a memory of themselves; she sang hair onto his head and his old mans' wavering croak to a boy's piping.

She couldn't sing his soul young, but it was hidden inside a body young enough to fool the greedy Coco.

'I'll make you a deal,' she cried out to the Coco. 'This young man for the life of the baby. What do you say?'

The Coco wasn't stupid, but it *was* greedy. It had seen the old lady making Luis Garrido a child again, but the Coco thought that was fine. It thought that magic made the young flesh potent, which it did, but not in the way the Coco was thinking.

'It's a deal, sure,' croak-hissed El Coco, but it was thinking, 'sure, I'll eat the magic in that one and still get that baby.'

The Coco ate Luis, who raised his arms and accepted his fate. El Coco, the stupid hell-thing, didn't reckon on the power that sacrifice holds, even sacrifice from the one who called it. Old Senor Garrido was full of his own sacrifice, and his wife's too, because she was too old to do that kind of magic without paying. She died when her husband did, and the double sacrifice wrapped around an old soul that couldn't be digested by the Coco sent the monster howling into a void.

One minute, Dragonsbane were witnessing the destruction of the Coco, and the next moment, utter silence.

'Let's go tell Bridget they're safe,' Rodrigo said quietly into uncanny hush, and the band set off on foot to find their car.

They found it, smashed to pieces, front end bent to a ruinous V around a tree.

Pablo Carrasco's body was behind the wheel. The crash hadn't killed him; that was the work of a row of bullet holes that extended through the car doors to his shoulder, chest, head. The strafing had caused the crash.

Marta found Bridget half a mile away, shot in the head. She was curled protectively around a hollow baby-sized space. Of Catalina Carrasco there was no sign.

Bridget McNair was not alone in death. Beside her were three men from the same little Valdivian village. They had knives and rifles in their hands, but they had each been shot – head and chest – so quickly they'd had no time to defend themselves.

Steve was speechless with horror. Letitia was the one who suggested that the villagers were the ones to murder the Carrascos.

'Maybe they thought if they gave the baby to El Coco, it would save their own children.'

'Cowards,' snarled Steve, as though he'd like to kill them all over again.

'Where's the baby, though?' asked practical Marta.

The earth was soaked in blood, but none of it, Rodrigo swore after he'd sung to the earth, belonged to the infant.

'Well, she didn't crawl away,' Marta said.

'Someone took her,' Steve said, finding tyre tracks further from the scene.

'Someone else wanting to offer her to the Coco?' Letitia asked.

But search as they might, Dragonsbane never found Catalina Carrasco anywhere in Chile, and they never saw that Coco again.

Chapter Thirteen

'My grandparents *shot* three people?'

Steve wondered if this was the right part of the story for Kitty to cling to, though so much of it was terrible and strange that he supposed the girl had to start somewhere.

'It seems to me that your grandparents did what they had to do, to save and protect you. Their son and daughter-in-law had already been murdered by these men who wanted to feed their granddaughter to a monster.'

'Why were Grandpa and Grandma even there?'

'I think Pablo must have called them after Bridget got in touch with Finlay. Your grandparents must have flown in from Melbourne and been on their way to the village when they encountered your mother's murderers. There's no doubt they're the ones who rescued you and took you to safety, because you've been here ever since, haven't you?'

'But the Coco was killed. I've been safe from it all this time.'

'They didn't know that.' Steve's tone was gentle.

'Right.' Kitty swallowed the tumult of her heart down. *Grandma and Grandpa killed people to protect me. They lied to me to keep me safe.*

I felt so trapped, and now I'm free, but I don't feel free.

Kitty had a whole life to see in a completely different light and it was too much to swallow all at once. And that bombshell was only half of the puzzle.

'If the Coco is gone, what was that today?'

'Unrelated,' Yuka said in her sharp fashion. Yuka continued, the words reconciliatory even if the tone wasn't. 'The dead have stirred three times since we arrived in Melbourne. At the markets, by the railway and with you. The railway dead woke the dead near you. Drawn by your power, perhaps, but you are not what woke them.'

Kitty liked Yuka's straightforward style. She might be blunt, but she got to the point a lot faster than Steve did.

'What woke them?'

'I do not know.'

'We need to find out soon,' Sal said worriedly. 'If it's going to be a zombie outbreak-'

'They ain't zombies, rightly speaking,' countered Steve. 'I mean, actual bodies, sitting up, that's serious territory, but zombies aren't usually laid back down so easy.'

Kitty considered questioning the 'easy' portion of that statement, but truly, it hadn't felt difficult.

'Besides, zombies usually have hunger in 'em, and bitterness. Zombie magic makes for resentment against the living, and I ain't feeling the rage.'

'I do not detect malice in these ones,' agreed Yuka.

Kitty was thoughtful. 'Maddie and the others didn't have any particular emotion. They acted like they were looking for something. They didn't mean anything by it. No more than a CCTV camera does, anyway.'

'The dead don't get restless for no reason,' Sal said. 'We've got to find out what's setting them off.'

'Oh, hell.' Aaron gulped his beer and wiped his mouth on the back of his hand.

Steve cast the young man a wry glance. 'Are you having second thoughts about joining the band?'

'Well up on eighth and ninth thoughts by now.'

'And yet, you're here.'

Laszlo laughed unexpectedly into the tension. 'I fought vampires with a melody on an old violin, no magic of my own at all. I pissed myself I was so frightened. I'm on hundredth thoughts, and I'm still here. Do you know why?'

Despite everything Aaron had seen and heard in the last few

hours, his pulse was racing with excitement, thrumming with adrenalin even as he kept his breathing even. Aaron knew why he and Laszlo were here. He couldn't articulate it yet, but he knew, and it showed in a tilted, self-deprecating smile.

'I thought you might.' Laszlo raised his glass in a salute and drained the last of it in a single swallow.

An irritating, almost universal chime interrupted the moment.

Steve frowned at the unknown number, clearly originating outside Australia. He answered the call.

All the colour drained from Steve's face.

He impulsively – almost involuntarily – threw the phone down. It clattered to the table and in the circle of silence, everyone in the booth heard an odd laugh: loud and sharp and suddenly gone.

'Sal.' Steve's expression went from shock to fury. 'What have you done?'

Sal's phone rang. Sal pulled it from his pocket and stared at the number, swallowing hard. He began to shake.

'Don't answer it,' Steve snarled.

But it was too late. Sal lifted the phone, thumbing the answer key as he did, and pressed the phone to his ear. Eyes huge and round and stricken, he listened, and he made no attempt to stop the tears that fell in a great flood from his eyes, as though a tap had been turned on.

Kitty reached out to him, her instinct to comfort kicking in, despite the fierce rage in Steve's face; the dawning realisation in Yuka's.

Even with the speaker pressed hard to Sal's skin, everyone could hear a muffled, rhythmic sound. Like a chant. Like a song.

'I. I, I,' Sal tried to speak into the phone. 'P-p-please. No. I. I…'

'Who is it?' muttered Laszlo, but the expression on his face showed that he was afraid he knew exactly who it was.

Steve reached out and pried the phone ungently from Sal's curled, tense fingers. Hand trembling, he placed the phone on the table and put the call on speaker. A cold voice sang, unaccompanied, down the line.

And we have no home
But the places we stay

While the man sang, Kitty and Aaron watched this little group, this band, shatter to pieces.

'No,' breathed Laszlo. 'No, you said-'

'How could you do this?' Yuka had risen from her chair, her tiny body looming over Sal, her hands clenched into tight fists that she might use at any moment. '*How could you?*'

And the cold voice kept on singing.

Anchored awhile
And we sleep where we may

'I didn't- I couldn't- I.' Sal closed his eyes but the tears wouldn't stop. He ground his fists against his forehead, as though that would help. 'It was *Alex*. Don't you understand?'

Laszlo was shaking his head. 'But he's dead. They're dead. We burned down the whole factory. Sal, you said you killed Alex before he could rise. You said. You *said.*'

The song held a lilt of cruel humour as the singer listened to the chaos unfold.

Our burdens are heavy
And the light is grey

'You said you dealt with Alex,' Steve snarled at Sal. 'You said it was done. You should have got me. You should have got Yuka. Hell, Sal, you should have got Laszlo if you couldn't do it yourself.'

When the end comes my home
Is wherever you bury my heart

A sob broke free from Sal's chest. 'No. I couldn't. I couldn't. I couldn't. Alex begged me and I couldn't. I loved him and I couldn't.'

'That was the *vampire* in him begging you, not *Alex*; our Alex.'

'You don't understand.'

My voice is my armour,
Blade and shield

Steve lurched out of his seat, hands closing around Sal's wrists to drag the fisted hands down, so that he could glare into Sal's face. Sal kept his eyes screwed shut.

'Don't you *dare* tell me I don't understand, Salvatore D'Souza. I have said goodbye and buried people I have loved for over 40 years...'

These words, these tones
Are a weapon I wield

'But you never had to kill one of them, did you?' Sal snapped back, eyes flying open at last. 'You didn't have to murder them, did you?'

'You don't know what I've had to do,' snarled Steve.

They herald our war
Lament what we've lost

'Alex, stop it! *Stop singing.* **Stop.**' Yuka shrieked, but Alex continued to the end of the verse.

And they give comfort
When we count the cost

Then Alex laughed. 'I have someone here with me. Kurt, say hello.'

'Hello,' said another familiar and horrifying voice.

Yuka spoke into the terrified silence. Her tone was even, bland, but the tendons of her neck were standing out, betraying the effort it took. 'Kurt. Alex. You are frightening everyone. You shouldn't do that. We are your friends. We love you.'

'Hello Yuka,' Alex said, his chilly tone made uglier with amusement. 'We were friends, I know, but haven't you heard? Friends don't let friends get made into vampires. When they took me, you should have known Kurt was the one who made me. But you didn't know, or you didn't want to know, and then Sal couldn't bear to finish it, could you pet?' Sal flinched. 'And see where love gets you?'

Steve leaned over the phone, his jaw clenched hard. 'You're right, kid. We should have done better by you both. We should have made sure you were gone, Kurt. I should have seen to you properly, Alex. I know how much Sal loved you, how hard he'd find it, but he said he wanted to be the one.' Steve's glare at Sal was unforgiving. When he turned back to the speaker, though, his expression was more complex. Sorrow, weariness, loss, guilt and despair vied for room on his lined face. 'I'm sorry,' he said to Alex.

'Too late for sorry,' Kurt said. 'We are what we are and you owe us for that.'

The myriad expressions were chased away when Steve scowled. 'Ain't nothing we can do for you, Kurt. We did wrong by you, and I'm sorry. We loved you, but you're dead. Undead. And we're not in Europe any more. How you gonna find us to hurt us?'

'We have ways to find you, even in a land down under, and you have something that belongs to us.'

Kurt began to sing. Alex harmonised, but the lullaby was grave-cold, death-rotten.

Heave a sigh, baby girl,
Don't you cry, baby girl
Your daddies are guarding the door

Finally, even Yuka's cloak of calm and rage cracked right in two. Eyes wide, burning and broken with bright tears, she shook her head in little jerks, saying 'no, no, no' in Japanese, a chant that she knew could not protect them.

Laugh out loud, baby girl
Be strong and proud, baby girl
Keeping you safe is what your daddies are for

'Get our baby Gretel ready for her Daddies,' said Alex. 'See you in Melbourne soon.'

The line went dead.

There was no sound among the people in the booth, until Sal began to moan, as what he'd done, and what it meant, finally came home to him.

CHAPTER FOURTEEN

Laszlo was the first to recover his wits.

'We have to warn Harper,' he said to Steve with fearful urgency. 'Are they safe in London?'

Steve's expression kept shifting. Determination. Fear. Guilt. Defiance. 'Harper and Gretel ain't in London.'

'But you told her to take Gretel there.'

'I changed my mind. Vladimir had turned Kurt before we got to the nest. He might've made Kurt tell him about Gretel, and he was a vengeful asshole with a sick sense of humour. If Vladimir knew Gretel existed, he mighta sent someone after her, just because he could. Soon as we were done burning the nest, I told Harper to leave London but not go to the States either.'

'Where are they?' Yuka demanded to know.

'Here in Melbourne.'

'*What?*'

Steve rounded on his bandmate in a fury. 'You think you're the only one who can organise things, Yuka? You think you're the only one who makes plans? Harper can babysit, but she can't be a mom to Gretel. She's got university and her own life to get on with, and I ain't stealing that off her, even if she was willing. There's others who care. I've been fixing things.'

'*Fixing* things?'

'Gretel needs a *family*. She needs people who are stable and safe, and can take care of her. That ain't us.'

'Of course not,' snapped Yuka, 'but who else is?'

'Angus and Taylor,' Steve said defiantly.

'Your nephew and his husband? Can they keep Gretel safe?'

'Yes. And they can love her like her Dads would've wanted.'

'Your nephew is an unemployed arts graduate.'

'Angus is a mighty successful freelance costume designer and Taylor is an IT consultant,' snarled Steve. 'They can take care of her. What's more, they *want* to. They *want* that little girl, unlike *some* people who were meant to be her fathers' *friend*.'

Steve and Yuka glared at each other. Laszlo looked stricken.

Sal, who had pulled his notebook out and scrabbled through the pages, searching desperately for something to salve his pain, was muttering to himself from the book's contents. They heard snatches of languages, among them the Buddhist phrase 'purity and impurity depend on oneself; no one can purify another'.

Aaron cast a helpless look at Kitty.

Kitty was sick to the back teeth of life just *happening* to her.

'You said Harper and Gretel are in Melbourne,' Kitty said briskly. 'Where's Angus, if he's taking her?'

'On his way,' Steve said immediately. 'He and Taylor emailed me this morning before they got on the plane. They land here tomorrow.'

'And your friends – Alex and Kurt. How do they know you're in Melbourne?'

'No idea. It makes no sense. We thought they were *dead*, so we lit out of there fast as we could. We drove over the Tatra Mountains to Poland, and swapped the old van for a new one and drove to Berlin, and we freighted Yuka's drum kit over here, and we sang customs blind to our trunk and got it on board and we got a flight with six different connections to get here. We made our track muddy with song magic and sheer bloody mindedness and came to the ass end of the world to fetch a little peace and try to mend what got broken in us in Budapest, and *they still found us*.'

Steve stopped suddenly, the torrent of panicked words halted by Kitty's gentle hand on his arm. He stared at her fingers on his skin; then into her calm, serious eyes.

'Damned if I know how they managed it,' he said.

'That's not the important thing right now.'

'No,' he agreed. 'It ain't.'

Kitty was thinking of Gretel, suddenly orphaned through violence and magic – exactly like she had been. Kitty knew she was going to help, for Gretel's sake, and somehow, for her own as well.

'We will have to leave the hostel,' Yuka said grimly. 'We have checked in under our names. If Alex has agents here, it is more likely he and Kurt will find us.'

'I have plenty of room at my house,' offered Kitty.

'You serious?' Steve was both hopeful and dubious.

'I am. We'll get your stuff and you can come around.'

'What about the show?' Laszlo asked, hollow with shock.

'The show?' Aaron asked.

'Saturday's gig,' Steve said. 'Our name's up on the board already.'

'You'll have to cancel,' Aaron said.

'Can't,' Steve said shakily. 'We gotta play.'

Aaron was astonished. 'You really intend to play a gig with all this going on?'

Steve dragged up a rueful smile. 'Gotta get paid, kid. Saving the world pays very badly.'

'You're still making this offer to join your band look really shit,' Aaron scowled.

Yuka's own expression darkened further. 'Steve thinks he is funny. We must play, but not for the money. We have money.'

'Yeah. Scads of cash. Just rollin' in it.' Steve sounded weary.

'We have enough,' Yuka said coldly. 'What we need is *reiki*.' At Kitty's bemused expression, she continued: 'Qi. Prana. Ruah. *Life energy*.'

'The Force,' explained Steve with a shade of his old humour.

Aaron nodded sagely. 'You kind of recharge your magic batteries with the audience, huh?'

'If they don't boo us off the stage,' Laszlo said glumly. 'There are only four of us now, and we have had no time to rehearse properly.'

'Four of us and those two.' Steve indicated Aaron and Kitty.

'Minus one.' Aaron nodded at Sal.

Sal was still trembling, mutely ignoring the entire exchange. He looked like he would never speak again.

For the first time since the phone call, Steve's expression softened. 'Maybe.' He returned his gaze to Aaron. 'Does that mean you're in?'

'Sure,' Aaron shrugged, a little manic. 'Why not? I've been rained on by magic rain, seen zombies, and heard a creepy vampire calling about his missing daughter. Four days to learn a whole set for a completely new band is the least of my worries, eh?'

'How about you?' said Steve to Kitty. 'You with us?'

Kitty didn't know the first thing about being in a band. For that matter, she didn't know the first thing about fighting vampires. Or singing the undead back to sleep. But the latter she'd managed without too much bother and the band thing was, apparently, in her blood.

As for the other – she was the daughter of magic musicians who had escaped from a baby-eating monster; the granddaughter of two people who had killed to save her from the cowards who murdered her parents. She would, she decided grimly, learn how to fight vampires.

If this band needed to sing to power up and protect an orphan girl from the undead, Kitty was damned well going to help them. So what if she'd never even played an actual instrument. She could sing; she could do that much.

'I'm with you.'

Laszlo was less convinced. 'Four days for two new people to learn the songs? Are you mad?'

'It'll be fine,' Steve waved his hand dismissively. 'It's always fine. The magic makes it fine. Doesn't it Yuka?'

Their fight was momentarily forgotten. 'The magic has its own agenda,' she agreed.

'Cool,' Aaron said, edgy and excited and, by the way, terrified. 'The gig's sorted, the magic's got the agenda sorted. I guess you need a van to move all your gear. I've got the van; Ms Carrasco has an address. Let's get this fucked-up show on the road.'

Aaron, armed with Kitty's Parkville address, went with Yuka and Laszlo to clear out the youth hostel. Kitty took the silent Sal by the elbow. 'I'll look after him,' she said, daring anyone to protest. 'See you at my place.'

Steve, turning his back on Yuka's steely glare, went to collect Harper and Gretel.

The band had precious little luggage: a rucksack each with changes of clothes and a few personal items, their instruments and the small trunk they had magicked past customs. In the passenger seat, Laszlo directed Aaron towards Kitty's home with the aid of a directory. In the back, Yuka sat on the trunk and fiddled with her jewellery, rubbing her thumb over and over the instrument fragments sewn into leather at her wrist, and the splinters of white and black keys she had strung onto guitar wire and hung around her neck.

As they came to the intersection, Aaron spotted Kitty waving on the corner. He slowed the van and, at her gesturing, passed the tram shelter and some bright graffiti painted on her outside fence, before steering the van into a small garage at the rear of her property.

Kitty ducked into the space behind the van and wrestled the rusted roller door down. Laszlo came around to help.

'I had so much trouble getting it up and now it's stuck,' she said apologetically as they struggled with it. 'I don't use it much. No car.'

With a squeal of metal, they managed to close the door. Between the four of them, they carried the rucksacks and trunk through the back door into Kitty's house and into her grandparent's old room.

Kitty withdrew to the kitchen to put on the kettle and gaze through the window at the graveyard opposite.

'Doesn't it give you the creeps?'

Aaron was side-eyeing the rows of headstones rising behind the cemetery fence.

'Why should it?'

'All those dead people.'

'There's nothing wrong with dead people,' she said. 'The dead are just empty houses. They're not usually scary.'

Aaron huffed a dry laugh. '*Not usually*. Our whole framework for talking about the world's changed, hasn't it?' He folded his arms and looked into Kitty's lounge room. Laszlo was studying framed photographs on a sideboard, doubtless realising that these were Kitty's parents and grandparents, whose terrible story belied the mundane facsimiles trapped inside glass and wood.

'The world changed for us today,' Kitty said. *Second time for me*, she realised.

'For him too,' Aaron replied quietly, nodding at Sal.

Sal had settled onto Kitty's sofa in a miserable stillness. Yuka was inspecting him with an angry frown. Whatever she concluded, she sat beside her bandmate, radiating a ferocious protectiveness that couldn't have been comforting. She placed one small, callused hand over his and his fingers twitched, but that was all.

The kettle boiled and Kitty made a plunger of coffee and a pot of tea, carrying them both into the lounge room on a tray with cups, sugar, milk. Yuka poured a small cup of tea for Sal and held it under his nose. When he didn't move, she wrapped his hands around the warm crockery. 'Drink, Salvatore,' she said, gentle despite her expression.

He drank.

For a short while, the room was filled with the quiet, civilised sounds of liquids being poured, the faint crunch of sugar granules scooped into cups, spoons clanking on the sides of ceramic.

Laszlo, perched on the edge of an armchair, nodded at the large boxes propped against a bookshelf. A receipt was sticky-taped to the top of one, which evidently held a new keyboard. The other contained a stand. 'You bought those on the way back here,' he said.

Kitty nodded. 'I've been wanting it for ages, but I thought it best to actually buy it today, with the gig coming up.'

'Your old one is fine,' Yuka said.

Kitty hesitated before replying. 'It doesn't work properly.'

'We should start,' Laszlo said after a sip of coffee. 'There's a lot for you two to learn.'

Yuka squeezed Sal's unresponsive hand. 'You have the playlist?' she asked Laszlo.

'Yes.'

'Magic songs?' asked Aaron. 'Like the rain song Steve played for me?'

'No,' Yuka said. 'Songs like that are *weapons*.'

'For audiences, our songs are just songs,' Steve explained. 'Our voices and instruments have magic in 'em but undirected.

'They are not *dangerous*,' Yuka said.

'Good to know,' muttered Aaron.

Laszlo began reading from a notebook in his pocket. 'I have *Reforged, Better Man. Swift. Copper Beaches. Listening.*'

'*Afraid of the Dark.*'

'That is a dark song,' Yuka said.

'It's my song.'

'I'll put it on the list,' Laszlo placated him. 'We'll decide later.'

Sal, satisfied, subsided.

Yuka left Sal's side long enough to burrow through their belongings in the spare room. She returned with the violin for Laszlo and a notebook filled with pages of neatly printed lyrics. She handed the notebook to Aaron and took her place beside Sal again.

Laszlo and Kitty examined the notebook over Aaron's shoulder.

'I know most of these,' Laszlo said. 'I've been studying since we left Budapest. We'll start with the melody, then harmonies. Instruments later. *Copper Beaches* first, I think. Yuka?'

Yuka placed the flat of her hands on the coffee table, ready to slap out a rhythm.

Laszlo tucked the violin under his collarbone, swiped the bow across it a few times to warm up the strings and his fingers, then played a fast, sweeping melody. He began to sing.

A seaside in rain and a hollow in the heart
And sand is a grave for rocks and bone
Smashed up by the tide and time
An ancient stage
Where we'll go with age
And we always go alone

Yuka's rhythm rose underneath it, gifting the bittersweet melody a defiance that made Kitty's heart jump. Yuka joined with Laszlo.

And the sun's going down and it's bleeding into
An ocean to swallow the sorrow down
And the bronze on the water and silver horizon
In the blazing light, I keep my eyes on
The copper that's staining the place where I stand
I'm on firmer ground in this copper sand.

Sal was suddenly sitting straight up, alert, coming in softly at first, but growing stronger.

It's nothing to anyone how old is the earth
It's nothing to the sea that my mother gave birth
And the sun doesn't care if I live or die
But it's such a beautiful sky
And everyone's bleeding and lonely and scared
And the world wouldn't notice if anyone cared
But we do
And we're too small to matter to oceans and skies
And our hearts are too broken to love after lies
But we do
But we do

Another verse, another chorus, and the song ended. Sal's expression was troubled, but he had come back from wherever he'd been hiding.

'You sing with us, this time,' Yuka instructed Aaron and Kitty.

Laszlo began to play the piece again. Aaron and Kitty exchanged dubious looks, but when the lyric began, they each took a breath and… it happened. Having heard it once, the melody and words had taken seat already.

The magic makes it all right, remembered Kitty.

They used the notebook to help with the lyrics, but after two runs they were able to put it aside and focus on the harmonies.

Yuka frowned at the end of that first attempt. She jabbed a finger at Kitty. 'Try the lead. I will sing your harmony.'

Kitty wanted to protest that she was not at all ready to sing lead on a song she'd just learned. She wanted to point out that this was the first time she'd sung in front of living people: she normally only sang at work, to the judgemental dead.

'Sing,' ordered Yuka again.

Kitty, more intimidated by Yuka than her inexperience, decided to try. She sang and ignored the way the others regarded her, as though she was a surprise.

CHAPTER FIFTEEN

By the time Steve Borman knocked on the front door, Kitty and Aaron knew the basics of three songs. Kitty was singing the lead on two of them, to Yuka's guarded satisfaction and Kitty's puzzled pleasure.

Kitty left off singing to open the front door. Steve stood there with a woman, younger than Kitty, holding an infant of almost a year old

'You must be Harper and Gretel,' Kitty said, smiling. Harper's harried expression softened in relief at the warm welcome. 'Come inside, I'll get tea.'

'Iced tea?' Harper asked hopefully, going in ahead of her uncle. Gretel clung to Harper's neck, her fist in her mouth, as she regarded Kitty with concern.

'Uh...' Kitty frowned. 'I could try making it with cold water, I guess.'

Harper threw a slightly desperate look to Steve. 'What is it with this country and all the hot tea?'

Steve followed her in, a small suitcase in one hand and a carry bag of infant paraphernalia in the other. 'Hot tea is how the rest of the world does it, Harper. They think *we're* weird.'

When they reached the lounge room, Yuka dashed up to see them. For all her reserve, her expression on greeting the child was gentle and sweet. 'Hello, Gretel,' Yuka said, waving her fingers slowly at the baby, soft and flowing, like fronds of waterweed. 'You are so big! Our lovely Gretel.'

Lovely Gretel giggled, grabbed Yuka's index finger with her own spit-sticky ones and held tight. Yuka kissed the little fist, pursed her lips and huffed into Gretel's hair to make the baby giggle again.

'Hi Yuka.'

Yuka dragged her eyes away from the baby to Harper. 'Hello. Thank you for looking after her.'

'She's no trouble.' She kissed Gretel's hair. 'I'm just so sorry about Alex and Kurt.' Tears choked her to momentary silence.

'I know.'

Harper opened her eyes wide, trying to dry out the tears. Across the room, Laszlo, who hardly knew her, nodded hello. Sal, whom Harper knew well, stared fearfully at Gretel.

'Sa! Sa! Sa!' cried Gretel happily, letting go of Yuka's finger and stretching out her arms for him.

Sal shrank away. 'I… can't. I might. I might. I might…' His shoulders collided with the bookshelf. 'I don't want to hurt her,' he finally said, almost inaudibly.

'You can't hurt her, Sal,' Steve said.

'I might.' Sal sounded lost and small.

Harper hugged Gretel close, angling her away from Sal's anxious gaze. 'Gretel needs a change, actually. Where could I-?'

'Oh, through there,' Kitty took the bags that Steve had put down and showed Harper into her grandparents' empty bedroom.

'Sal's a mess,' Harper observed as she laid Gretel on the change pad she'd placed on the bed. The baby burbled at her and Harper bent to kiss her nose. 'They're all a mess,' she continued.

'I know,' Kitty said, because of course they were. She'd seen families go to pieces like this before. Cold and quiet and battling among themselves because the fabric of their lives was torn by loss. Perhaps Kitty didn't know much about magic or the terrible danger that had brought them here, but she knew all the manifestations of grief.

'They'll keep her safe, though, won't they?' Harper had removed the wet nappy and was cleaning Gretel's soft skin. Gretel kicked her legs and grabbed one foot, which she promptly hauled up to her mouth so she could gnaw at her toes.

'They will,' Kitty said. 'We all will.' She stretched out a finger to stroke the back of Gretel's free hand. Gretel gave her an uncertain look.

'Dadda,' she said. 'Pappa. Dadda, Pappa.'

'Your daddies aren't here, sweetie.' Harper tried unsuccessfully to hide her distress.

Gretel's little mouth twisted unhappily. 'Dadda. Pappa.'

Harper fastened the clean nappy and scooped the baby into her arms, as much for her own comfort as the child's. 'Your daddies love you, Gretel,' she said. 'They love you and they won't hurt you. I promise. We promise.'

Gretel didn't understand the problem or the promise, but she began to cry anyway.

Gretel doesn't know she's an orphan yet, thought Kitty. Well, as a kid it hadn't occurred to *her* that she was an orphan either, until she'd met other children.

'I'll make tea,' Kitty said, 'or cordial, if you prefer?'

'What's cordial?'

Kitty was too dumbfounded by the question to answer.

'Never mind,' Harper said. 'Steve's always telling me how everywhere else is so different to Texas. Whatever you make'll be lovely. I'll stay with Gretel for a minute. See if I can get her to settle.'

'All right.' Kitty cleared the bed. 'Lie down if you like. The linen's all fresh.'

'Thanks.' Harper sat on the bed and cuddled the softly sobbing Gretel.

'Back in a tick.'

Kitty returned to the lounge room on her way to the kitchen, where she found Laszlo and Steve setting up the new keyboard on its brand new stand.

'Hey, kid,' Steve said. 'Yuka said you got this new today. Nice. Play us something. I want to hear what you got.'

The keyboard was shiny and gorgeous. It was enticing and exactly like she thought it would be. It was also positively menacing. Panic set in.

'Hey, don't sweat it, kid,' Steve said encouragingly. 'We don't shoot you if you miss a note.'

'I–'

'Yuka says you're a natural with the songs. Just want a feel for how you play, before you start learning that too.'

Kitty stared at the challenge of the virgin machine. Keys ranged in four octaves. *Real* keys, not ones painted on wood and in her imagination. Keys that would move and make sounds when she pressed them.

She could do this. She could. She was not a fraud, simply untested. Her parents had been magic musicians. She had sung the dead to sleep again. She could damn well press a key and make a sound. She could.

Kitty pressed a key, a simple C, and the note rang out. She licked her lips nervously. She placed her thumb lightly on the C and her index finger on E, stretching her middle finger to the G. Then she pressed.

The C Major chord vanished under the yip of shrieked excitement as Kitty jumped away from the keyboard. She kept her fingers on the keys, though, and further obscured the chord with a fit of giggles. Her eyes crinkled in joy.

'They sound exactly like I thought they would!'

Steve's expression effectively conveyed that he thought she was barking mad. Her giggling subsided, burst out again, subsided once more. 'It's all right. Really. I'm excited to hear what it sounds like outside my head.' She released the combination and tried the ones for an E Major. Oh, it was lovely. Perfect. Better than it had ever sounded in her mind. She giggled again.

'Are you telling me that you've never played a keyboard before?' said Laszlo, behind her.

She sobered and took her hand from the keys. 'Grandma and Grandpa forbade it. We never had music in the house. Ever. Not even the radio.'

There was a collective gasp of horror.

Kitty drew herself up, suddenly needing to defend her grandparents' choices.

'They probably thought they were keeping me safe from the Coco.' She scowled. She understood her grandparents at last, but she also knew they'd been wrong. 'But I heard music anyway, and I taught myself.'

'On what?' marvelled Laszlo.

Kitty threw back the cloth on the breakfast table to reveal the painted octaves. 'And I can sing,' she said fiercely. 'You've heard me. And I *can* play.'

Into the stunned silence, Steve clapped his hands and rubbed them together, attempting to overcome the rising sense of panic with bluster. 'Right. So. *Right*. It's fine. Everything is *fine*. Kitty is Bridget and Pablo Carrasco's daughter! Granddaughter of The Piper. Descendant of Senora Garrido. All y'all've seen what she did with no training at all. She's a *natural*. It'll be **fine**.'

Kitty fled from all the appalled stares to hide in the kitchen. For the next half hour, whenever someone came in, she pretended to fossick for things in the cupboards. Finally, the back door opened and closed several times in a row, indicating everyone else had retreated to the garage.

Well, everyone but Harper and the baby. Harper wandered in, jiggling a grizzling Gretel on her hip.

'Oh, God! I'm sorry! I forgot your drink!' Kitty started pulling cups out of the cupboard.

'I heard the hullabaloo. Sounds like you've got your hands full.'

Kitty sloshed the dark red concentrated raspberry cordial into a tumbler, poured cold water from the fridge into the fluid, and shoved the resulting beverage at Harper like her life depended on it. Then she apologised some more and used a tea towel to mop up the liquid that spilled over Harper's hands. 'Sorry. God. Sorry.'

'Oh, so this is cordial,' Harper sipped with a great show of interest. 'We don't have this in Texas. It's a bit like Kool-Aid, or Snapple. You know. Iced tea. But it's powdered. Kool-Aid is, I mean.'

Kitty looked at Harper like she had two heads.

Harper sighed. 'Australia sure is weird.'

Kitty's round-eyed gaze grew even rounder, and then she giggled, one explosive snorting laugh she tried to stop and then let go. Harper began to giggle too. Gretel forgot to grizzle, instead smacking Harper on the arm and making curious noises at them.

'It's okay, sweetie,' Harper kissed Gretel on the forehead. 'Auntie Harper has had a long day and your new Auntie Kitty's had an even longer one.'

'Yeah. It's been a big day.' Kitty smiled ruefully at her visitors. 'And on top of everything, they think I'm a fraud. I think they're right.'

'Oh, *bullshit*,' Harper said vehemently. Gretel stared at her, affronted, and Harper kissed her on the nose this time. Mollified, Gretel grabbed a handful of Harper's hair to suck and stared at Kitty.

'Hey, they all got a few cobwebs in the attic themselves,' Harper said by way of explanation. 'Actually, Uncle Steve's a lot less crazy than Poppy and Nanny Borman led me to expect, with all their cussin' him out for changing to a boy's name and all. Tell the truth, he's got more sandwiches in his picnic than they do, if you know what I'm saying.'

'I think so.'

'And all the rest. Steve's brung all sorts home since I was little, including the band before this'n. I heard so many stories about what they did on the road. Cleaned up for a kids' ears I know, but my brother Angus says even if only half of it's true, it's twice too much crazy to be getting on with. So Kitty, if you grew up with music not allowed and you can sing anyway, and if you taught yourself the piano without a damned piano, that will not ever be the weirdest thing this band has done. Trust me.'

Kitty found this speech oddly reassuring.

'And if Yuka gives you the wall-eye again,' concluded Harper, 'you give it right on back to her and ask her to tell the story about the flute. See if she doesn't sit right on down and shut the hell up.'

'The flute story?'

'Yuka's a drummer, right? But she played the flute on spec when she had to. No trainin'. It was a-' Harper waggled her head in a dismissive gesture, 'a *thing*. A magic making it right thing. It didn't have to last long, way I heard the story, but where there's need and a will, it seems things happen. They don't think you're a fraud, Kitty.'

Harper wound down, her gaze coming to rest on Gretel. 'They're hurting and I think they're scared. I know I am.' She kissed Gretel's face again and Gretel nestled into Harper's hold.

Kitty straightened her spine. 'Okay then.'

She squared her shoulders and jerked her chin up and decided to hell with doubt, and with Yuka's wall-eyed glares, and even with Steve's brittle enthusiasm.

'Better get them back inside for rehearsals then, hadn't I?'

Chapter Sixteen

Early the next morning, Kitty was rummaging for breakfast supplies when Steve padded in, phone pressed to his ear.

'Uh-huh. Yeah, bitch of a flight. You can get the bus if you… oh, okay. Sure.' He smiled into the speaker. 'I'll text you the address. See you soon.' After texting, he greeted Kitty. 'Morning. Angus and Taylor landed half hour ago. They're gonna get a cab.'

'Two more for breakfast.' Kitty dumped extra bowls on the table.

'You did real well yesterday. Yuka was right to give you those song leads.'

Kitty absorbed this comment. 'I'll get better with the piano, I promise.'

'No sweat. The voice is as important as anything else, maybe more at this stage. Anyway, it'll be great, you singing up there and Aaron on backing vocals. It ain't like we need two bassists at this point, though he's picking it up real quick.'

'You've given up on the idea of him playing the didgeridoo?' asked Kitty with a smirk.

Steve grimaced. 'I think Aaron made it clear that he is a guitarist and not a didge player, and nobody ain't got any right to think otherwise just cos he's a Yorta Yorta man – did I say that right?'

'Yep.'

'So, yeah, I learned a lesson in not being an asshole, so that was ten minutes of yellin' well spent.'

'Aaron didn't yell at you.'

'He did with his *eyes*, Kitty girl. Those eyes shouted plenty loud, even if he spoke low. My mom used to yell like that. All growlin' and daggers in her eyes. Sometimes I preferred it when Pa or Uncle Joshua straight up walloped me.'

Steve frowned, stretched his neck like he was twitching something off his shoulder. 'Never mind that, anyhow. Y'all set for today?'

Kitty put the kettle on and pulled cups and teabags out as well. 'I've called in to say I'm taking the rest of my bereavement leave. Trudy was kind about it, which makes me feel awful for lying to her. She says Maddie's funeral went well, though. Thanks for helping me with her. It wouldn't have been fair for her family to have to deal with what happened.'

'Happy to help, Kitty. That poor kid.'

'Yeah. She seemed like she was lovely. I'm always meeting the nicest people that it's too late to get to know, in my job.' Kitty took a bag of ground coffee from the fridge and a large coffee pot and plunger from the cupboard. 'I haven't taken time off before. I haven't been sick a day in my life. Is that a Minstrel Tongue thing?'

'Yup. Either hale and hearty or bleedin' to death, that's us. Aw, shit. Sorry kid.'

But Kitty was laughing. 'Aaron's right, you're appalling at selling this whole band thing.'

'Well, there's no point in asking you to join us on a lie. You have to know what it's gonna be like. What it's gonna cost.'

'So where's the upside?'

Steve watched her scoop aromatic coffee into the pot. 'Saving the world is pretty neat. Well, parts of it at a time. Using the song inside you to keep the balance. Doing something with your life beyond working at Walmart or diddling with numbers in an accounting firm.'

'That's not it though, is it?'

Steve smiled at her insight. 'No, it ain't. Partly, but mainly I've stayed because it was the only place in the world I could use my music to do something that means something, and be who I am with nobody to tell me who I should be, and who I shouldn't.'

'That sounds wonderful.'

'Dangerous and exhausting and there ain't never a place to call home except the road and the people you're with. I love it.'

'But you want to leave it.'

'I get tired, I guess. I'm nearly 60. Kind of old for this life. Time to retire, I figure. Go sit on a porch and be the crabby ol' man who shakes his fists at clouds, kind of thing.'

Kitty gazed at him steadily, and he cleared his throat. 'You do this to everyone?' he asked.

'What?'

'Stare the truth right out of 'em with those big eyes?'

Kitty poured the just-boiled water into the coffee pot and rested the plunger on top to let the coffee brew. 'I don't mean to. I try to understand people. It's important in my job. And I think... I think I must have known I've been lied to all my life.' She fixed him with that piercing gaze again. 'You still haven't told me why you really want to leave the band. You love it. You love your friends and you love what you do.'

'I'm gonna get those people I love killed,' he said at last. 'The magic can do an awful lot, but it can't make me younger. I'm slowing down. I'm making bad judgement calls. Like letting Sal finish Alex off, wanting him to be able to so I wouldn't have to do it. It's a hard life, Kitty Carrasco, make no mistake. It's good, but it costs, and I've lost a lot of people I love. And one day, I'm going to make a worse mess, or I'm going to be too slow, and I'm going to get these good people killed. Maybe it's too late, and we're going to die because I failed Alex and Kurt and Sal. Maybe those vampires are going to get that little girl, and it's my fault.'

Kitty pressed her hand over his.

'We are going to keep Gretel safe,' she said with conviction. 'You and Yuka and Laszlo and Aaron and me. Sal, too, even if he isn't at his best. I think he'd do anything to keep her safe. Don't you?'

'Yeah.' Steve looked into those steady hazel eyes. 'I think he would.'

'Right then.' Kitty pushed the plunger down and the earthy scent of it rose. Kitty poured two cups and passed one to him.

Steve was wearing that expression again: the one that said he knew an exciting secret.

Slowly, the household awoke. Kitty had slept in her own room and Harper had claimed the second room with the baby. Almost everyone else had slept haphazardly on sofas, in arm chairs, in sleeping bags on the living room carpet. Aaron had elected to sleep in his van with some extra blankets.

Kitty determined who were the natural early risers (Steve and Yuka) and who were the grumpy layabeds (Aaron, Laszlo and Sal). Her grandparents' house – her house now – had never been so full.

Laszlo was emerging from the bathroom, greying hair in a wild mad-genius frizz, when a taxi pulled up outside, expelling Angus and Taylor onto the quiet urban street. Steve strode outside to hug his nephew.

Angus crushed his uncle in a tight embrace. 'I'm so sorry about Alex and Kurt.'

Steve's jaw worked, as though he kept starting to say something and kept giving up. Finally he said: 'Thanks. You best come right in. We gotta lot to talk over.'

Steve introduced his nephew and Taylor to everyone and went to fetch Harper and Gretel.

'This is a big decision,' Yuka said from the side of the room, her arms folded. 'Newly wed. Now you come to Australia to fetch a daughter.'

Taylor met her challenging glare. 'Angus and me would've been paper-married ten years ago if it had been legal. We've been married all that time anyway, except without all that government sanctioned bureaucracy.'

Yuka hitched herself off the wall and poked at a shelf of ornaments while she fiddled with her necklace. She didn't see Angus smooth his hand down Taylor's arm, kiss his cheek, though she may have heard his murmur: 'Deep breath, baby. She don't mean anything by it. She's worried about Gretel.'

The child in question babbled happily as she was brought down the hallway. Gretel clung to Harper as they entered the living room to meet the newcomers.

'Hi there, honey.' Angus spoke gently, not reaching for Gretel, not doing anything to startle the baby. 'Do you remember me? Taylor and me met you when you were itty bitty and again this year. You've grown so much!'

Gretel sucked her knuckle and stared at him, saucer-eyed. She clung closely to Harper.

Angus cast a round-eyed look of his own at Steve. 'You know we want take Gretel home and love her as our own. But what about her mother?'

'Alex is her biological dad, but I'm not even sure *who* the mom is, let alone where she is. Alex and Kurt didn't tell us. They thought we'd talk them out of having a kid, so maybe by their lights they weren't wrong to keep it secret.'

'You can't, I don't know. Track her?'

'Tried. Didn't work. Even if we could find her, Gretel's mom is a stranger to all of us.'

'Would you have talked them out of it?'

Steve gazed at Gretel, as besotted as any grandfather. 'They sprang that little angel on us out of the blue; two weeks old and the most beautiful little thing I'd ever seen. Who couldn't love her? We tried to be a family on the road, even doing what we do. And now look. Not a year old and orphaned already. Yeah, we would have. But woulda-coulda-shoulda's no use to anybody. All that matters is we keep her safe from her daddies.'

Angus squeezed his husband's hand tight. 'About those two. First you said they were dead, and now they're... not?'

'Ah, turns out, yes, but no. Alex and Kurt are vampires.'

'Shit.'

'They're coming for Gretel. They mean her harm, Angus. You gotta take her home.'

'But is it right for *her*?'

'Can't be *wrong* for her, Angus. Her daddies are gone and she needs people who'll be there for her, who won't put her in danger. That ain't us.'

'Is it *us*?'

Yuka rose up, her spine ramrod straight. 'You will love Gretel,' she declared. 'You will be the fathers she should have had. You will protect her and care for her and keep her safe and be the family we cannot be. You must.' Her lip quivered, before she bit it and scowled more fiercely. 'You can tell her who she is, and who her fathers were. No-one else can do it. No-one else can be trusted.'

Steve put an arm around Yuka's waist and she leaned into him. 'This is right for her,' Steve said. 'It's right for you too.'

'Gretel is the only important thing,' Yuka said.

Taylor kissed his husband's cheek. 'Isn't Gretel the perfectest little girl?'

Harper carried Gretel over to the two men. 'This is Angus and Taylor,' she said soothingly to the child. 'Do you remember them? Angus is my brother and Taylor is his honey-pie.'

Gretel reached out with a saliva-slick hand to bump it against Taylor's nose. He held his finger up for her to grab. 'We are going to love you so much,' he whispered to her, 'and we are going to tell you how much your first daddies loved you too. Every day.'

'There's a–' Steve faltered, cleared his throat. 'There's a song they wrote for her. You should learn it, sing it for her. It's...' He swallowed. 'It's all the heirloom we've got for her. Their instruments got smashed up, they hardly had anything worth keeping anyway. Just the music and each other, and Gretel.'

Taylor continued to chat to Gretel, who warmed to him cautiously, then with increasing enthusiasm. 'Your daddies wrote you a song, Gretel? You sure are a special little girl. I'm gonna learn your song and sing it to you. I am. Yes I am.'

Angus beamed at the pair of them. 'My honey-pie sings like Dolly Parton,' he teased fondly

'And my sweety-cake sings like Macy Gray, but don't you hold that against him. He's got a good heart.'

'Uuuh!' shouted Gretel cheerily.

'What do we do about the paperwork?' said Angus, booping Gretel on the nose with his finger as she giggled.

'That'll all be fixed up right soon,' Steve said.

A peculiar sound drew Steve's attention to Sal, who had materialised to watch the proceedings with haunted eyes that were bruised from lack of sleep.

'I thought we could have this,' he murmured, threadbare as a ghost. 'Family. Children. I thought Alex and Kurt had changed the rules. But they didn't.'

'Sal, man, I'm so sorry. I know how close you and Alex-' began Angus.

Sal never took his eyes off Gretel. 'The rules don't change because you love someone. You just... have to do better. Love better. Be better. *Make* yourself better.'

He disappeared. The bathroom door banged shut.

Taylor was puzzled. 'Was he in love with Alex?'

'Not like you think.' Steve shook his head with a troubled frown.

Kitty could read the guilt in Steve's expression. A gentle deathside manner, tea and biscuits that would remain untouched weren't going to help a man who felt responsible for making the wrong call, with such a devastating effect on everyone he loved.

'Gretel needs a change,' Harper said suddenly, jogging the baby in her arms as the girl began to cry. 'Want to come learn the basics?'

'I know the basics,' asserted Taylor as he and Angus followed her to the bedroom. 'I'm the eldest of eight and had to change my baby sister all the time when Mom was working.'

Steve, troubled and unhappy, followed his kin down the hall.

The living room fell into a strange silence. Laszlo dropped onto the sofa and wiped his face with the damp towel. Aaron, at the kitchen table for the entire exchange, poured milk into a third bowl of cereal. Yuka fiddled with her necklace.

'I need air,' Yuka said, and she stalked out the front door.

For a short time there were only the sounds of Aaron rapidly shovelling down his third breakfast and the beep of his phone as he sent a dozen text messages, presumably to his old bandmates; and from down the hall, a lullaby.

You are strong, baby girl
Life is long, baby girl
Your daddies will sing you to sleep
You are smart, baby girl
You have heart, baby girl
And the hearts of your daddies to keep.

Eventually, Steve returned to drop onto the sofa next to Laszlo.

'How is she?' Laszlo asked.

'Harper?'

'No. The little girl. Gretel.'

'She's fine.'

'Too young maybe to miss her daddies?' Laszlo was unaccountably sad.

'Harper says otherwise. I guess she'd know. Better'n me anyhow. But Gretel seems to like Angus, and Taylor especially. Taylor's a sweetheart with kids. She'll be okay.'

Laszlo nodded. 'Yes. She will adjust.' The hint of bitterness was as unaccountable as the sadness.

'We're not going to let her forget her real dads.' Taylor came into the room, holding Gretel, who was thumping a bee-shaped rattle against his shoulder.

Laszlo regarded Taylor sternly. 'Good. She should know her true fathers.' Gretel grasped Taylor's ear with chubby fingers. 'She likes you. Be good to her.'

Taylor, besotted, kissed Gretel's hand. She tugged his earlobe and he laughed.

'His biggest temptation will be spoiling her rotten,' chuckled Angus, returning to the living room with Harper in his wake.

'It's hard not to,' agreed Harper, as the bathroom door banged open again. 'She... oh my god, Sal. Are you all right? What have you *done*?'

CHAPTER SEVENTEEN

They met over a book of poetry.

A shadow fell across Sal's precious copy of *Selected Poems of Joseph Furtado*, which he was reading in an Edinburgh café. The clammy Scottish rain outside was a depressing contrast to the lush, fragrant Indian heat of his father's orchard. Homesickness was in his heart, a comma made of stone in the shape of a cashew.

'Is that Nellie Furtado's dad, then?' she asked.

Salvatore D'Souza looked up into the pale face of a Scottish girl. He knew her from a class or two at the university, though they'd never spoken.

'Joseph Furtado was a poet,' Sal corrected her.

'Are you saying Nelly's nae a poet?' Her challenge was accompanied with a friendly laugh. 'Read me something?'

Sal wondered if she was flirting with him. He never could tell with people. He closed the book, though, and recited from memory.

'In the valley as I rambled, sad with thoughts of childhood days, though the birds sung loud about me, how could they my spirits raise? All they sung was Never, never, will return your childhood days.'

'Well, that's depressing,' she said, and sat beside him. 'I'm Claire.'

'Pleased to meet you, Claire.' Even though she didn't like the poet who made him feel less homesick, Sal found that he was pleased. He hadn't made many friends yet.

'So what else has your boy Furtado got for me?'

He recited the poem of the Brahmin girls "so fair, upon their nose the ring of pearls and jasmine in their hair".

'Not a fan of the Scottish lassies, then?' Claire asked, amused rather than offended.

'I like poetry,' Sal said earnestly, and Clair laughed like that was delightful.

'You've never had a girlfriend then?' Claire asked Sal a week later in the Edinburgh University library, while they worked on their crop and soil assignment together.

Agricultural Science was not Salvatore D'Souza's heart's true calling, but he accepted that his family needed it from him. He'd dreamed of entering the University's Arts stream: Portuguese and English Literature appealed. He had enrolled in a few language electives for fun: Spanish, Italian and French to augment the English, Portuguese, Konkani and Hindi he already spoke. He carried a notebook in his pocket to jot down phrases and quotes he particularly liked.

Sometimes he jotted down ideas for song lyrics too. In his few free hours each week, he wrote music for the words on his lovingly maintained Alvarez guitar.

Sal had fantasised, too, about switching to the Acoustics and Music Technology program. It was a fascinating field for someone with his skills in mathematics and music, but his father wouldn't believe that being a more accomplished musician could help the orchard thrive.

Sal suspected the music program might have been more useful than soil science, considering the peculiar things he made happen in the orchard. The kitchen garden would grow literally as he watched when he sang to it. The family cashew orchard was the most abundant in the region, perhaps because his Uncle Joki had taught Sal since boyhood to walk with him among the trees and sing to them. After he earned his degree, Sal would support the orchard in both ways, with science and song.

'No girlfriends, no.' Sal curtly tried to head off this unwanted conversation. He liked Claire as a lab partner. Why couldn't friendship be enough?

'Oops, shoudnae make assumptions. Boyfriend, then?'

'No.'

'That's a shame, that is.'

Sal hated these conversations. *But you're a good looking guy. There's someone out there for you. How do you know you don't like sex if you haven't tried it?*

'Unless it's not,' Claire continued. 'The whole "you complete me" shite's a bit much, eh? Not every lad needs a lassie or even another lad.'

'No.'

'And not everyone's gantin' for it, either.'

Sal regarded her sideways, curiosity warring with irritation.

'Ye think I'm gettin' too personal? Sorry. It's just. I don't... meet many people. Like me.'

'Like you?'

'Y'know. Ace.'

He hadn't known a word existed for what he was. Claire took it on herself from that moment to teach him all the words, a spectrum of possibilities that explained him without judging him. *Ace. Asexual.* He had never desired another's body, though he could appreciate beauty. *Aromantic* was another word. He could love, and did love, but not with desire.

Words existed for who he was, which meant there was nothing wrong with him at all. He was just at one end of a curve. Sal was so grateful to Claire for showing him this truth. He'd sort of loved her for it, with one of the other kinds of love the Greeks talked about.

What a pity that half of what she said was lies. Claire wasn't like him at all.

'D'ye know how hard it is to find a virgin at this university?' she said as the blood dripped down his back.

Sal didn't know which was the worse betrayal: that she'd lured him to the basement of her house to have her boyfriend overpower him and string him up, naked, to a beam across the ceiling, or that she'd never been his friend at all. Her affection for him had been that of someone for a pet; or for the lamb destined for the pot. A short, kind life. Then the blade.

Sal had tried to scream, but Claire's boyfriend Iain had stuffed his mouth with rags to block the noise.

'What d'ye think, love?' Claire gestured towards her handiwork – the circle carved in Sal's back and the smaller markings surrounding it.

Sal whimpered in pain and fear.

'Ye've a steady hand,' Iain said. 'Will it work?'

'It's like ploughing a field,' Claire said impishly to Sal, as though he'd appreciate the joke. 'Prepare the soil, plant the seed, and och, lad, what a crop we're raising. The devil himself!'

Sal believed her. He felt evil burning in the shapes carved into his body. The bad seed planted there. What a paper he might write on it, if it weren't the seeds of his own destruction.

Claire intoned words as she walked widdershins around Sal, Iain's voice intertwined with hers as they chanted. The language was alien to Sal, yet he understood what they meant.

Sal's future on the orchard was slipping away from him, leaking out with the blood from the sign carved on his back. He had ceased to be a seed himself, full of potential. He was only a vessel. Something empty for others to fill.

Sal coughed and probed at the rags with his tongue until they fell onto the floor. He tried to cry out but he only croaked.

The marks on his back burned like acid and he felt it like poison in his body. Sal could track the progress of it into his flesh, into his organs. He didn't have the energy to be astonished that witchcraft and devils existed. The last of his vitality was bound in a fierce desire to hang onto his sense of self.

Without conscious thought, a song rose to his cracked lips. From his hoarse, dry throat came his last defiance, his attempt to remain himself, in English and Konkani, Portuguese and Hindi, mingled together, his mind so muddied with the coming possession he couldn't separate them. All language was one language.

Sal knew his song was a source of salvation, because Iain stopped chanting long enough to stuff bloody rags back into Sal's mouth.

The devil burned in the lines carved in his back. The world diminished. Sal saw only what other, bestial eyes saw, which revelled in destruction. Through those eyes, Sal saw the figures entering the basement of Claire's house, bright eyes full of courage and resolve. Their mouths were open and Sal could *see* the sound as a distortion in the air.

Unbind thee from this vessel
Unbind thee from this blood
Unbind thee from his innocence
Unbind thee from his good.

Iain took to the intruders with a hatchet, but one of the men sang and twisted his hand. The little axe flew away and into Claire's chest.

Sal fell to the floor, a puppet with cut strings. Iain fell too, shrieking. Sal saw the sound Iain made as a jagged shape in the air. The jaggedness shattered and disappeared like fog.

Then Sal raised his head to glare at the intruders and flickered his long, forked tongue at them.

I will eat your souls, he said to them, or thought he did. He spoke in a language made of corruption and cruelty that hurt his throat and tongue.

'We can't save him,' said one of the people, the shape of his damnation made with breath from his mouth.

Another said, 'It's too late.' The words hung heavy in the shape of blood and granite.

Sal watched with the demon's eyes; he laughed with the beast's voice. His vanishingly human heart cried out for help.

Sal remembered the songs of growing he and Joki used to sing to the trees, and though his throat and tongue and eyes weren't his own any more, what remained of his heart tried to sing. He reached a clawed hand out the intruders, palm up, defying agony to offer this plea.

"We can try,' said another, whose words were a futile shape of hope.

'You'll free the demon, *sötnos*,' warned one. 'We can kill it if it stays inside him.'

'I want to try,' the kind one said. 'Be ready.' Then he took Sal's hand and he *sang*. Blade in hand, he cut a line across the pentagram carved in Sal's back as he sang. Sal screamed. He screamed. He screamed.

'Please. *Por favour*! Help me! *Madat kar*! *Meree madad karo! Me salve!*'

The air rang with screaming, with shrieks of rage, with a desperate song. A roaring wind became part of the music. It pulled at him and anything not fixed spun around them. Great, bloody claws dug into his back but a small person singing a high note stabbed at the gnarled hands with a pair of drumsticks.

A spray of blood arced past; a skinny person swung a guitar at the weight of the something at his back.

The man who held Sal in his arms sang and scored the lines of the pentagram and sigils on his back, rendering him unfit as a vessel for the devil.

Suddenly, the basement wind stopped howling and a bruised silence hung over them. The hands and voices that had battled with the demon softened, and the shape of their singing wound around him like a vanilla vine, roots strong, fragrant and full of love.

Sal's voice became his own again and, rasping, he joined it to theirs, entwining his will with his own redemption.

'You're safe,' crooned his saviour like a lullaby as someone pressed cloth to his lacerated back, soaking up blood.

Sal's human eyes saw Claire and Iain dead in pools of their commingled blood. His angel saviour gently turned Sal's head from them, so that Sal saw into his eyes only.

'I'm Alex,' the man said.

'*Dev borem korum*,' gasped Sal. '*Te abençoe*. Bless you, thank you, thank you.'

Chapter Eighteen

Sal held a vegetable knife in his hand, and blood dripped in a steady stream from his head to his bare shoulder and thence to the floor.

'Sal?' Steve darted up to meet him. 'Jesus, Sal…'

Taylor shielded Gretel from the gruesome sight, while Angus and then Harper stepped between them and Sal too. Kitty and Aaron took involuntary steps towards them then halted, wondering what to do.

As Sal took one slow step after another into the living room, Laszlo rose and pressed the damp towel he'd been using against the bleeding wound in Sal's freshly shaved scalp.

'You silly boy,' Laszlo held the reddening cloth firmly to his head. 'You silly, silly boy.'

Sal allowed Laszlo to administer aid as he raised his chin to look placidly at Kitty. 'I'm sorry about the blood. I'll clean it up.' He gazed at Laszlo. 'I'm all right. It will heal.'

'What have you done, Sal?' Steve's hand hovered above Sal's, which held the blood-stained knife in a tight grip.

'Waste no more time arguing about what a good man should be. Be one,' Sal said, matter-of-factly.

'Don't you. Don't you go quoting Marcus Aurelius at me.' Any anger in Steve's response was lost under his anguish.

'I must be better,' Sal said. 'To protect her, I must be pure.' He let Steve take the knife from his hand.

Kitty rummaged frantically through the kitchen drawers and shoved handfuls of tea towels at Aaron before resuming her search.

Laszlo pulled the towel away to examine the damage. Through the blood, he could see that besides shaving his hair to the finest fuzz, Sal had carved a symbol into the thin skin above his left ear. A circle surrounded by triangles: a stylised sun. Blood began welling up in the shallow grooves again.

Aaron handed Laszlo the pile of clean tea towels and took the bath towel, damp with water and blood. He looked helplessly at Steve, but Steve simply laid the knife down on top of the mess and wiped his hands on the corner of the towel.

'Rumi the poet says "be like the sun for grace and mercy".' Sal explained simply. 'It'll remind me. To be better.'

'Aww, Sal.' Steve's mouth quivered. He took Sal's face between his hands and rubbed his thumbs over the younger man's cheeks. 'You shouldn'a hurt yourself like that.'

'I have to be better.'

'We all have to be better, Sal.' Steve was crying, his thumbs gently caressing Sal's skin. Skin stained with blood embedded with tiny fragments of fine black hair. 'I have to be better. I'm sorry, kid. I should never have left you to finish Alex. I should never have done that to you. I'm so sorry.'

Sal's placidness cracked at last. His eyes filled with tears. 'I loved him so much. He saved me, Steve. He saved me when nobody cared. He saved my soul. My *soul*. He thought I was *worth* saving, and I wasn't.'

Steve pulled Sal close. Sal sank down, his face buried against Steve's neck. Steve patted the denuded fuzz at Sal's nape, gently pressed down on the cloth absorbing the blood.

'It's not your fault, Sal. It's mine. You're a good man. There's no taint in you.' He rocked the taller man gently in his arms, petting his shoulders and his head. 'You were worth saving.'

Sal sobbed and clung to Steve.

Gretel began to cry, tiny frightened gulps. Taylor cuddled her close, but she reached for Harper. After a reluctant moment, he handed Gretel over. Gretel clung frantically to her babysitter and wailed.

Sal straightened up suddenly, dragging his arms across his wet eyes. 'I'll clean up.'

Kitty held up a first aid kit. 'Let's clean you up first.'

'You don't have to do that,' he said dubiously.

'We're going to be bandmates,' Kitty said with an encouraging smile. 'We're going to take care of each other, yeah?'

Sal nodded slowly.

'Good. Sit down, then, Steve'll be right there with you. Aaron, chuck that stuff in the bathroom, we'll deal with it later. Can you get the antiseptic cream out of the cupboard in there? I think there are some painkillers there, too. Sal's going to need them. Laszlo, there's a linen press in the hall next to my room. Would you mind getting out some towels and face washers for me? I think there's an old sheet there too. Toss it over the mess in the hall. Harper, maybe you and the guys can take Gretel to the back yard. It's a sunny day, she'll like that.'

In minutes, it was arranged. Steve sat beside Sal at the kitchen table, holding the younger man's hand and squeezing it for reassurance. Kitty filled a bowl with lukewarm water. From the first aid kit she plucked a half empty bottle of antiseptic, some of which she added to the bowl. When Laszlo returned with an armful of linen, she grabbed a flannel from the top and swished it in the bowl of water. She sponged the wound on the side of Sal's head carefully. He flinched at the contact. The bleeding had stopped.

Aaron brought cream and tablets. Steve helped Sal to take the painkillers. Sal's hands were shaking too badly to hold the glass steady.

Kitty had doused a ball of cotton wool with antiseptic. 'This will sting,' she warned, and dabbed it on the cuts. Sal hissed sharply but grit his teeth, squeezed Steve's hand, and let her clean the lines he'd carved into his scalp. She dabbed cream over the top.

She wasn't sure how to wrap him afterwards, but Laszlo took over the task. He made a pad from a wad of gauze and wound a bandage around Sal's head to hold it in place.

When they were done, Steve lifted Sal's hand and kissed his knuckles. 'It's gonna be okay, Sal.'

Sal turned haunted eyes on him. 'How?'

Steve swallowed, unable to answer.

Kitty rested her hand on Sal's shoulder. 'Angus and Taylor are going to take Gretel home and raise her and love her,' she said, with so much confidence for one so new to all of this. 'The rest of us will deal with the monsters. That's what we do, I'm told. We're the cure for the poison. Aren't we, Steve?'

Steve was aghast at being asked to confirm his blithe assurances.

'Sure we are,' interjected Aaron suddenly. 'This light in me, this stuff I've always been able to do. It's *for* something, isn't it? It's for something good in this bad world? That's what my gran always said. That's what Steve says. And damn me, if I don't reckon so too.'

Laszlo regarded them all as though they were crazy, and like he was so proud of their combined lunacy. 'We will make it right,' he asserted, 'or at least, better. I believe that. I believe it is possible to make things better than they have been, to make up for our mistakes.' His gaze took in both Sal and Steve. 'It's as Steve says. We can do better. All of us.'

Hope was beginning to glimmer in Sal's eyes, and Steve's too, when the front door banged open and Yuka took three jerky steps into the house. She was tugging anxiously on her necklace.

'Steve!' she shouted as she entered. 'The graveyard is-'

Yuka paused, seeing suddenly the white sheet spread down the hall, dotted with the blood it was absorbing from the floor; smears of blood on the wall and in the living room; the huddle of people and Sal with his head shaved and bandaged.

'I was gone *twenty minutes*,' she said, in horrified wonder.

'What was that about the graveyard?' asked Steve, getting to his feet.

Yuka's large eyes snapped back to him 'The dead are rising.'

'But it's only half eleven,' Aaron blurted. Yuka rolled her eyes at him.

'They headed over here?' Steve went straight to the instruments they'd left in the living room overnight.

'Yes.'

'Laszlo, tell the kids to get Gretel out of here.'

'Tell them to take the van.' Aaron threw his car keys to Laszlo, who raced to the back yard.

Sal was on his feet too, going for his own guitar, while Yuka dug among the pile for her drum sticks and djembe drum attached to a strap, which she slung across her shoulders.

Laszlo returned as Aaron pulled out his acoustic bass.

'You don't know any of the songs,' Laszlo protested suddenly.

Aaron looked at the guitar, at Laszlo, at Steve. 'I can still hit things with it.'

Steve grinned ferally at him. Laszlo retrieved the violin from the trunk.

Kitty curled her hands into fists and followed the others outside. Taking a keyboard wasn't practical: she'd have to hope her voice was enough.

Over the road, a haze of dirt and dust hung over the gravestones. Something dirty and desiccated and *wrong* undulated near the fence line.

Cars hummed past left and right, oblivious to the wrongness happening in the cemetery. The small team of minstrels, clutching instruments – and some of them, their courage, too – waited for a break then darted to the fence.

Yuka struck a rhythm against the fence with her drum sticks. Hands flying fast, she beat the tattoo against both the fence and her drum. It was a rattling rhythm, like a bundle of dried bones ricocheting down a long staircase.

Beyond the fence, the stone caps groaned. The terrifying sound of burrowing things rose up, bringing with them the reek of the grave. The earth along the paths heaved. Hands appeared; and the skeletons of hands. Heads with the flesh clinging on, and the bare bones of skulls. The recently buried and the long dead, scores of them, were shaking off the earth that had been taking them back to its heart, and began to stagger towards the people on the footpath.

Steve plucked out notes on his bass while Sal played melody over it. Steve began to sing.

Scratching your way up
And out through the soil
You'll never quench the morbid
Thirst in your veins

'This is awful,' whispered Kitty. 'Those poor people.'

Yuka was drumming furiously. 'They are the undead.' She tossed

her head in irritation then raised her voice into the refrain behind
Steve.

Sleep now and behave
Down in your grave

'They don't mean anything,' Kitty protested, sure of her intuition
despite her lack of experience. The dead were rising, but they felt
the same as Maddie and the others at the funeral home. 'They're not
conscious, there's no malice. They don't *feel* anything.'

'She's right,' Sal said, fingers flying over the strings. 'There's magic
in it, but not zombie magic.'

Slide away into
Meaningless clouds of smoke

'Thank God,' muttered Laszlo, holding the violin under his chin.
He dragged the bow across once, twice, finding a simple harmonising
note, waiting for inspiration to strike.

Steve kept singing, though he glared as if to say: *a little help here?*
Yuka and Sal launched into the verse with him, while Laszlo found
the key and played long, low notes underneath.

Shake loose the cobwebs from your
Hungry sighs and go
Sleep now and behave
Down in your grave

The fence stood between them and the rising bones. The nearest
dead were falling back as the song wound into their animated bones,
dried flesh and clods of earth. Dozens faltered and stumbled away,
sinking back down into the mounds of soil from which they'd
erupted – going back to their graves, to behave as bones ought.

But further down the street, other bodies were coming. They
rattled along the fence, pressed against it and packing in close. Some
reached through, others scrambled over the top of the pack to topple
over the fence and onto the footpath.

Stoplights at further points created a lull in the traffic flow. The
vehicles that did pass slowed to see then suddenly accelerated away.

Inside the cemetery, a lone wavery scream rose. The pounding of that person's feet on an escape path added its own syncopation to Yuka's drumming.

The first of the bodies to make it over the fence shuffled towards them. Kitty stared at the wrongness of it – bones able to move without muscles, progressing as though they remembered how muscles once worked. Some were held together with gristle and shrivelled meat, some apparently by lichen and scraps of cloth. The bodies may not have been motivated by malice, but it was terrifying nonetheless.

Aaron grabbed Kitty's hand in his free one, as much for comfort as to pull her back. He clutched his guitar by the neck in the other hand. 'Shit,' he was muttering. 'Oh, shit, shit, shit.'

'We need to sing,' Kitty said.

'I don't know the words.'

Kitty glanced at Laszlo and his simple bowing. 'Harmonies?'

'Yeah. Sure. Ah. Sure.' Aaron hummed notes, found one that worked, and opened his mouth to push it out, mingling with the song.

An advancing corpse stopped and listened.

Kitty found a note that fit between Aaron's and Laszlo's and sang that.

The corpse cocked its head to one side, which was deeply alarming, but then it shuffled away from them. It began to climb the fence back into the graveyard. Its bony feet pushed through the gaps, stepping on those trying to exit the other way. It used them to clamber over the fence and back into the cemetery.

That was one body gone, but a dozen more had tumbled to the footpath and were shambling towards them.

Steve took up a position between them and the advancing dead.

Take your dust and
What remains of your bones

A skeletal hand reached out for Steve's guitar. Steve jerked out of its reach. Beside him, Aaron took the neck of his own guitar in both hands and raised the instrument, ready to strike.

The corpse, and the corpses behind it, stopped then began rattling their shambolic way across the street towards Kitty's house; towards the sound of the rusty roller door shrieking in protest as Angus and Taylor tried to force it up so they could get the van out. Behind them, Harper was clutching the baby close to her chest, staring in shock at the horrors crossing the road.

One car slowed, saw, sped up, slamming into a decaying body dressed in a fouled and gruesome bespoke suit. The cars behind it didn't bother to slow. Drivers with their eyes and mouths in appalled 'O's took one look at the scene and tried their damnedest to get away as fast as possible.

Angus and Taylor struggled with the garage door.

The dead stumbled towards them.

The dead who were approaching Gretel and her protectors weren't neutral any more. Anger radiated from them. Their jaws worked; what teeth they had snapped together in dull clicks.

Yuka threw a desperate glance over her shoulder, but she didn't dare leave her post, drumming along the metalwork. She was keeping the dead at bay behind the fence – many burrowing back into the ground to return to their graves, as the music instructed. Sal, at her side, was playing and singing the magic too, while Laszlo, more confident in his playing now that the steady melody had been repeated so often, was striding along the footpath, letting the old magic in the violin send the rattling bones back from the street.

The dead behind the fence were going back to sleep, in ones and twos, then in tens.

Steve stepped up to confront the corpses advancing across the street. These angry dead ignored him, aiming instead for the house. Steve followed them, playing and singing, his expression wild with a dangerous determination.

Take three lonely steps and turn
Your cold dead face from this home

Those nearest him faltered, fell back towards the cemetery. Others continued on. With a final groan of metal, the roller door finally shifted up and clear of the van's height.

Steve, fingers flying over the strings, voice rising strong and loud in the air, strode into the middle of the road.

Sleep now and behave
Down in your grave

Angus yelled a warning.

The speeding car smashed into Steve and then one of the undead. The bone man crumbled. Steve was thrown into the air, his body spinning one way, his guitar flying another, before both crashed to the bitumen.

Angus ran to his uncle. On the footpath, Sal's playing fumbled and halted. Yuka stopped drumming. She ran to Steve lying in the road on his back, face to the sky, left arm at an unspeakable angle, blood trickling from his mouth.

The car had slewed to a halt. The driver – a spindly young man, dark hair in spiky disarray, brown eyes enormous with fear – stumbled out. 'I didn't, oh god, he wasn't... I didn't see him. I saw. I saw. Oh god. What the fuck...?' He backed away from the shuffling things on the road, though they ignored him. Five of them still shambled towards the house on the corner.

On the tar, Steve coughed, moved, groaned. He opened his eyes to stare at that terrified boy.

'S'okay,' he croaked. 'Not... not... not your... fault. Not.... Go. S'okay. Go. Better go. Go.' Another coughing fit sprayed blood over Steve's shirt.

'You. Go,' ordered Yuka, pushing the young man towards his car. 'Leave.'

The fellow fumbled his way to the driver's seat and slammed the car door shut. He stared at the broken man on the road. Then one of the walking dead, on a teetering spine of bone and gristle, snapped its teeth at him, and the driver sped away.

'Gretel,' Steve moaned as Angus dropped to his knees at his uncle's side. 'Get. Gretel. Go. Go. Go.'

'Steve...'

Coughing blood, despair in his eyes, Steve glared at his nephew. 'Keep. Her. Safe.'

Angus rose. Taylor was wrenching open a door to the van and cursing about the *'wrong side, wrong **fucking** side of the car in this country, with its crazy fucking left-hand driving, damn it to hell.'* He ran to the opposite side of the car – the driver's side – and yelled for Harper to get in the passenger seat: 'no, the *other* side!'

The five malevolent skeletons advanced, although their brethren behind the fence had given up, had lain down, gone to sleep, gone to their graves.

But there were Aaron and Kitty, Laszlo on their heels, taking up position between the dead and the garage. Laszlo swept the melody of the song out of his violin and into the air. Aaron hefted his acoustic guitar and played the bass-line he'd heard, missing notes, fumbling the flow until he could settle, and there was Kitty, her hands upraised, spread wide, as though appealing to the bones' better nature.

Take your dust and
What remains of your bones

She sang, loud and clear, Aaron's voice beside hers, picking up the melody again, the strings of violin and guitar weaving through it all.

Take three lonely steps and turn
Your cold dead face from this home

Four sets of bony feet stumbled to a halt, the malice draining out of them. Four forms of dirt and bone clattered as they made a tremulous, rattling return to the graveyard, back to the mounds of earth that had spat them out.

One continued to walk towards the van. Harper curled her body over the baby in the front seat. The corpse's gruesome arm was outstretched, bony fingers beckoning.

Sleep now and behave
Down in your grave

Aaron stopped playing, unslung the guitar and smashed it into the relentless thing.

Sal appeared, fisting his hand in the corpse's ruined scalp, yanking on its hair to throw it off balance. The fistful of hair ripped free of the skull but Sal, undeterred, drove his fist into the delicate, thin bone of its temple, crushing it to splinters.

Yuka joined Sal with a sharp shout, stabbing first one drum stick, then the next, into the corpse's ribs. She flicked her wrists to beat the rhythm directly against the cage of bones, while Kitty's song rang high and clear with the violin to back her, both sounds wrapping strong around the moving carcass and squeezing.

Sleep now and behave
Down in your grave

The bones splintered, collapsed and fell to dust as the final note of voice and violin faded to silence.

In the uncanny quiet, the only sound was of Steve's ragged breath, laboured and worryingly wet, in the late morning sunshine.

Chapter Nineteen

The question Steve Borman asked himself as he stood in the darkest part of the alley, was whether to put his guitar case against the wall and lean against it to keep the guitar safe while he slept; or to cram himself into the least stinky corner of the alley with the guitar in front of him to keep himself safe from the rats while not sleeping a wink.

Protecting the guitar from thieving bastards was usually his first instinct when forced to sleep rough. Rats weren't fun but not likely to beat him up. But this lightless alley was full of red eyes, scuffling noises, and ominous squeaking. His skin prickled with the sense that these critters were not your average street rat.

A red-eyed rat lumbered out from under a pile of boxes and scraps. This was not a rat that scurried. By the distant street light, Steve could make out the hulking silhouette, large as a well fed cat. The red eyes regarded Steve unblinkingly.

'Git outta here, y'uppity mouse,' Steve snarled at it with more bravado than conviction.

A second enormous rat joined the first.

'Y'all don't scare me, you big-ass sum'bitches. Why, in Texas, I seen fleas bigger'n you.'

Steve was a dab hand at playing with the truth, but that was the biggest lie of his young life. He was plenty scared. Giant rats in a stinking 3am alley in downtown Los Angeles was way beyond his experience, and Steve had experienced a whole lot of weird in his 15 years.

The two red-eyed rats with their cold, cold stare were joined openly by a third. The detritus all around rustled with the twitchings of others of their kind. Steve saw their eyes. Twenty, thirty pairs of 'em. More coming.

Steve warily put his guitar case on the ground and eased the locks open. Slowly, slowly, he took out his guitar, held it ready to play. He tried to think of words that might work. They'd have to be different to the ones that came to him that night on the Greyhound bus as Uncle Clement stalked down the aisle, intent on dragging him home "to beat the tomboy outa ya". Fear and anger had given Steve words and a melody he never knew before. They made him invisible while Clement cussed, and the whole time the security folks had escorted Clement off the bus.

Steve strummed and began to sing.

I ain't afraid of no pitter-patter
Your nasty little feet are gonna skitter-scatter
Your beady red eyes are gonna shut real tight
When I tell the darkness to bring on the light

Light began to glow around Steve's hands, crazy bright. Brighter than they'd ever been when he spent days hiding in the barn from Jed Tully's boys.

Right here! A brighter blaze
Right now! Like the brightest days

The light burst forth, searing white, from Steve's hands, his arms, his face, his legs and feet. The rats flinched as the beams struck them, their tails lashing with pain and fury.

I'm shining a light on you, burning like a sun
You're blinded by the light, you better run, run, run.

The three rats and all their shifty companions skitter-scattered all right, furious and afraid, teeth clicking and chittering.

Steve kept singing, stalking up and down the alley to drive them all away. He thought maybe forty of them altogether, huge and raggedy, with malevolent eyes squinting against the bright light as they ran. When they were all gone he let the guitar and his voice go silent and he leaned against the brick wall, trembling and struggling to breathe. Between adrenalin and the power from the song, his binder felt like it was crushing his chest and lungs.

'Well, that was something to see.'

Steve jerked upright, hands returning to the guitar strings as he strained to see who'd spoken.

A silhouette at the mouth of the alley resolved into a woman as curvy and dark as he was skinny and pale. She held a pool of pale blue light in the palm of her hand.

In the palm of her hand.

'Y-you.' Steve stared. 'You're like me.'

'Seems so,' said the lady, her smile like a beam of light all on its own. 'Question is, why'd the rats come chasing after you? Did you call them here?'

'Hell, no. But I think they followed me.'

'They do tend to follow blood.' She peered at him intently. 'But you don't have an injury, do you kid?'

'No ma'am.' The muscles of his jaw twitched.

'Hmm.' The woman tilted her head to one side, scrutinising him further.

Steve shifted uncomfortably, calculating whether he could duck past her, outrun her. His squashed-feeling chest said no. His fear said he had to try. Steve knew that expression, and it had nothing to do with the magic he'd just done. No sirree. That was the look he got a lotta days and a lotta nights, while someone figured out why he was different. Usually, their conclusion was followed by him getting the shit beat out of him. Or worse.

Any minute now, this lady who made light with her hands (just like he could) was going to ask the question (*you a girl or a boy?*). She would hate the answer (if he bothered to give it). Tonight's trouble had begun with the problems that arose from that question. Steve had decided against the men's shelter, since his body was doing its monthly thing, whether he wanted it or not. The women's shelter though, they got an eyeful of him and said no way, you go to the men's shelter.

133

He'd made that choice that once before, though, during his monthly time. He wasn't ever making that mistake again. He'd escaped before they hurt him too bad, and locked himself in the bathroom till he sang himself invisible, like with Uncle Clement, and slunk away again.

'What's your name?' the woman asked.

'Steve.' He jerked his chin up in defiance.

'Good to meet you, Steve. I'm Anna. I think you should meet my band.'

Steve felt wrong-footed by this unexpected conversational direction. He backed away.

'You don't have to if you don't want to,' Anna said, 'but I think those rats might come back this way. It'd be safer for you with us.'

'I can look after myself.'

'I can see that,' Anna said, not a hint of condescension in her tone, which was another new thing for Steve. 'I guess I should add that this rat pack isn't easy to sing into submission. AnnaTomic – that's my band – this kind of thing is a speciality of ours, but an extra harmony makes the magic stronger. You clearly have Minstrel talent, and we could sure use another voice.'

Minstrel talent. Magic. Crazy ass shit, for sure, but the words rang true. Anna knew things that he needed to know, for certain. But then he remembered why the rats had stalked him in the alley. 'I'm bleedin',' he said. 'Won't that bring those monster rats after me?'

'True. We can keep you safe in our squat, if you like, though if you're willing to help, that's a plus for us. The rats aren't the real problem, you see. It's that bastard from Hamelin. We have records hundreds of years old that show us Minstrels keep putting him down, but every hundred years, regular as clockwork, someone wakes him up again. Then it's all plagues of rats that can eat your cat, and that little shit demanding wealth beyond paying or child sacrifices.'

'That's not how that story goes,' Steve said uncertainly.

Anna snorted. 'That's not how the Piper tells it, but he's a trickster, a thief and a goddamned liar.'

'Three of my least favourite kind of people.'

Anna held out her hand, the one without the ball of light.

'Come join us tonight, Steve,' she said. 'It's a hell of a life, though. You won't have to stay if you don't want to.'

Steve, his guitar in one hand, took Anna's hand with his other.

'I got a hell of a life already,' he said. 'Might as well try a different one.'

Chapter Twenty

Angus dropped to his uncle's side, one trembling hand stroking Steve's forehead. Steve coughed more blood, whimpered, then grimaced in an approximation of a smile as his friends gathered around him on the street. Blood coated his lips, his teeth, dribbled from his mouth as he dragged in another agonised breath.

'Damn,' he wheezed. 'I really hoped to live long enough to quit.'

'Shh, shh,' Angus said. 'We'll call an ambulance. You'll be fine.'

'I'm all... all br-broken...' Steve began, but the effort was too much. He wheezed and blood bubbled.

Yuka, kneeling next to Angus, took Steve's uninjured right hand in both of hers and squeezed his fingers. Her dark eyes were wretched with tears, her face crumpled with anguish. 'No,' she said. 'Don't go. Don't leave us. Don't leave me.'

Sal knelt at his head, a hand cupped over Steve's cheek. He was crying, tears dripping down his cheek, falling into Steve's blood-smeared hair. Laszlo and Aaron waved cars around them.

Taylor ran out from the garage and Harper, holding Gretel, stood by the roller door, watching.

Kitty was never able to identify the impulse that made her do it. She only knew it felt right to go to Steve and kneel opposite Angus and Yuka. Careful of his shattered arm, she gently undid the buttons of his shirt and pulled it back to reveal torn skin, trickling blood, the horribly warped shape of his chest, where ribs had broken and shifted.

Steve had scars on his chest from long-ago surgery. Knowing what they meant wasn't important. Only Steve, living, *staying*, was important.

Instinctively, Kitty held her hands over the torn skin and broken bones. She hummed a single perfect note then pressed her hands against Steve's bloodied skin.

Steve groaned, high, agonised, but when Taylor tried to grab Kitty and drag her away, Sal seized his wrists. 'Let her.' Sal's body was taut as a guitar string, breathlessly hopeful.

Kitty began to sing.

It's easy to go away
To leave the sorrow and the pain

The song sank into Steve's body. She could feel the ruin under the skin; the jagged bone piercing his lung; the twists and shards tearing at the blood vessels and soft tissue.

But you still have so much to learn
I'm asking you to stay
She sang to the life trying to leave him.

The earthquake in your body
Broke the walls that hold you up

She sang to broken bone and flesh, telling it what she knew.

The tributaries of your veins
Spilled over
Every breath that leaves you
Is one that won't come back
She sang, asking that body and the spirit in it to hold on.

But there is so much more for you to learn
Please stay
Please be with me another day

Her song descended deep into his body, and what she found was not what she expected.

As this thought coalesced, Steve's spirit began singing to her, a harmony in her head.

Born one person on the outside, someone else on the inside, he sang to her in something other than words. *Never was Momma's little girl. I'm me. I'm me inside; partly outside too.*

Kitty understood the chest scars now. The late Lionel Browne had scars the same. Lionel's mother had wanted him to be a *her*, to be Lucy, dressed in a frock and eye shadow. Lionel's daughter and girlfriend had said *No, he was Lionel*. Lionel's truth succeeded despite the bitter row. Kitty learned a lot about how love wasn't necessarily the same as acceptance.

They know me, sang Steve's not-words. *My family, band and blood, know all of me.*

Kitty detected other magic meshed deep in his tissue: not Steve's magic but a gift from long ago.

Arkady's gift, lilted his harmony, *to bring together inside and outside.*

The song Kitty sang into Steve's cells gathered up the threads of that gifted magic and wove it in to keep it strong. The harmonies of three magics were combined in her head, as she asked Steve's body to be whole and it responded.

Bridges building in your bones
The river banks inside of you are holding

She sang and sang, never having heard the words or made the tune in her life, but which rose up at the need.

The rips and tears close up again
Your walls are strong
You will live on
Live on
Please live on

Under her hands, bones shunted, slid, found their proper place again. Steve whimpered. The healing hurt him, but even his cries were somehow the right notes, a harmony, a counterpoint.

Steve's magic and the magic that was Arkady's gift fused with Kitty's magic to knit bone, muscle, skin. Kitty sang to the rhythm of blood pulsing through the riverine system of arteries and veins; to the strange tempo of membrane, collagen and calcium reforming.

The rivers flow, the earth is whole
Reunited with your soul

Lung tissue knitted up and the blood trapped in all those cells, flooding the chambers and suffocating him, found its way back to the vessels from which they came.

Breath streams in
Sweet oxygen

And the feeble thud, thud of his heart grew steadier.

Your heart is beating
Calm and strong
You will live on
Live on
You will live on

Kitty's teeth were chattering. She'd never been so exhausted in her life.

'Hey kid.' Steve's voice was thin, but it had lost that awful wet, bubbling sound of blood filling his chest.

'Hey,' Kitty managed to reply, a high-pitched and teary syllable.

'Knew you were the one,' he said weakly. 'Minute I saw you.'

Kitty's answering laugh was half a sob. 'I've no idea what you're talking about.'

'We must get them off the street,' Laszlo said, choosing practicality over wonder.

When everyone was too afraid to touch him, Steve struggled to sit up. He hissed at the tenderness and ran a hand over the unbroken skin of his bare chest and stomach. He flexed the fingers of his good arm, and those on the one that had been broken and was now straight, mended, but still sore.

'Pretty sure I can walk,' he asserted, 'if I can get up.'

Yuka wrapped an arm around his back and held him steady while Sal hooked hands under his armpits. Angus carefully wrapped his arms around his uncle's waist and the three of them helped Steve to his feet.

Steve swayed then steadied. He took a step. His knees buckled and his three props grabbed hold of him. Steve managed a wheezy laugh. 'Gimme a second.' He tried again, and his knees locked this time. With their help, he walked away from the blood pooled on the road.

'We gotta get out of here,' Steve said as they steered him into the house. 'We got no idea how they're finding us, but they got us pegged here. We have to go.'

'Let's get you cleaned up first, mate,' Aaron said. 'You look terrible.'

Steve caught a glimpse of himself in the hall mirror. Wet blood was matted in his hair and smeared over his face and chest. It was in the gaps in his teeth and streaked down the arm that had been broken. He was candlewax-pale, he wobbled when he walked, like he might fall over again any second.

The observation made Steve laugh again. 'You should see the other guy.'

'Don't laugh, Uncle Stevie,' Harper said. She and Gretel were clinging to each other. 'It's not funny.'

'Sure it is,' he said, sinking gratefully onto the sofa. 'I oughta be dead and instead we find we've got a wielder of flesh magic in the band. If that don't give us something to smile about in this whole sorry mess, I don't know what does.'

'Hell, Uncle Steve. When you told us you had a freaky-ass job and a freaky-ass life, you weren't telling the half of it.' Angus addressed his uncle with a combination of awe and irritation.

'I never even told you the story about the asshole piper from Hamelin and his fat-ass rats.'

Harper's discomfort at Steve's continued levity prompted Angus to pat her on the shoulder. 'Let's get Gretel's things together, sis, since we gotta go.' He held out his other hand to his husband. 'Come help?'

Taylor took Angus's hand firmly in his. 'And to think I thought *my* family was weird.'

'Gotta say, I think I'm a lot less scared of Thanksgiving with them now.'

'Go off and pack.' Steve took the glass of water Aaron handed to him. 'We'll leave soon.' He sipped, swilled the water around, swallowed, grimacing at the diluted taste of blood.

'I should pack,' Kitty said, but instead of doing something useful she wobbled onto the sofa beside Steve. 'Flesh magic, you reckon? That sounds gross.'

Yuka had fetched a clean cloth from the pile of tea towels left over from Sal's injury. 'He means spirit magic. It alters flesh as well,' she said as she tenderly wiped the blood from Steve's face and chest. 'It is the rarest magic. Very hard on the user.' She regarded Kitty warily. 'Usually.'

Sal helped Steve take his shirt entirely off, leaving the older man's scars and wiry musculature on show. While Yuka used a wet cloth to clean the blood from Steve's hair, Sal used another to wipe blood from Steve's arms, ribs, back. Steve submitted to their care with serene gratitude.

'I ain't seen someone with the gift for wielding spirit magic on flesh in a long time,' Steve said with genial wonder, growing stronger with every unimpeded breath. 'Senora Garrido was your great auntie. That gift's from her line, through your daddy. Arkady did spirit magic too.'

Steve ran a hand over his scars. He glanced up, sensing eyes on them. Laszlo was there, averting his eyes as he offered a clean shirt he'd dug up from the luggage.

'Who is Arkady?' Laszlo asked, clearly wanting to distract Steve from noticing his awkwardness.

Steve took the shirt. 'Guy we met when Anna took me to Europe to find a reconstructive surgeon.' He grimaced. 'I haven't had to explain all this in a long time.'

Yuka squeezed his shoulder supportively. 'You don't need to.'

'We got new people in the band,' he countered gently. 'And no use for secrets.' He addressed Kitty, Laszlo and Aaron. 'Arkady helped me after the operation. He sang magic into my body to get it to produce the hormones I need; it's too hard for me to get injectable supplies on the road, the way we live, especially back in the 70s. Half killed Arkady to do it, though. It's a rare magic and it takes from you, hard.'

'I could feel his magic inside you,' confessed Kitty.

'And now he has your magic in him too, Kitty,' Sal said. 'You persuaded living cells to accept instruction from you. Maybe this binds Steve to you somehow.' The idea plainly worried him.

'All I did was ask them to become whole,' replied Kitty, alarmed. 'I didn't force Steve to do anything!'

'Hey, hey!' Steve held a hand out to her, wiggled his fingers until she took it. 'It's okay, Kitty. Everything's okay. You're the one.'

She still didn't know what he meant by that. She would ask him, as soon as they had found somewhere safer to stay.

'And thanks, for asking my body to mend. Thank you.'

'We're the band,' she said. 'We look out for each other.'

'You sure you're okay?' Aaron said thickly. He hadn't stopped staring at Steve's no-longer-smashed bones.

Steve flexed his fingers. 'Ache a bit. Reckon I'll be back at the strings in no time.'

'Oh.' Aaron sounded disappointed; heard himself – began to rectify the error. 'I mean, yeah, cool. That's good. I'm glad. But I can… while you're recuperating, you should teach me the songs. I didn't know what to play back there.'

'You did great, kid. Does that mean you still want me to teach you the songs?'

'Well, yeah.'

'After all that?'

'I'd rather use music magic to sing the little buggers to dust than clobber them with my favourite Fender, yeah.' His tone verged on indignant. 'It's *dented*.'

'That is what offends you?' Yuka asked. 'That you dented your guitar on an animated corpse?'

'It's my favourite Fender,' Aaron said, as though Yuka were the one having problems with her priorities.

'You intend to join us, then?' asked Sal.

'Cos if you're going to drop out, now might be the time to do it,' warned Steve.

'Are you kidding? That was *brilliant*. Well. Not you getting run over by some galah in a hatchback, that was fucked. Thank God Kitty sings better than she plays the keyboard, eh?' He was oblivious to the twinge of irritated anxiety that twisted Kitty's face. 'But sending that mob back to their graves? Stopping them from hurting anybody? That was… was… *shit…*' Aaron struggled to find the words. 'Bloody *brilliant*! I should be terrified. I know that. If I had half a brain I might be. But it's what I've been waiting for all my life. My gran was right. The things I can do are important. And using music to save the world from monsters? How fucking rock and roll is that?'

He was so wide-eyed, bright-eyed, wonder-eyed with it all, so filled with adrenalin and relief, that he was bouncing on the balls of his feet.

Steve positively *beamed* at his old bandmates. 'We got a new line-up.'

Yuka cast a calculating look at Kitty. 'And you are thinking we have a new lead singer?'

'Might be. Might be I'm thinking that.'

Kitty was confused. 'That would be Steve, wouldn't it? Or one of you?'

'I am not a leader,' Yuka said.

'Steve?'

'Don't you worry none, Kitty. I'd say you best pack some things. We'll stow your keyboards, load up the van, talk about this later.'

'Is that what you mean with all that talk of *The One*?'

'Talk later,' Steve said cheerfully, doing up the last of his buttons. 'Pack. We gotta be gone from here before something else comes hunting.'

That was spur enough. Kitty ran to her room to drag down a backpack and stuff it with clothes and personal items. She ran out again to find Angus rocking Gretel in his arms while Taylor helped Harper with their few bags. Angus was singing Gretel's lullaby to her. *Heave a sigh, baby girl, Don't you cry, baby girl, Your daddies are guarding the door.*

Yuka stood with her arms full of bags, her hourglass drum slung over her back, spare drum sticks jammed into her belt. 'You will still take her?' she asked Angus solemnly.

'You need to ask?'

'What you saw today is her heritage. The music. The magic. The darkness of the world.'

'Steve said the gift isn't always inherited,' Taylor said warily.

'The Minstrel Tongue may skip a generation, it may not, and not everyone with the gift is called. We can't know what Gretel will be.'

'She'll be loved,' Angus said, cuddling the dozing baby close. He kissed her head. 'She'll know who she is, and she'll be loved.'

'This is her heritage.' Sal repeated Yuka's warning, spreading his arms to take in their surroundings: the bloodstained bandages around his head and the blood smeared on Kitty and Steve; the pile of scant belongings in the living room; the impending flight for safety. 'Are you sure you want to take it on?'

Taylor put a protective arm around both his husband and Gretel. 'Of course we do.'

'You had best be sure,' Yuka threatened.

Taylor hugged Angus and the baby closer and answered for them both. 'Gretel's our daughter now. We're her Dads, and we're going to keep her safe.' Then Taylor's unflinching gaze met Yuka's. 'You'd better keep her safe too.'

'We will,' Yuka promised him. 'If I have to die to do it.'

'Oh, hey, none of that,' Steve said. 'One near death a day is enough by anyone's reckonin', don't you think? Let's load this stuff and get on the road.'

'Where are we going?' Laszlo asked.

'I got a mate has a place,' Aaron said. 'It's not too far either which, considering how crowded that van's going to be, is a good thing.'

'Good. That only leaves two big problems to solve,' Steve said.

'Those being?' Laszlo asked.

'How the hell are Alex and Kurt finding us all the time, and how the hell are we going to stop them?'

CHAPTER TWENTY-ONE

Aaron made a phone call from the drivers' seat while everyone piled instruments, bags and then themselves into the van. Taylor and Harper sat in the front beside him, Harper holding onto Gretel. Everyone else was jammed into the back with the luggage.

Aaron drove carefully out into the road and idled while Laszlo wrestled the roller door shut. The road was stained with blood, dust and dirt. Police sirens wailed in the distance. It wouldn't do to loiter if they wanted to avoid impossible explanations.

Once Laszlo had squashed himself into the van, Aaron drove eastward to Thornbury. Half an hour later, he parked outside a low brick warehouse and jumped out to greet the man waiting outside.

'Here you go, Macca,' Aaron's friend said, tossing a set of keys at him. He folded his arms and watched as people poured out of the vehicle, like some kind of silent comedy sketch. 'Man, you were right about having a whole mob to stack away for a night or two.'

'Ta, Mitch,' replied Aaron, opening up the graffiti-splashed roller door to the warehouse. 'I've had a helluva day, yeah? I owe you big time.'

'Nah, it's all good. Consider it payback for helping with the old man.'

'Anytime, cuz, you know that. And hey, if the jacks come poking around, you haven't seen me or the van, eh?'

Mitch frowned. 'Trouble with the cops isn't usually your game, mate. What'd you do?'

Aaron smiled lopsidedly. 'Nothing yet, but the day's young.' At Mitch's unimpressed expression, he elaborated. 'Someone nasty's got it in for Kitty and her mates, made a ruckus at hers. They need to be under the radar a while, yeah? No trouble for you, I swear. We just don't have time for it, you know?'

'Yeah, I know. Need to borrow another car, then? Uncle Stu's in hospital with his kidneys again, so you know, it's there if you need it. Parked around the side. Keys are inside on the kitchen hook.'

'Cheers, Mitch.'

Mitch regarded the mismatched group: the Indian man with a blood spotted bandage around his head; the small Japanese woman and the white guy with wild, greying hair were hefting bags and musical instruments from the back of the van to stow inside the warehouse. The olive-skinned girl, Kitty, was helping while a skinny older white guy with blood-smeared jeans inspected the premises. A couple of white blokes and a woman were fussing over a baby.

'I'll bring over the old cot this afternoon too,' Mitch suggested. 'Auntie Mona's boy's graduated to a big boy bed.'

'You're a lifesaver, Mitch.'

'Yeah. I'm a saint, me. Make sure you let me Mum know next time she's ragging on me for not taking out the rubbish.'

Aaron grinned. 'You should take out the rubbish for your mum, Mitch.'

'Saint Mitch, if you please. And I'll bring some more bedding around for you later. Oh, and watch out for the kettle in the kitchenette, it's on the blink, you'll have to use the microwave.'

Aaron and Mitch exchanged a few more words before Mitch strode off, hands in his pockets and whistling, to his car parked further down the street. Aaron drove the van into the warehouse garage, pulled the roller door down then entered the main building through the connecting double doors.

In the warehouse proper, the group were settling in. The garage was flanked by a large room, comfortably cluttered with boxes of clothing, toys and soft furnishings, all stock belonging to Mitch's family's distribution company. In a far corner, a couple of fold-up camp beds, three inflatable mattresses and a box of blankets took up some space.

Through the back was a kitchenette and shower area, and a couple of offices. A third back room had a camp bed in it. Aaron informed

Taylor and Angus that a cot for Gretel would be coming, and more bedding.

'We can unpack that lot too.' Aaron nodded at the beds and blankets in the corner. 'They're not too dusty. Auntie Mona broke 'em all out for family last month for Uncle Stu's birthday.'

'Big family, huh?' asked Steve.

'Big extended family, yeah.'

'Must be nice,' Laszlo said wistfully.

'When it doesn't drive me nuts,' grinned Aaron. 'What now?'

'I guess we regroup,' suggested Kitty. 'I suppose we need to rehearse some more.'

'After everything you've been though today?' demanded Harper, incredulous.

'Especially after that,' Steve told her. 'First up, though, I need a shower.'

He fetched a towel and clean clothes and disappeared while Laszlo and Yuka began moving boxes and setting up instruments in the cleared space. When Sal winced and prodded at his bandage with his fingertips, Harper insisted on checking and redressing the wound. Gretel was fretful, so Angus and Taylor sang her lullaby to her.

Eventually, Angus unpacked the groceries they'd brought to find a jar of something suitable for his new daughter while Harper rummaged around the kitchen for a plastic spoon.

Mitch returned with the promised cot, extra bedding and more groceries. He raised an eyebrow at the music set-up. 'You going to explain this whole thing some time, Aaron Maclean, or am I going to let Auntie Mona bully it out of you?'

'I'll explain when I've got my head around it. Promise.'

'Okay, cuz, I'll leave it with you then. Give us a call if you need us. Oh, and watch the bub out the back, eh? There's no fence between the yard and the creek down the hill.'

'Gotcha, Mitch.'

Kitty waited until Mitch had gone before she sought out Steve. He was in fresh clothes, his hair clean and spiky. He looked good for a man who'd been a gasp from dying mere hours ago. He leaned with crossed arms against the kitchen wall, watching a mug of water go round and round the microwave.

'How are you feeling?' she asked.

'Oh, I'm fine and dandy,' he said mildly.

'Because I'm still waiting for an explanation about this lead singer business.'

The microwave pinged. Steve dropped a teabag into the mug of water. The hot water fizzed as the surface tension broke. 'I grew up on iced tea,' he said, 'but I got a taste for the English stuff. Microwaving the water's just wrong.'

'Stop stalling.'

Leaving the teabag to steep, he said, 'Thing about the band is when the one that leads the band leaves, we gotta get a new leader.'

'When you say 'leaves' you mean 'dies', don't you?'

Steve grimaced. 'Mostly. Not always. But being honest with you, yes. I joined AnnaTomic in 1970, when I was fifteen. Anna was our lead singer. When the dragon killed her in '88, Rodrigo took over and we became Dragonsbane. A witch poisoned Rodrigo in 2003. Alex stepped up and we became Rome's Burning. Now Alex's gone. We need a new leader, and the leader will give us a new name.'

Kitty's dawning realisation was mingled with horror. 'So, you and Yuka thinking I should sing the lead – that's not actually about *singing*, is it?'

Steve removed the teabag and added milk from a small box of long-life milk. 'Well, the singing's pretty important.' He sipped. 'This is godawful tea. Want some?'

'No. Thank you. And when you kept calling me *the one*, you meant I should be the next leader of this band?'

'It's in you,' he said simply. 'It feels right. Since I saw you in the funeral home singing down those dead folks, keeping your cool after, finding out who you really were: yes, Kitty. I think you're the one.'

'That's ridiculous,' Kitty scowled. 'I can't even play an instrument.'

'For someone who taught herself on painted lines who touched real keys for the first ever time yesterday, I reckon you may be a prodigy. An instrument ain't a pre-requisite anyway. And Kitty girl, you can *sing*. You got a voice to make a world sit up and pay attention.'

'Oh...' She waved her hand dismissively, flustered. 'I–'

'All that, and you have the Minstrel Tongue too.' Steve rubbed a hand over his healed chest, and regarded Kitty so intensely she felt his gaze singing inside her.

'Right out of the blue, you sang that girl Maddie and the others back to quiet,' Steve said. 'You sang the animated dead back into the ground. You sang my body whole. You did all of that, Kitty Carrasco, without anyone ever telling you how. Without anyone teaching you the old songs. You sang words and tunes out of the clear air, singing the dead down and the life right up in me. Believe me. You're the one.'

'But I don't know anything!'

'Leading a Minstrel band ain't all about experience. It ain't even all about power. I keep seein' you take charge and get things done. You got the qualities of leadership, is what I'm saying, as well as all that magic.'

'What... what if I don't want to... to sing lead?'

Steve put down his neglected cup of disappointing tea. 'Then there's nobody going to make you take on a life you don't want, Kitty. It's a hard enough thing to do when you choose it.'

'What will happen to you and the others if I don't?'

'It ain't your problem to be bothering with, if you don't want to step up.'

'That's no answer.'

'It's all the answer you get if you don't want this life. We'll do what we have to till we find someone.'

'Or your old leader and his boyfriend will kill you and take Gretel.'

Steve scowled. 'They ain't the people we loved anymore. They are not *touching* her.'

Kitty believed him. At least, she believed that he'd die rather than let anyone hurt that child. So would Yuka, and Sal. Maybe Laszlo too. Aaron, she didn't know about, but she found it hard to imagine him giving up. He seemed so excited, so proud, to be part of this.

Kitty was calm, now that she knew what Steve and Yuka meant. She felt proud, too. Excited. Terrified. Her grandparents had kept her from knowledge of this life and this danger, but they were gone and she knew who she was. She knew what she wanted.

'You're right,' Kitty said, raising her chin. 'They're not touching her. I won't let them.' It was a big vow to make, knowing so little of how this worked, but she made it anyway. 'You're going to teach me how to keep her safe.'

Steve's scowl gave way. 'You with the band then?'

'I've already said I am.'

'As the leader, I mean. Are you stepping up, Kitty Carrasco?'

'I am,' she said. 'And if I'm supposed to lead, I need to know the songs we're performing. So does Aaron, and he and I need to know a lot more than we do about fighting vampires.'

'Laszlo can help with that. Anything else?' Steve was grinning fit to burst.

'We need to know how Alex is finding us.'

'That we do.'

'And I need to think up a band name, you reckon?'

'It'll come to you,' Steve said. 'No hurry.'

'There might be a *bit* of a hurry. I think I'd better go practise.'

'Never hurts,' he conceded. 'You warm up. I'll see if Angus and Harper'll do the honours of making lunch while we get back to into it.'

'Lunch. Oh god, yes, I'm famished!' She said it as though her hunger surprised her. She felt suddenly dizzy with it.

'I'll make sure they feed you up big, then.'

Laszlo waited until Kitty had gone before entering the kitchen. He spared the briefest glance for Steve before pulling out tins and jars out of the cupboard.

'You right there, Laszlo?'

'Fine, thank you Steve. I thought I would make food for everyone. Magic makes everyone hungry.'

'So does the fact of it being lunchtime.'

'Yes.'

'You sure you okay?'

'Yes.'

'Only, it seems to me you don't want to look me in the eye.'

Laszlo locked gazes with him. 'There, Steve. I look you in the eye. All is well.'

Steve crossed his arms and glowered at Laszlo. 'If you got a problem with me, you state it outright.'

Laszlo was the first to drop his gaze. He rubbed a hand over his eyes. When he lifted his head again, every line of troubled weariness showed.

'I don't have a problem with you, Steve. I don't *understand*, but that's not the same thing. You are still the same m…' He stumbled. 'Person… the same *person* I knew yesterday. You are the same person who taught me how to fight vampires.'

'The same *person*,' Steve echoed back, angry and hurt. 'Sure sounds like you have a problem with me, Laszlo.'

'No,' Laszlo insisted. 'It's not a *problem*. It won't *be* a problem. There's a lot in here.' Laszlo tapped his own forehead with a long index finger. 'There's been a lot in here for a while, and this is something new, that's all. I need to make a place for it.'

'You made a place for vampires in there,' Steve said.

'Yes. I don't understand them either.' Laszlo stretched tension out of his neck. 'Steve, I respect you. I admire you. But today I have two new things too many and my brain, it's telling me, no. Enough. It will catch up. I need time.'

'Time's something we're kinda short on.'

'I *know* this,' snapped Laszlo. 'Do you think I don't know this? I am *trying*, but every other day is something new I have never seen or done, and every other day is something else I struggle to understand. My whole life has become one unending struggle to *understand*. I don't understand how a political system can become more important than people. I don't understand how a career I worked for and loved all my life could become in a single day something I could not stand a second longer. I don't understand how the intention to do right turns into doing so much wrong. I don't understand how a family can walk away and never forgive a mistake. I don't understand how the world is not what I thought it was all my life, or how suddenly there are more and *worse* monsters than the merely human ones I thought were gone for good when the Communists fell.'

He spoke raggedly, the torrent unleashed. 'I chose this life with you because it gave me a chance for something new, something I did not spoil, but it's just another life I don't understand. I don't understand how vampires are real, or how music turns into a weapon against them. I don't understand how a violin knows more about music than I do. I don't understand how Kitty, a mere *child*, is so unafraid of death, or how she can use her voice to make it leave a dying body. And although it seems the very smallest of things to not understand in this life I have now, I don't understand why someone born a woman would want to be a man. I don't understand much, it seems.'

'Not *want*. I *am*. I *am* a man, always have been.'

The silence between them was thick and buzzing with challenge. Laszlo was the first to back away from it, huffing unhappily between pursed lips.

'I have read things, you know,' he said. 'I have heard of people like you. Do... do you mean...' Laszlo groped for the right words, read once in a magazine, '...who you are inside did not match your body, outside?'

Steve's mouth twisted into a troubled *moue*. 'That's one way people describe it, yeah. It's not the only way. Does that description make it easier for you?'

Laszlo eyes narrowed then widened as a realisation awoke in him. 'I... I think perhaps... yes. Sometimes who we feel we are inside is not how we seem outside. And one or the other must change or... or the conflict will drive you mad.' He nodded. 'Yes. I see that.'

'Uh...'

'My conflict is different but... perhaps a little the same. I am trying to fix it.'

They stared at each other, Laszlo like something in him had broken; Steve like he was sorry to have been the one to break him.

'Laszlo, man, if you want out, you...'

'I don't want out,' Laszlo said. 'I want to *stay*. I want to do something *right*, and one day for it all to make sense.'

Steve grimaced sympathetically. 'Can't say for sure that'll ever happen.'

That elicited a bark of dry laughter. 'That is true, I suppose, for any life.'

'I reckon so. Maybe this one more'n most.'

'I wouldn't say that. Living under communism is in many ways much stranger than anything I have done since I met you. And that includes staking vampires and settling the walking dead. At least with those two, it was clear who the enemy was.'

'It's not always that cut and dried, but yeah, I guess the lines are usually easy to see when it comes down to it.'

'I'm sorry that I… caused offence.'

'You are far from the first, and even further from the worst.'

'Nevertheless. I will do what young Salvatore says we must do. I will do better than I have done. That is the promise I make myself daily. And you are a good person, Steve. A good… a good *man*. I think I at least understand *that*.'

'Okay. Well. I guess, if you got questions I can send you to some internet sites. Personally, I'm *way* over teaching Trans 101.'

Laszlo nodded. 'All right. Yes. Please. It would be good to understand at least one new thing.'

'Sure. When this blows over, if any of us survive, I'll send you the web addresses.'

'Aaron is so right. You make this vocation so unappealing.'

'That's why it's a vocation and not a job.'

'You should be the leader, you know,' Laszlo told him. 'Not that girl. She's too young.'

'It ain't youth or age makes you fit to lead a Minstrel band,' Steve replied. 'Alex was nineteen when he stepped up, and he led us for near ten years before it went to hell in Budapest.'

'Hmm.' Laszlo was not convinced.

'We'll see, I guess. She's been leading us fine since we met her so far, and she didn't even notice she was doing it.' Steve grinned at Laszlo's surprise. 'Mostly we didn't either. She's a natural. I've been doing this more'n forty years, Laszlo. Trust me. I ain't leader material, and Sal ain't ready. Aaron might, one day, but not yet.'

'Yuka is formidable.'

'Yuka got burdens of her own about being responsible for us. She don't want it yet. Kitty's the one gonna do this for us, if anyone can.'

From the band area came the sound of Kitty's exasperated huffing, a thump and Angus saying: 'No, see, you haven't locked the legs in place.'

'If you say so,' Laszlo said, dubious.

'I do. What say I help you get lunch together. Then we rehearse.'

'It's kind of you, but no. Any fool can dump canned vegetables into a bowl and heat them up. You go help that girl learn how to set up her keyboard.' As he said this they heard a second, more irritated huff that transformed into *sotto voce* swearing.

Steve laughed. 'That's what roadies are for.'

'This roadie can either make lunch or set up a keyboard.'

'Lunch. I'll send Angus in to give you a hand. Sounds like he can't set up either.'

An hour later, the ten of them were ranged about the main warehouse room on chairs and unfolded camp beds and air mattresses. Gretel had been rocked to sleep in Taylor's arms. Angus gazed at them both like they were made of spun gold and fluffy kittens.

'Don't know how long we've got before Alex and Kurt track us down again, so we gotta make the most of the time we have,' Steve was saying. 'The band needs to rehearse for the gig, and before you ask, Angus, yeah, we gotta do the gig. Now more than ever. We got used up this morning, and I gotta say, personally, I feel like I've been hit by a hatchback.'

Everyone looked at him, aghast, except Yuka, who scowled. 'You're better,' she said. 'You're telling bad jokes again.'

'You like my jokes.'

'I hate your jokes.'

'You love me, though.'

She broke into a rare, affectionate smile. 'I do. So what now?'

'We can take Gretel back home,' Angus said. 'Keep her out of harm's way.'

'Trouble is, we don't know where harm's way is, yet,' Steve said grimly. 'Alex and Kurt know all about you two and Harper. I don't even know where they are right now – heading Stateside to waylay you, or flying down here to waylay us. I don't want you going home and being undefended.'

'Staying here doesn't seem so safe,' Taylor said. 'Not after this morning.'

'Maybe you could stay in a hotel. One of those short stay apartments,' suggested Aaron. 'Lay low while we work out what's going on.'

Yuka began to protest this, but Kitty spoke up: 'You told me the dead had been following you guys. When you came to the funeral home, you said it wasn't me – that it had been happening to *you*.'

'At the markets first,' agreed Yuka, 'and by the railway station, near the music venue.'

'Then at the cemetery over from my place, but only after you guys were all there.'

'Maybe they are following only one of us,' Sal said, troubled. His fingered his freshly bandaged scalp.

'But it's you lot, not Gretel. So if Angus, Taylor and Harper take Gretel somewhere in Melbourne that Alex and Kurt don't know, they should be all right. And if anything happens, we won't be far away.'

Yuka was unconvinced. 'That doesn't tell us how Alex and Kurt are using the dead to find us.'

'Is that what you think's happening?' Laszlo asked.

'The dead we encountered have no malice or volition,' Yuka pointed out. 'They are conduits for something else.'

'Some*one* else, you mean,' Steve said.

Sal covered his eyes with his hands.

'We have some time before they find you again, don't we?' Kitty asked.

'Some,' agreed Steve. 'Assuming we're not sitting on a cemetery here, or a morgue, or the site of some multiple fatality.'

'I'm pretty sure this was always just a meeting and hunting place for the Wurundjeri people,' Aaron said. 'I couldn't tell you more than that, though. It's not my country.'

'Then let's get some rehearsal time in, because we need it, while Taylor phones around for a place to stay.'

'And checks his bank balance,' Taylor said. 'We spent an awful lot getting here on short notice.'

'I can cover that,' Kitty said. 'I had heaps in my account. I've never had much to spend it on.'

'We can't ask you-'

'You don't have to ask. We're looking out for Gretel, right? Besides, it might even be my job.'

Steve's eyebrows rose in surprise. 'It may be, at that. Tell the truth, we're none too used to anybody having much in the way of cash flow.'

'We'll sort it out later,' Kitty decided. 'Right now, Aaron and I have to learn some songs.'

'Fine.' Steve turned to Laszlo. 'Got an old one here. Thought you might like it, Laszlo. It seems fitting.'

'Oh?'

'I wrote it after I joined Anna. We've updated it couple of times since the '70s. I don't think it'll be much of a problem to add a violin part.'

'All right,' Laszlo nodded.

The old and new band members took their positions and followed Steve through the music and lyrics several times. On the third step-through, Kitty played a few harmonising chords while Laszlo wove a simple line of violin notes through and around the melody. Aaron echoed Steve's bass line, and on the fourth time through they sang without stopping.

The shifting sand beneath my feet
Gave way to solid ground
I push, push
I push against it
Running at the world

Yuka's rhythm echoed the sound of running feet and a joyfully thumping heart. Sal on lead guitar sang the main melody along with Steve. While he did so, his grief and anxiety gave way to a remembered fire.

The slap and sting
Feet on the road
To and not away from life
I'm running at the world

When they sang it through again, Steve pulled back from lead vocals to give Kitty free rein on the chorus.

My lungs burn from all this precious air
This life I nearly missed
Nearly left unsung
But I found it, or it found me
This gift you gave me

Aaron's growling bass matched and then counterbalanced Steve's, finding something to add rather than simply echoing the original part.

This city at my feet
The life in my lungs
Light in my eyes and blood in my veins
Joy in my heart
On the edge, on the edge
Of the wide, wide world
Sometimes even when I'm falling
It feels like flying
This gift you gave me
Stopped me dying

And Laszlo played, the old violin tucked under his chin like it belonged there, his expression lost in the music and hope.

My lungs burn from all this precious air
This life I nearly missed
Nearly left unsung
But I found it, or it found me
This gift you gave me

CHAPTER TWENTY-TWO

Not everything went well at rehearsals. Learning a single song in a day was a hard enough, but Kitty and Aaron had only a few days to learn enough songs for a supporting set. They wouldn't be able to play instruments for all of them: even someone with the Minstrel Tongue needed time.

Then there was the new song Steve and Yuka were writing in fits and starts. A part would be learned, an alteration would be needed and the new version learned in its place. The lyrics, too, were taking a toll, given the nature of and reason for the song. It was hard going. They hadn't even begun on Fighting Vampires 101.

By dinner, there had been two hissy fits, one ferocious swearing session, and a bout of frustrated tears.

But they had four songs down. Another four, Steve decided, would be enough. If an extra song was necessary on the night, the newbies could clap their hands and dance.

Taylor had found a serviced apartment to rent. Aaron helped him load Uncle Stu's station wagon and Gretel cried constantly at yet another move. She only settled when Harper held her, and Angus reacted like a kicked puppy then retreated.

Kitty walked in on Taylor giving his husband a reassuring cuddle.

'Aaron said we're ready to go when you – oh.' said Kitty. She averting her gaze while Angus wiped his teary eyes.

Taylor kissed Angus's forehead. 'She needs time, baby, and it's been an awful day.'

'That's the truth. I'm tired as hell. Can't imagine how she must be feeling, poor thing.'

'We've got us a nice, quiet, warm place to stay, where she can have a bit of calm for a few days, isn't that right, Kitty?'

'Yes. A bit of calm is just what the four of you need.'

'You going to be okay?' asked Taylor with genuine concern.

'If I don't beat myself or Steve to death with that stupid keyboard,' Kitty said with a pout.

'You'll be fine, Kitty. You're *The One.*' Angus said it with that dramatic intonation that Steve loved to use.

Kitty wrinkled her nose at him. 'I might have to put you on the list for pummelling as well.'

'Don't you even think it, or my hubby will challenge you to a duel.'

'You see if I don't,' added Taylor, arms wound around Angus's waist. He kissed his man on the cheek. 'Come on then, Gusling, time to get Harper and our little girl out of here.'

Out at the car, Kitty took the front passenger seat beside Aaron, while Angus and Taylor joined Harper and Gretel in the back.

'You don't have to come if you're tired,' Aaron said.

Kitty waved her wallet at him. 'Little Miss Credit Card has to be in attendance.'

'You're taking this being *The One* thing seriously, aren't you?'

Kitty thumped him in the arm with her purse, then sighed. 'I have to, I think.'

Aaron pulled a face. 'Rather you than me, kid.'

'That seems to be the consensus,' agreed Kitty.

Once Angus and his family were settled in and Little Miss Credit Card had done her duty, Aaron and Kitty returned to the warehouse to find the others in deep conference.

'We could go back to Hungary,' Yuka was saying. 'Finish it there.'

'That's supposing Kurt and Alex are still in Budapest, and I don't have a lot of faith in that supposition,' countered Steve. 'They said they were coming for her. We gotta assume they're on their way.'

'How do they even know where to come?' Sal protested.

'I'd have thought the waking dead were taking care of that end of business,' Steve replied. 'What was it Kitty said about the funeral home? That the dead were watching her like CCTV cameras. We know there ain't animosity in most of 'em, except those few today that got close to the house. I can't even say if it was their anger or somethin' else's I felt.'

'How do they get the dead to move?' Kitty asked, a step ahead of Aaron as they joined the group. 'Is that a vampire thing?'

'No,' Yuka said.

'I don't think we've ever had vampires that used to be Minstrels, though,' Steve said. 'I have no idea what kind of magic that might make, or how it might warp the Minstrel magic they had.'

'There's nothing in the journals?' asked Sal, reaching for the battered trunk.

'I read them all the time,' Steve said. 'I don't recall seeing anything there. But I'll check.'

Kitty sat with her back to the keyboard that was giving her so much trouble. 'Maybe you should go through them tonight, while I practise.'

'I think you should rest up,' Steve said. 'We appreciate you working so hard, but you're gonna drop like a stone on us if you keep going at this rate. You sang my nigh dead ass whole again this morning and you been galloping ever since. You have to be half dead on your feet.'

'I'm bushed,' she admitted.

'Oh, you'll be fine,' Aaron elbowed her playfully. 'You're *The One*.'

She rolled her eyes, elbowed him back, but they both froze at Steve's grim expression.

'You may be The One at that, but you only learned about the Tongue and this business two days ago, and you can't push yourself like this. This is the start, Kitty. You ain't seen things yet but mostly empty vessels and a wounded man that wanted real hard to live. You have not fought a real-life, gold-plated goddamned monster yet, and you are going to need to be strong and awake when those monsters come. D'you hear me?'

They sobered. 'I'll get some sleep,' promised Kitty.

'You do that. You too, Aaron. We got a lot of work to do tomorrow, besides learning songs. You need to talk to Laszlo about what happened in Budapest. We need to teach you some basics about vampires, how to not get bit and where to stake 'em.'

On that sombre note, the six of them found beds and bedding and burrowed down to get an early night.

Kitty awoke from a dream full of furtive footfalls and sinister shapes looming at her from the shadows.

Heart pounding, she lay in the camp bed in one of the offices. She had to make herself believe that nothing evil lurked here. No Coco was waiting to eat her. No shuffling, dried out corpses were snapping their teeth at her in the dark. All was peaceful and silent…

Or… not. Kitty was suddenly aware of the faint strains of an unknown song through the walls. It was nothing more sinister than a guitar and a low voice, singing softly, note for note of the melody but a fraction of a beat afterwards, a ghostly echo. She couldn't quite hear the words.

With a blanket pulled around her shoulders, Kitty padded out to see who was singing in these small, secret hours of the night.

Steve snored gently in the second office; in the warehouse, Yuka tossed fitfully on a mattress while Aaron slept on his belly, one arm dragging on the floor. In another corner, Laszlo lay curled on his side, the pillow over his head.

Kitty followed the sound to the garage, then stepped through the connecting door, which she closed before the music could wake anyone. Cool air moved about her shins and feet as she passed Aaron's van.

The garage's roller door was half way up. In the gap she saw a chair and the legs of the person sitting in it. She recognised Sal at last, singing a half beat after the note on the guitar.

Standing in the lamplight
Cast by a reflection of the truth
No longer does it comfort
For I fear illumination
Of the shadowed motivation
I have used for all I do

He'd seemed better, last night, but Kitty knew grief didn't work like that. At the Schumacher Funeral Home, she'd seen all kinds of grief in a few short years. Sadness, disbelief, rage, denial, numbness; even guilty gladness. There were other kinds of guilt, too, in the grieving.

Sometimes I'm scared
Of what I'll find
Behind the shadows in my mind

Kitty was only 21, but she'd worked at the funeral home since she was eighteen and her grandfather had arranged for her to apprentice with the Schumachers. At the time, Kitty hadn't even thought it strange. It some ways, the funeral home had been happier than the melancholy house she shared with her grandparents. The Schumacher siblings were kind, compassionate people. They never minded her singing while she worked, and it had never occurred to them to tell her grandparents that she did.

From the time I could perceive
My own willing to believe
In words like faith
I could feel them there

Kitty was not going to tell Sal that he didn't have to feel guilty or how to grieve.

And though I'm old
I know my soul
Is still afraid of the dark

She waited until the last note faded and then said softly: 'Sal?'

His feet moved sharply on the driveway, betraying his surprise, but then Sal pulled up the roller door.

He'd taken the bandage off his head. She could see the scabs over the lines he'd cut in his scalp.

'I didn't mean to wake you,' he said.

'You didn't. I was having bad dreams.'

'Hmm.' Sal propped his guitar beside his chair.

'You too?'

Sal shrugged. 'I've been having nightmares since Budapest.'

Kitty stepped outside and looked up into the clear sky. The Southern Cross shone, bright, above them.

'The stars are different where you're from, aren't they?' she asked.

'Do you mean India, or Europe?'

'Either, I suppose.'

'Some of them are different.'

'Are you from India or Europe?'

'I was born and raised in Goa. I went to Edinburgh to study. Then... then some bad things happened.'

'I'm sorry.'

'Alex found me. He saved me.'

'I'm sorry about him, too.'

Sal closed his eyes. 'Laszlo thinks I was in love with Alex. He thinks I was jealous of Kurt.'

'Steve doesn't think that.'

'Steve and Yuka were there when Alex decided to save me. Kurt was the one who wanted to kill me.'

'Oh.'

'I didn't blame him. It would have been safer if they had.' Sal fingered the buttons at the top of his shirt, then undid the top three. Twisting and stretching his neck to one side, he tugged the material over. In the dim glow cast by the nearest streetlight, Kitty could make out the curve and line of a design on his back, written in scar tissue.

'I'd been taken prisoner, by these... terrible people. To be a vessel for a demon they wanted to summon. They cut a pentagram into me.'

He pulled his shirt straight again.

'The demon was in me when Alex found me. Killing me would have destroyed it. Alex cut it out of me instead, and they had to banish it.' The fingers of Sal's left hand drifted to the new symbol carved into the skin above his ear. 'Alex thought I was worth saving. I loved him for it. Like plants love rain and the sun.'

His hand curled into a fist that he tucked in close to his diaphragm. 'And I let him down. I let him die. I let him rise as a monster. He saved me, and that's what I did to him.'

'My grandparents saved me,' Kitty said. 'Then they kept me in a kind of cage for 20 years. I get angry about it sometimes. But they loved me. They did their best.'

Sal frowned at the sky. 'Is that an excuse?'

'It is what it is. Loving someone doesn't stop you making mistakes. Really big ones, even. I think the thing is that afterwards, you have to take what you've got, mistakes and all, and keep doing your best for whoever's left behind.'

'I have to do better, for Gretel's sake.'

'Then do better,' Kitty said, 'and remember you're not alone.'

Sal's troubled gaze softened to something that was almost a smile. 'Steve might be right about you.'

Kitty shrugged. 'It's not about me. It's about *us* – everyone, the whole band, together, isn't it?'

'Yes,' Sal said uncertainly.

'That song you were singing...'

'I wrote that after... after Edinburgh.' That dark, unhappy tone was back.

'I was afraid when I woke up a few minutes ago,' Kitty said. 'On my own, in the dark, having nightmares about the Coco.'

Sal lifted his gaze to meet hers.

'But then I saw everyone sleeping around me, and I followed the music and found you. So I stopped being afraid of the dark. I remembered I wasn't alone any more. You're not alone, Sal.'

She leaned over to place a cautious kiss on his forehead. He allowed the unsought but welcome benediction with a sense of bemusement.

'I'm still afraid,' he whispered.

'That's okay,' she said. 'We'll just do our best.'

Chapter Twenty-Three

Being sprawled inside a container of optical and surgical apparatus was not the most comfortable of places to spend almost a day. Alex Torni supposed it was less uncomfortable than if he'd been alive for it, but that wasn't saying much.

Kurt had made the expedient arrangements, calling in a few favours, making a few threats. Kurt always was the practical one. There was no reason that should change simply because they were undead.

The soft crack of the container opening was loud to Alex's ears. Kurt grinning down at him through the darkness. Kurt's grin had changed, now he had those pointy teeth. Fangs didn't have to be on show like that, but Kurt liked them that way.

Kurt had always been the brash one, too.

'Time to rise, precious boy.' Kurt Stefan's lilting Swedish accent remained. Alex had always loved it, though Steve teased him about it sometimes: *bork bork bork.*

He wondered if Steve Borman would still find it funny, the way Kurt talked.

The bastard.

Alex disentangled himself from the boxes of machinery. 'Where are we?'

Kurt helped him out of the container, even though such assistance wasn't at all necessary. 'Australia.'

'That's a big place.'

'We're in Melbourne,' Kurt said, taking no offence. He never did, when Alex teased.

'They're still here?'

'If not, we'll find them soon enough. Now we're back on the ground, we can find them anywhere.'

'As long as they're not flying.'

'They don't know that.'

'No.' They smiled at each other, comrades and co-conspirators, as always. Death hadn't changed them that much.

Alex took Kurt's hand. 'How do we get out of here?'

They fell silent at a footfall in the distance. The security guard had heard them, possibly. Kurt's grin became more feral.

'Best not,' whispered Alex, lips pressed against Kurt's ear. 'If we leave a body, they'll know we're here.'

'I'm *hungry*, Alex.'

'I know, *amore mio*. When we're away from here. I promise.'

Kurt nipped him on the shoulder, harder than playfully, drawing a sluggish bead of dark blood, then lapping it up lavishly. Alex buried his fingers in Kurt's hair, holding him close while Kurt licked the wound clean and it closed up again. 'Time to go,' he whispered.

Kurt swiped his tongue over his lower lip, capturing a smear of Alex's blood from his skin, before leading the way through the dark freight warehouse. Alex followed, their vampire senses leading them unerringly over, around, past obstacles.

At the door, they watched the guard step through the newly unlocked door and make his quick round of the floor. He didn't lock the door behind him. When the guard turned down the first aisle, Kurt and Alex, treads as soft as a mouse, went outside.

The stars of the Southern Cross twinkled overhead, proof of the distance they'd travelled inside the crates. Neither had ever seen this sky before. Neither of them much cared for it, either. To their unnaturally acute senses, every peculiar scent of plant, earth, air was unpleasantly alien. The less time they had to spend here, the better.

Kurt tugged on Alex's hand. *This way.*

They ran faster than watchful cameras could record except as an inexplicable blur. Their steps took them over the tarmac, past freight and passenger aircraft, across expanses of grass surrounding concrete aprons and long, flat runways. They ran west, silent and untiring, leaping fences, then south, following the sound of running water to a creek. Nearby was a road. Beyond it was a golf course, the lines of it unmistakable to their uncanny night vision.

Kurt kneeled and put his hand flat to the earth. Alex sat beside him and looked at the stars.

'Well?'

'The earth,' Kurt said. 'The usual decay. Plants and animals. Nothing we can use.'

'Can you sense her at all?'

'I'm so hungry, Alex.'

'Soon, sweetheart. I promise. Take what you need for now.'

Kurt pressed the fingers of one hand into the dirt and took Alex's hand in the other. He bit into Alex's wrist. Beads of dark blood welled up. Kurt lapped at them then sucked at the wound. When he was done, he kissed the already healing skin in apology.

'Yuka is still here,' he said. 'Somewhere east. I can't tell more than that yet. If I can find human remains, it will be easier.'

Alex kneeled beside Kurt and wriggled the fingers of his free hand into the soil. He had always been more attuned to the earth, while Kurt had more affinity with the air.

'A little way south and east from here,' he said at last. 'There's an old graveyard, too. That will give us deep roots for finding them.'

'We'll find them,' asserted Kurt, getting to his feet and pulling Alex up with him. 'You're never far from the dead in a city like this.'

Alex kissed his lover's cold cheek. 'Let's find you someone to eat, *cicci*. Then we can find our *friends* and get our daughter back.'

Chapter Twenty-Four

The day's rehearsals were intense, but by the end of it the band had eight songs. Three of them even sounded halfway good. The new one was coming together, too.

Yuka was the core that kept them strong, her command of the percussion ensuring that their rhythms were tight. The songs wove around the framework built by her flying hands and drum sticks.

The sound was still lop-sided: although Sal knew the lead guitar parts, he struggled to be consistent. But then Kitty would look at him encouragingly, almost expectantly, and he'd throw himself into it anew.

Fortunately, Laszlo proved adept at filling out the sound with the antiquarian violin. Long, exquisite notes underneath the melody; quick dashing notes above it; the sigh and hum of melody, counter-melody, harmony and even silence, compensating for the changed balance of the band.

'You're amazing,' Kitty told him during a short break.

'I used to be brilliant, the best,' he replied, immodest but without boasting either. 'I haven't played in a long time. Most of what you hear, that's the violin itself. It has a lot of magic in it.'

Laszlo felt foolish even thinking it, but he had the impression that the violin *liked* him. He certainly loved the instrument – how it felt under his hands, the base of it tucked perfectly under his chin or, when he was singing, against his collar bone; the neck of it under his nimble fingers; the bow sliding across new strings on that old wood. The rich notes rose up like a tide, like an ocean – secret and deep and wild and dangerous. When he played it, Laszlo remembered what it used to be to love making music.

Aaron was hampered by the fact that, in Steve, the band already had the bass covered, but he was clever too, pulling together a counterbalancing bass line that worked with the harmonies he was learning as well as fitting in with the overall song.

Kitty kept it simple with the keyboards. Her frustration warred with her delight that at long last she was making music, out loud, where anyone could hear.

Taylor dropped by in the mid-afternoon to report on Gretel, arriving in a hire car and bringing extra provisions. Yuka cornered him in the kitchen and grilled him like a suspicious police interrogator on Gretel's moods, sleep patterns, appetite and clothing options. She kept him there for fifteen minutes, tugging on her necklace and bracelets in agitation, before Steve came to Taylor's rescue.

'Give the boy a break, Yuka.'

'He is not a boy. He is a man who should be looking after his daughter.'

'Harper and Angus are doing some shopping for her,' Taylor told Yuka, half annoyed and half amused.

'You have let them go out *alone*?' was Yuka's horrified response.

'Yes, because Gretel needs food and diapers, and more clothes before we head back to the States. She and Angus have to get used to doing things together too.'

Before Yuka could explain to him why all of these were valid and yet irrelevant points, Taylor's phone beeped. He held it up to show Yuka and Steve a picture of Gretel dressed in an adorable outfit covered in cartoon giraffes in jeeps. The child was chewing on the ear of a fluffy toy koala. The picture was accompanied by the message:

> *Safe and sound back at HQ. Gretel chose this toy herself. Stuck it right in her mouth and bit. Today she either said Gus or burped. I think 1 Harper says 2. <3 u bb.*

'Wind,' asserted Yuka.

Taylor texted back:

> *I say 1. <3 u2.*

He received another:

<3 u and Gretel <3 u 2

and three lines of xxx's in response. Taylor thought Yuka would have something scathing to say about that, but it seemed to mollify her.

'You go back to your family,' she said gruffly. 'Watch them.' Her fingers were tangled back in her necklace.

'She means thank you for the groceries,' Steve said, 'and call us if you have any trouble.'

'Send me that picture,' Yuka added, staring hungrily at his phone. Taylor promised to forward it.

'And you're okay?' he asked Steve outside, by the hire car. 'You were... I was going to say pretty banged up, but...'

'I'm good,' Steve assured him. He hauled up the bottom of his shirt to show off his unblemished ribcage. 'Good as new, see?'

'That is maybe scarier than seeing you all smashed up on the road.'

Steve tugged the shirt down again. 'Not from my end of things, it ain't.'

'I didn't mean anything. But it's all...'

'Yeah,' Steve nodded. 'It is.'

'I'm glad you're okay. Angus and Harper are too. I guess, if freaky miracles are going to happen, it's good they happen to someone you like, right?'

'The *good* freaky miracles, sure.'

Taylor wasn't comforted by the clarification. 'Sure. And... look, I have no idea what's coming for you guys, but take of yourselves. You call us if there's any trouble.'

'If there's any trouble, you take that baby, your husband and his sister and you get the hell out of Dodge, you hear me?' Steve told him grimly.

'But-'

'No 'buts' about it, Taylor. If we can't handle it, you sure as hell can't either. First sniff of trouble, you take care of Gretel and your family or I will personally beat you to death with my favourite guitar. If you have to run, *you run*, and if anyone here is left standing after to ask if they can have some quarters for bus fare, they will be in touch. Am I understood?'

Taylor grimaced. 'Loud and clear, Steve.' He placed a reassuring hand on Steve's shoulder. 'I'll take care of them, I promise: Gretel, Angus, Harper… and anyone who calls for bus fare.'

'Good. We're counting on you for that.'

'Right. Well. I'd better go. Yuka's standing at the door giving me what Harper calls the wall-eye. I see what she means.'

'We can't have that. Get going, then. We'll be in touch. And send that picture along. Might help Yuka keep her calm intact.'

'Yeah, well, Yuka with her calm intact is what we want, right?'

'You best believe it, Taylor.' Steve's grin was another thing that Taylor didn't find especially comforting. With a final wave, he climbed into the car and drove off.

Steve walked back to Yuka, who stood at the open door, fingers curled around her necklace.

'Don't start,' Steve said, ready to push past her.

'You did the right thing.'.

'I don't need your approval to know that.'

'No.' Yuka's thumb stroked one of the white keys hanging from the guitar string around her neck. 'I approve anyway.'

Steve drew a breath and released it slowly. 'You'd think after all this time, you and me would be better at saying sorry.'

'You would think so,' she agreed, deadpan.

'Come on. Let's get back to teaching these kids how to remember more than ten notes in a row.' He back into the warehouse.

With a wry smile, Yuka followed him.

The day wasn't all frustration about rehearsals. Some of it was frustration about their situation. Sal was fractious and jumpy. On more than one occasion after a break he was late back. Someone would have to fetch him from the back yard of the warehouse, where he'd be found staring at the river.

'We have to find out how they're tracking us,' he muttered, or 'Why is it taking them so long to find us this time?'

'We should be thankful they *haven't* found us again,' Yuka berated him.

'We don't even know how they've been doing it,' Sal complained. 'How can we be ready if we don't *know?*'

They'd had the argument several times over, each time convincing Sal to deal with one problem at a time. Given they had no idea where Alex and Kurt were at present, the current problem was being ready to perform for the following night. The band had lost so much, they absolutely needed to get on that stage and get something back. Their survival, when Alex and Kurt finally caught up again, might depend on it.

When night fell, another short break found them once again a guitarist short. Steve started cursing, then sighed. It had been a long, tiring day, and Sal's concerns were far from misplaced. Instead, he went out onto the path and stood by Sal. Sal was leafing through his little inspirational diary, but he put it away and they both stared at the river.

'I don't know what to do apart from what we're doing, Sal,' Steve confessed. 'I don't know where they are. I don't know how they're finding us. I don't know how they're coming, or how soon, except that Alex always manages to do as he means to do. All we can do is try to be ready, and we need what this show is going to give us.'

The door behind them creaked on its hinges. Steve glanced over his shoulder to find Kitty, Aaron, Yuka and Laszlo coming out to join them, carrying folding chairs.

'I don't need to nursemaided by a ... a *pack*,' snapped Sal.

'Look who's got tickets on himself.' Aaron flipped his folding chair out, put it down and flopped into it.

Sal didn't know whether to be puzzled or offended. 'What does that even mean?'

'It means that it's not all about you.' Aaron tilted back in the chair to take in the stars.

'It's pretty out here, with the creek and the sky.' Kitty unfolded her chair and placed it beside Aaron.

'You can see a lot more stars up north,' Aaron said. 'Up by the Murray River. Not so much light pollution, not half so many clouds either.' He inhaled deeply. 'Smell that eucalypt, though.'

Laszlo was carrying extra chairs, and offered his spares to Steve and Sal while Yuka set up her chair too. He set up his chair beside hers. Soon all six of them were seated, pretending briefly to be absorbed by the view.

'We must find out how Alex is finding us,' Yuka said.

'Through the dead, somehow,' asserted Steve. 'There's no malice in the dead that keep rising up to us. They're just... tools.'

'Like CCTV cameras,' Yuka reiterated earlier thoughts. 'But surely they are not asking the dead all over the planet to search for us on the mere hope that we will be seen?'

'Why not?' Aaron asked.

Yuka checked her irritation at the question. 'Communicating with the dead is not easy, even for someone with the Minstrel Tongue. It is not... compatible with what we do. Our magic connects with life.'

'It's not impossible, though?'

'Not impossible, but communication with a dead entity takes focus.' Yuka sat forward in her seat. 'Every encounter so far has been concentrated in a single area. To ask the dead of the whole world to awake and seek us specifically is an extraordinary task. How would they find only us of all the Minstrel bands? How could they be alert to the reply of every dead thing? It would drive someone mad.'

'Didn't you say, though, that you didn't know what would happen if someone with the Minstrel Tongue became a vampire? Maybe they can do it.'

Yuka frowned. 'Perhaps the Tongue goes dark and speaks for the dead instead of for life.'

'Now there's a happy thought,' Steve said dourly. 'But magic has a cost. It tuckers you out, eventually. Even for the undead there must be a price to pay. I don't see how Alex and Kurt have the power to wake up the dead of the whole world to put us on a watch list.'

'The dead at the market were very *old*,' Yuka said. 'The bodies hardy remembered what they used to be. They were under many layers of earth.'

'Not to mention layers of asphalt and concrete,' Steve said. 'Beats me how they could even see you on your own like that.'

'Where was this?' asked Aaron.

Yuka explained tersely about the Victoria Markets and the old cemetery under the asphalt.

Kitty leaned forward too, keenly interested. 'You were on your own?'

'Yes.'

'And the second time was with everyone else in the park next to the rail bridge.'

'Yes.'

'But what about what happened at the funeral home? It was only me there, that time.'

'You were close to the disturbed spirits at the station, and the freshly dead remember more easily than old bones,' Yuka said.

'So, you think that whatever reacted to you at the station sensed Maddie nearby and tried to use her and the others to... to look for you.'

'Makes sense,' Steve said.

'That's horrible,' Kitty blurted out. 'They had no right to do that to Maddie. What if it had been her funeral service? What if her family had been there?'

'I don't expect they care much about that.' Laszlo's eyes lingered on Yuka's tense posture.

'Too right they don't care,' snapped Kitty, outraged. 'What about all those dead people from Melbourne Cemetery and their families? It's awful. It's stupid and it's selfish and it's cruel.'

'That's vampires for you,' Steve said.

'I'm not having it.' Kitty stood up, jaw set. '*I'm not having it.*' She glared at everyone staring at her. 'God, I sound like Grandma.'

'You sound like your Mom, too,' Steve said.

'Good.' Kitty pushed the heels of her hands into her tearing eyes and sat down again. 'Okay. So Alex found Yuka through the layers at the old Vic Markets cemetery; he found the rest of you at the site of an old train crash. Then he latched onto the freshly dead nearby to look for you – and you lot came haring on in on cue. How did you know to come, anyway?'

'We could feel it.' Yuka's fingers were once more curled around her necklace. 'My necklace pulled towards you.'

'Your necklace?'

'Yes, it-'

Yuka froze, staring down at Alex's old guitar strings tangled around her fingers; at the pegs from an instrument that had spent years imbued with Alex's magic. She stared at the remains of Kurt's magic-imbued keyboards which she had drilled and threaded onto the necklace.

She tugged, hard, but there was no catch to snap, no weak point. She'd made the clamps strong when she'd made it, crying soundlessly over the shards of her dead bandmates' instruments, singing her grief and rage into the necklace that she'd made to remember them by, to avenge them by.

Yuka tugged desperately and fruitlessly at the necklace. 'Get it off me. Get it off!' The join where she'd clamped the wires together was as solid as if it had been soldered.

Sal seized the necklace and pulled so hard his fingers bled, but it wouldn't break. It was full of magic and rage and love and loss, and it didn't want to let go.

'I saw scissors in the kitchen,' Laszlo said, rising to fetch them.

'Wait!' shouted Steve.

'No.' Yuka was frantically trying to drag the necklace over her head. The strings sawed against her skin where they were snagged on her ears and chin. 'No. I have put Gretel in so much danger. I have-'

'You gotta keep it on, Yuka.' Steve closed his fingers over her left hand. 'We ain't gonna find Alex and Kurt on our own. We gotta bring them to us.'

Yuka stopped tugging. Her wide open eyes were filled with torment and tears. 'If I have brought them to Gretel-'

Laszlo's placed a reassuring hand on her upper arm. 'You haven't. Gretel is away and safe.'

'Maybe you've brought them to *us*, the band, but we can deal with it,' Steve said urgently. 'It's what we're *for.*'

'This is my fault.'

'You didn't turn them into vampires, Yuka.' Steve squeezed her hand. 'It ain't Sal's fault, either. It's nobody's fault 'cept that damned skunk asshole Prince Vladimir and his damned nest of leeches.'

Yuka's free hand twitched towards the necklace. She made herself rest it on Laszlo's hand on her arm.

'I should have known it was cursed,' she said. 'I should have felt them using it.'

'Why would you know?' asked Steve. 'It would just have felt like their old magic in the wire.'

Yuka's right hand twitched necklace-ward again. She rubbed her fingers against one of her bracelets instead. 'I have put so much anger inside it.'

'Not only you,' Sal said. 'Dying makes you angry. I *know*. Alex had his guitar when they turned him. His rage is there too.'

Steve took Sal's hand too and held tight.

'We can do this. We will put Alex and Kurt to rest. We'll do it right this time, and we will keep Gretel safe.'

Yuka swallowed hard, bit her lip, nodded. She leaned into Laszlo's warm hand, gripping her shoulder.

'And me,' Laszlo said into the tense quiet. 'Whatever I can do. My hand is yours to use as you need.'

'Don't forget me.' Kitty's chin lifted, determined and fearless.

'While we're at this whole *Fellowship of the Ring* thing,' added Aaron, 'you'll have my Fender, too.'

Yuka's eyes narrowed, but that did not conceal how moved she was by the declarations, nor how much dread remained.

'This is all very *Super Sentai*,' she said, struggling to maintain her usual brusqueness. 'But what are we supposed to *do*?'

'Can you tell if they're using the necklace now? If they're near?' asked Aaron.

Yuka gave Steve's hand a squeeze, and he released both her and Sal. Yuka nervously pressed the pads of her fingers to the wire. 'I don't know how to tell.'

'Earlier, you said it pulled you towards Maddie and me,' Kitty said.

'I felt it pulling east in the Markets, too.'

'How about now?' Steve asked.

Yuka closed her eyes and pressed both hands to the necklace. A faint vibration buzzed against her fingertips, though thad could have been the result of her own palpitations.

She pushed her fear behind a door and calmed her racing heart. With a slow exhale, she held her hands lightly over the keys and pegs rather than the strings.

A slight vibration. The ghost of a *pull*.

'I can't be sure.'

Sal regarded the necklace quizzically, one hand resting on healing cuts in his scalp. He tentatively reached for the necklace but halted before he made contact.

'When Alex pulled the demon out of me, his song was deeper than my blood,' he said. 'I still feel it, sometimes, almost like spirit magic. I think I would sense it in the wire if he is... not alive, but... present.'

'You want to try?' asked Steve.

Yuka held herself tense while Sal touched a broken black key threaded onto the guitar string.

Sal couldn't feel anything except plastic and metal, but he'd felt Alex's songs soul-deep once. Perhaps he had to take this in deeper too, to detect its essence.

Slowly, he slipped the necklace into his mouth until both key and string rested against his tongue.

He closed his eyes and hummed a collection of notes, not a melody, but they served to focus his mind. Stroking the cuts in his scalp with one hand, the other a fist pressed into his diaphragm, Sal tasted the plastic and metal. More, he tasted the magic in them.

Yuka and Steve were unfazed by this novel approach. Laszlo, Aaron and Kitty were fazed as hell.

'Sometimes we improvise,' explained Steve softly. 'Gotta go where the moment takes you, yeah?'

'This band is madder than a box of frogs,' whispered Aaron in reply, grinning.

His grin vanished as Sal suddenly keened and began to choke. Fear spiked in Sal's eyes but instead of spitting out the necklace, his teeth clamped shut. His wordless keen rose in pitch, except for the growl of the trapped retching at the back of his throat.

Steve snatched at the protruding parts of it and pulled while Yuka tried to force her fingers between Sal's teeth to make him release the necklace.

She and Sal fell towards each other, as though Sal was swallowing the whole necklace first, Yuka next, even though his jaw was compressed firmly shut. Instinctively, Laszlo and Aaron wrapped their arms around Yuka and Sal respectively, and held tight against the dangerous magnetic tug.

Kitty went where the moment took her. She wrapped her hands around Sal's head. She kissed the side of Sal's mouth then whispered against his skin: 'Let. Him. Go.'

The pressure lessened slightly, but the sound of his choking was terrible.

Kitty threaded her fingers between Sal's on his skull over the sun carved into the skin. She placed a hand over his chest. Kitty's face was so close to his, her hazel eyes a handspan away from his frightened brown ones.

'I've got you,' she said. 'I'm not letting go.'

He whimpered.

'You're stronger than the dead. He can't tell you what to do,' she said to him. 'And you're a good man. You made a sign to remind yourself of that.' She squeezed his fingers over the symbol in his skin.

His eyes lost their fear. His brows drew down and he hummed new notes.

Kitty once more kissed the corner of his mouth and spoke, her lips dragging against his skin. 'Sal doesn't belong to you. He belongs to himself. *Let. Him. Go.*'

With a horrible, gagging cry, Sal's mouth opened and the necklace flew from it. He staggered backwards into Aaron's arms, while Yuka flew back into Laszlo's. Steve followed, his hand clutching the necklace. Kitty stumbled to her knees between them.

A hand gripped her shoulder. Sal. His skin was flushed but he was calm. He held a hand out to her. She took it and used his strength to regain her feet.

'They're here in Melbourne,' rasped Sal, 'but they haven't found us yet.'

'But-' began Aaron.

'They're within twenty or thirty kilometres, to the north-west, but they don't know our exact location.'

'I guess the inside of your face isn't exactly a Melway's map reference.'

Sal arched an eyebrow at him.

'So now? Kitty?'

Kitty was startled to have her opinion sought. She tried to think of a plan. 'First – do you think they can follow the necklace if Yuka isn't wearing it?'

Sal exchanged a glance with Yuka. 'It's hard to tell. It's so full of your magic, Yuka.'

Yuka looked like she wanted to cry, which was unsettling. 'Then we'll cut it off.'

'If we do that, can you repair it?' Kitty asked.

Yuka nodded. 'It is held together with copper tubing. If I cut it, I can use wire or cotton. Very easy.'

'We can do that later, then. We'll cut it off you and then move out of here, to be on the safe side. We don't want to face Alex and Kurt before the concert, do we?'

'We do not,' Steve confirmed earnestly.

'Right. So if we want to get them to come to us, it has to be after the show.'

'Alex and Kurt will be able to follow us to the concert through the necklace,' Sal said. 'The venue is near the rail bridge, and also your funeral home. There'll be so much energy coming to us through the audience, and with those dead nearby, they can't miss us.'

'That's okay.' Kitty sounded more confident than she felt she had a right to be. 'We need to confront them eventually. As long as they don't get to us before we're done. Oh.' A worrying thought occurred to her. 'There'll be so many people there.'

Steve shook his head. 'They won't try something on the crowd. It's us they want, to find out where Gretel is.'

'Right. We play the show, wait to see if Alex has found us, and then-'

'We fight,' Yuka said.

Half an hour later, Steve and Laszlo were still wrestling with the necklace. They had tried sawing at it with knives and twisting it with pliers. The kitchen bench was littered with broken scissors and bolt cutters. The necklace most definitely did not want to be cut, and Yuka's neck was raw with the attempts.

'Leave it,' she finally growled. 'Do it after.'

'What about the plan to leave the warehouse?' Aaron protested.

'We'll have to stay and risk it,' Steve said. 'No sense lighting out to some other hidey hole and have them follow that too. We stay here, rest up and tomorrow we go to the Corner Hotel.'

There was nothing for it but to agree. Yuka hunched in a corner, arms wrapped around her knees. She kept making abortive movements at tugging the necklace.

Kitty sat beside her, back to the wall, legs stretched out.

'Everyone else is in bed.' Kitty ignored Yuka's glare. 'Except Aaron. He's taking first watch.'

'They are not coming tonight,' Yuka said with deadpan certainty. She jerked her chin down toward the necklace. 'I am listening properly, now. I can tell. I thought it was because I missed them, that I felt them so often. I thought their magic was strong in the necklace because they were recently gone. I was wrong.'

Kitty sighed. 'Everyone keeps saying about how wrong they've been about things.'

Yuka's glare intensified. 'If you mean to tell me that everything will be all right, you are wasting your breath. People make terrible mistakes, and there is a price to pay. Then people you love die. Gretel is not an exception.'

'I know,' replied Kitty calmly. 'I've been working in a funeral home for years. I know that death comes to everyone, some much sooner than later. The saddest thing I've ever seen, I think, was a tiny white coffin with teddy bear stickers all over it. The baby was too little to even hold a bear, I think. I helped his mum dress him in this cute little brown jump suit with a hood, with these little bear ears on it. She was really calm the whole time, and she sang to him. *Teddy Bear's Picnic*, you know? I didn't have to do much. The dad put the stickers on the coffin, and he was crying and he couldn't stop. When they were done, they had a minute, and then Marcus came to put the lid on, and she lost it, the mum. She kept screaming. It was awful. So sad. In the end, Marcus left them a bit longer. There was no great hurry, after all.'

Yuka stared at her, aghast.

'All I mean is, I know there aren't any guarantees. I just found out my parents were murdered, not killed in a car accident like my grandparents said, but it hasn't changed much. I've known since I was little that losing people's got nothing to do with fair.' Kitty swallowed. 'All I wanted to say was… I'm going to do my best. I know there's so much I don't know yet, but I've got you and Steve and Sal who know all those things, and we've got Laszlo and Aaron too. I want you to know I'm taking this seriously.'

'It's dangerous,' Yuka said. 'Any of us could die. You.'

'I'm not scared of death,' Kitty replied. 'I see it all the time. I don't *want* to die yet, I've got too much I want to do, but it doesn't frighten me.' She shrugged. 'Half the time I don't know what I'm doing here, and half the time it feels like something I was born for. That doesn't matter much either. I'm here, and I'm going to do everything I can to make sure Gretel's dads don't hurt her, or anybody else. And I wanted to tell you that, and give you this.' She handed over a soft grey cashmere wrap. 'I'd stuffed it in my bag with some of my underwear. I don't actually need it, and I thought you might want to put it under the necklace. Give your skin a break. It looks sore.'

Yuka took the offered wrap, folded it, and placed it between the necklace and her skin. She instantly felt better, as though the buffer of it was more than wool and dye.

'I'm going to get some sleep,' Kitty said.

Yuka watched her leave, her hand sneaking up to the scarf round her neck. She rubbed the cloth between thumb and forefinger.

She dared hope that at the end of all this, Gretel would be safe – even if the rest of them weren't.

Chapter Twenty-Five

Kitty stood backstage at the Corner Hotel, peeping out at the gathering crowd, and tried not to hyperventilate. Death didn't scare her much, but apparently the idea of performing in front of that crowd terrified the living fuck out of her.

She ducked back into the cramped room. 'We should have rehearsed more,' she said, her voice rising in panic. 'You made us take the afternoon off, and you shouldn't have. I don't know the songs well enough! *Oh my god, I don't know the songs* **at all**!'

'You know the songs fine,' Steve told her soothingly.

'No I don't!' Kitty wailed. 'I've forgotten every bloody word and note! *Oh my god.*'

Aaron handed her a paper bag that had until recently held a takeaway burger and fries, then helped her breathe into it. Her hazel eyes were huge and disbelieving as they stared at him over the rim of the bag.

'Stage fright,' Aaron said confidently. 'It's a bitch.'

The bag expanded and contracted with every heaving breath Kitty took.

'Ignore the crowd,' Laszlo told her kindly. 'If you get lost, look to Steve. Take your lead from him.'

'I'm supposed to lead the band,' was her paper-muffled reply.

'That means you should know when to pass the reins to someone else for a bit,' Aaron said. 'You'll be fine.'

Kitty closed her eyes and tried to believe it.

A woman with short pink hair and a T-shirt decorated with zombie unicorns stuck her head in the room. 'Ten minutes, guys.'

'Thanks.'

Kitty breathed harder into the paper bag.

'I had a panic attack my first performance,' Aaron said, 'and I accidentally set fire to my amp.'

'Not helping, kid,' Steve said mildly.

'Not with magic,' Aaron elaborated. 'I knocked a candle over, it fell into the wiring, sparks went everywhere. It was brutal.'

'*Really* not helping,' Kitty said.

'The crowd loved it.' Aaron, patted her shoulder.

'How can you be so calm?' Kitty demanded, screwing up the paper bag in her fist.

Aaron bounced on the balls of his feet. 'That which does not kill you makes you stronger, yeah? That mob out there can't kill you. All they can do is make you try harder next time. And hey.' Aaron nudged her with his elbow. 'In the last couple of days your audience has been the zombie apocalypse. This'll be a doddle.'

'Not the zombie apocalypse,' Yuka corrected him sternly. 'The wakeful dead.' Yuka's now hated necklace rested over her neck. Her skin underneath it was raw and inflamed, despite wearing Kitty's cashmere scarf as a barrier. Yuka acted as though it didn't hurt.

Sal brushed his fingers over the scabs of his sun-shaped wound in his shaved head. 'Alex told me that before he even discovered he was a Minstrel, he decided about his first audience: *You're going to love me*. And they did. It wasn't magic, just Alex. He was like that.'

Sal looked Kitty in the eye. 'You have that spirit in you, too. When you take that stage, you'll see all those people waiting in the darkness to love you. You'll be where you belong.'

Kitty inhaled deep. Exhaled. Inhaled. Exhaled. She could do this. Her untrained father had sung to a Coco and kept it at bay. *She* could bloody well sing a couple of songs to a boozy crowd. Easy peasy. No worries.

Kitty jumped at the touch on her elbow. It was Steve, with kind eyes and a little of that slightly manic humour she expected.

'You do belong up there,' he said. 'You have the Minstrel Tongue. And we need you.'

'I'm not really The One am I?'

'Kitty, honey, you come from a long line of Minstrels and you have a talent for bringing everyone along with you when you get organised. Don't let two words said by an old fool who couldn't believe he wasn't dead spook you. You do what your heart tells you to do.'

'Right,' she said. 'Right.'

The pink-haired lady reappeared. 'Time.'

Kitty strode onto the stage ahead of the others: because she belonged; she had the Minstrel Tongue; she was The One, even if she wasn't; because it had to be done.

She stared out at the crowd from behind her keyboard as the rest of the band took their places on the Corner's side stage. Sal was right – with the lights focused on the stage, the audience were a moving mass of shadows in the darkness.

And they were going to love her, damnit.

Yuka hit the drums and Steve hit the bass line. Laszlo drew his bow across the violin and a sweet note sang out high over the top as Aaron's improvised counter-bass line thrummed underneath.

Kitty put her hands on the keys and the chord swelled from the amplifier. This time she didn't jump at the sound. She leaned into the microphone, mouth close to it as Steve had taught her, and began to sing.

They say love is hearts and honey
It's what we feel
We gaze at each other and sigh
At the altar of Eros, we kneel

Kitty sang strongly and steadily, and she remembered every word and every note.

But love is not a state we are in
Love is not a wailing violin
Love is an action, it is a force
Love is a battlecry
Shout it until you're hoarse

This had been Anna's song. Anna, whom Kitty would never know, but who had written this declaration of intent.

This is the world I love
I will fight for it
For wisdom and kindness
I will fight for it
Open my arms to the blood and the pain
And I will do it again and again and again

Other voices had joined with hers. Kitty heard them, heard the music, heard it all, each individual line but also how each part blended together in harmony and counterbalance, becoming larger than its component parts. It was glorious.

You cannot fight darkness with darkness, only light
The other side of fear is love and the end of night
For every act that is cruel, there is one that is kind
For everyone lost, there is someone to find
For every dark deed, there is one of grace
For the hope of all this, I will take my place

The crowd loved it. The energy the musicians threw out to the audience came back threefold. Fivefold. Tenfold. It was a spark and then a fire and it made Kitty's heart pound and her blood sing.

This is the world I love
I will fight for it
Compassion and courage
I will fight for it
And open my arms to the blood and the pain
Open my heart again and again and again

A part of her was thinking, *look at me Grandma, Grandpa. Look at me, Mum, Dad. Look at what I can do. Look.* The rest of her was weaving itself into and around the song: the notes and the instruments, her band. The unexpected and astonishing beauty of all those different and separate things meeting and meshing and becoming something new and unique and powerful.

Love is an action, it is a force
Love is a battlecry
Shout it until you're hoarse

The notes held, and held, and held, and faded. Kitty, eyes bright, face shining with the glory of it, shouted into the microphone:

'G'day all you beautiful people! You came for Rome's Burning, but we've changed our name. From now on we are Kitty and Cadaver. I'm Kitty. And we're here to save the world!'

Yuka crashed out a wild rhythm; the band played; Kitty threw back her head and sang. The audience roared acclamation back at them. They shouted and danced and filled the band up, filled them all up, with every bit of energy they had.

And outside, on the streets of Melbourne, two dead men loped along in the dark, led by the rage of their dying that was woven into a necklace, towards the hotel beside the railway tracks.

Alchemy.

The magic has its own agenda. Music in the blood as well as the soul. All ways of saying that the first ever gig by Kitty and Cadaver did everything it was supposed to do.

The eight songs were rough in parts. Steve had to take lead vocals half way through one song when Kitty blanked at the end of the first chorus, but they'd never played in front of a living crowd before, and the audience didn't notice anyway. With Aaron's encouraging grin and Sal regarding her as though he already trusted her with his fate, Kitty dismissed the misstep and stepped up to do better.

The wash of musical energy flowed out to raised hands, upturned faces, bodies that swayed and rocked, and the tide of it came back, a swelling wave that slapped onto the stage and surged over each musician. Out it went again, the rush of music and alchemy, feeding the audience, who sang and moved into it before sending it, swelling higher, onto the stage again. Back and forth. Mounting with each ebb and flow, until the room was awash in music and power.

No wonder the bands that played after Minstrels always did so well. When Kitty and Cadaver finished their set and the headline act came on, it walked into a space potent with creative vitality. To a Minstrel, they were fizzing with it as they unslung their instruments in the greenroom, practically bouncing on their feet.

Kitty hugged Steve deliriously, squeezing him hard instead of trying to articulate the buzz in her blood. Steve wrapped his wiry arms around her and held her tight.

'Told you,' he murmured in her ear, and she laughed.

The pink-haired woman stuck her head into the room again. 'Nice one, guys,' she said. 'You got some people waiting at the bar to see you.'

'Who?' Yuka asked, suspicious, fingers hovering over the necklace. The weighty tug in it slewed the necklace to one side, but she gave no indication that danger was any closer.

Pink-hair shrugged. 'Musos and a couple of Kooris.'

'My mob,' Aaron said. 'Mitch and his lot, and probably my band. My *other* band. I texted them all to come. Guess I need to go break up with them, eh?'

'Pack up first,' instructed pink-hair. The venue staff and Laszlo had brought their gear off stage. As the headline act launched into song on the main stage, the band all mucked in, winding amp cords, stowing guitars into cases, packing up Kitty's keyboard, disassembling the drum kit and stowing the lot in a corner, ready to load into the van.

The new onstage energy splashed against them as they reached the bar. Aaron's cousins were effusive in their praise, slapping his back and saluting the whole band with a round of beer.

Aaron's old bandmates were less impressed. Baz the drummer and the lead guitarist, Mace, were disgruntled but resigned.

'We've been waiting for you to find a better band to join, mate,' Mace said, making the best of it.

Pauly, the lead singer, was pissed off. 'You didn't tell us you had a side gig going on.'

'I didn't until a few days ago,' Aaron said.

'They're not bad, I guess. Except for the old dudes.'

'We were fucking *awesome.*'

'Your drummer's hot,' Pauly conceded, giving Yuka a slow, lingering once-over. Yuka scathed him from head to toe with a glare that would flay rats. Pauly looked hastily away and he caught sight of Kitty. 'Aaron. Dude,' he scoffed, waving his hands in front of his chest to suggest that Kitty's main failing was lack of bust. 'Chicks on keyboards shouldn't front bands.'

Aaron's intention to bow gracefully out of Firedog Brigade took a mortal blow to the head. 'Pauly, you're a prick. Find yourself a new bass player.'

'We only wanted you 'cause of the van, anyway,' sneered Pauly. 'You are *so* full of it.'

'I bet you joined this lot 'cause you're banging one of those chicks.'

'Hey man,' Mace interrupted half-heartedly. 'Don't be a dick.'

'Which one are you nailing?' Pauly persisted. 'Or is it both?'

Before Aaron could find an insult all-encompassing enough to reply, a bluff, overly effusive man pushed his way into the group.

'A six piece after all, eh Borman? Nice work on short notice. You got the crowd jumping.'

'Malone,' Steve acknowledged the promoter with an aggravated sigh. 'We told you it'd be fine.'

'So you did. My bullshit detector misfired, I admit it.'

'You got the cash, then? Or is *my* bullshit detector in perfect working order?'

Malone laughed as though that wasn't an insult. 'Well, you know there's a fee on cash rather than bank transfer.'

Laszlo stepped in behind Malone – effectively giving him nowhere to run – and leaned close.

'Mr Malone,' he murmured into the promoter's ear. 'I don't think you want to do that. What with your *professional standards* to maintain. We have a reputation too.'

Malone was irritated at being so oddly threatened and in such vague terms. 'You're hardly in a position to dictate terms.'

Yuka drew drum sticks from her belt and tapped against the rim of the bar. The almost inaudible rhythm immediately disrupted the flow of energy coming from the headline band. Sal sang something in a minor key, fracturing the energy further. Around them, the mood began to be restless, aggravated. Verging on the ugly.

'Y'all best pay up what we're due,' Steve said.

'How're you doing that?' growled Malone.

'Magic.' Steve's all-teeth grin was frankly alarming.

Malone hated brawls. Glass was a bitch to clean up. 'You have the wrong end of the stick entirely,' he insisted. From the pouch at his waist he drew two thick roles of bright red twenties.

'Some of those pineapples as well, I reckon,' Aaron said, checking out the bounty. Malone shot him a venomous look and included a thinner roll of mustard-yellow fifties in the bundle he handed to Steve.

Instantly, Yuka and Sal changed their rhythm and key. The bad vibe vanished in a wave of replenished enthusiasm from the crowd.

'Cheers,' Aaron cheeked.

Malone never wanted to see these people again. In order to facilitate this desire, he shouldered past Laszlo looming at his shoulder and went to sulk in his office.

'Well, that sure was easier than usual,' Steve said, jamming rolls of cash into his pocket. 'Oh, don't worry kid,' he said to Kitty's alarm. 'Venues hate to pay, musos hate not to be paid. Gotta have a little – what's that great word the Brits have? Argy-bargy. Don't feel we've properly earned our bit if we don't have to bump heads for it.'

'I don't suppose you could pull some strings,' Pauly said, shoving his face into the conversation, 'and get us a gig here?'

Yuka knocked Pauly aside with a sharp shove of her hip. Her hand was clutched in the necklace, the strings on the point of drawing blood as they pulled hard against her neck. 'They are here.'

Ignoring Pauly's irritated protests, the band turned as one to see two shapes moving towards the front exit. One of them was tall and slender, ash-blond hair cropped close except for the long fringe. The other was shorter, stockier, with darker, longer hair. They moved like slow liquid, like mercury, through the crowd.

'Gotta go, Mitch,' Aaron said to his cousin. 'Talk to you soon.'

'Still need the space for your mob, cuz?'

'For a day or two. I'll call.'

'No dramas.'

'Oi, you traitorous prick,' snarled Pauly. 'I'm talking to you.'

'Give it up, Pauly, you arsehole,' Baz said wearily. 'You blew it.'

At the stage door exit, the pink-haired roadie glared at them. 'Your instruments?' she said pointedly. 'You'll have to clear them out of the green room after the gig.'

'We'll be back,' Steve promised, perhaps rashly under the circumstances.

Laszlo stopped to collect the violin, so was the last out the door as the others dashed into the car park, where they dug into the van for their acoustic instruments and Yuka's marching drum. Yuka stood at the mesh fence on lookout.

A train rumbled across the overhead railway bridge. On the other side of the narrow side street was the park where they had sung magic into Yuka's new sticks. A few streets over was Schumacher Funerals.

Shadows detached from the darkness. Alex smiled at Yuka, light gleaming from his bared teeth. Behind him, diamonds of light accented Kurt's eyes as those of a predator.

'Hi Yuka.' Alex knelt and put his hand to the earth without taking his eyes off her. 'Where's my daughter?'

Yuka's necklace dragged groundward. The uncanny gravity tugged on her feet, those strings of sensation she'd first felt in Victoria Markets.

'We have to get away,' she murmured to Steve as he came up beside her.

'I can heaaaaaar yooouuuu!' sing-songed Kurt.

'I want my daughter.' Alex was tapping on the ground with the palms of his hands, knocking at the entrance of what lay beneath.

'You can't have her,' Steve told him. 'You're not her Daddy anymore.'

Sal joined his bandmates. There they stood abreast – Yuka, Steve, Sal – confronting two dead people whom they had once loved.

'Sal,' Alex's smile widened to a horrible approximation of something warm. 'How's my boy?'

Sal trembled, head to foot, a deer caught in the gaze of a wolf. He squared his shoulders. 'I'm sorry,' he said.

'You should be. Where's Gretel?'

'Safe.'

'She's ours.' Kurt's lip curled, revealing the point of a fang. 'Give her back.'

'Safe from you,' Sal elaborated. 'I'll always keep her safe from you. That's what Alex and Kurt would have wanted.'

'I *am* Alex, and I want my baby girl.' Alex loomed towards him. Sal took an involuntary step back.

'You *used* to be Alex and Kurt,' Steve said. 'Now you're just dead things that wear their memories.'

'Gretel needs her Daddies,' snarled Kurt.

'That ain't you no more. You can only hurt her now. And you – the people you used to be – wouldn't want that.'

'You always were a smart-arse, weren't you, Steve?' said Kurt. 'Smart mouthed girly-man. Whiny little ladyboy.'

Steve knew for sure that this was not the Kurt he'd known, because Kurt – practical, loyal, good-humoured and adoring Kurt – would never have said that to him.

Out of the dimly lit car park, Aaron took his place next to his bandmates. 'You're a bit of a shit, aren't you?' He had one hand on the neck of his guitar, the other poised over the strings.

Kitty appeared beside him. 'We're not doing this here,' she said, addressing the vampires.

Laszlo took his place, too, although he didn't speak. Alex's face lit up cruelly. '*Buanosera*, Laszlo, you bastard. Have you told the others what you are, yet?'

Laszlo grit his teeth. 'What I was and what I am are not the same. Like you. Only I am claiming my soul back and you gave yours up.'

'Oh, I didn't *give* mine up,' snarled Kurt in reply. 'I didn't *give* a thing. Vladimir *took* it from me, and I got vampire blood in exchange. What I am now, I was *made*. You gave up yours though, didn't you, Alex, *sötnos*. For me.'

Alex reached for Kurt's hand. 'You *were* my soul, *cicci*.'

'You're the one who made Alex.' Steve's eyes widened in shock. 'Kurt, how *could* you?'

Kurt and Alex exchanged conspiratorial and amused glances.

'I asked him to,' Alex said. 'Vladimir said I could try to survive turning or watch him behead Kurt. Vladimir always did have a cruel sense of humour. But I wasn't going to lose Kurt a second time. I *love* him.'

'You loved him. You don't love him now, in the way you think. You need a soul for that kind of love.'

'You don't know the first thing about love,' Alex snarled. 'You never had what Kurt and I have, and you never will. Who'd want you? Anna? The pity fuck?'

Steve lifted his chin. 'You can't hurt me by twisting Alex's memories to be cruel. I know who I am, and I know who you ain't, and you ain't Alex. Your soul is dead. You *think* you're real. You ain't. You're an echo.'

Alex's mouth twisted in savage outrage. 'I'm real enough, you little shit. Kurt and I risked everything to have our baby, and then I surrendered everything to keep Kurt. All we need is Gretel, and we'll be a family again.'

'Told you, ain't gonna happen.'

'Told you,' mimicked Alex nastily, 'give me my daughter.'

'*I* told you,' interjected Kitty sternly. 'Not *here*.'

Alex grinned, showing off his sharp teeth. Kurt laughed, a low and unpleasant sound that morphed into a low note, resonant and swelling.

Four things happened.

The ground beneath their feet surged and buckled with the sound breaking from it: the scream of metal, failing breaks and century-old ghosts remembering when death was upon them.

Yuka sang a note in reply, pure and high, as she raised her drum sticks and crouched into a battle stance.

Sal, his guitar slung untouched across his back, spread his arms wide and sang a harmonising note. He walked towards Alex, determination in his eyes.

Kitty Carrasco set her lips in a firm line, scowled and grabbed both Sal and Yuka by their shirts and shoved them in the direction of the underpass that was cast into shadow by the railway bridge. 'Not *here*! Run, like we **said**!'

Instead of standing to fight on ground full of the blood memory, Kitty and Cadaver took off as one. They ran full pelt towards the main road and the underpass, clutching their instruments, then down the footpath heading towards the sports park and the Yarra River.

A group of people trying to cross a busy intersection against the lights, burdened with instruments and trying not to get run over, will never be as fast as two angry vampires. The band's only advantage was the unexpectedness of their sudden flight while the vampires were busy summoning old pain from the earth, and probably trying to summon the recently dead from the Schumachers.

With a snarl, Alex and Kurt abandoned their first plan and dashed after their prey. They flung themselves into the stream of traffic in pursuit, causing drivers to brake hard and spit curses at the 'drunk morons'. By the time they'd crossed the road, the others had passed the rental car yard and the car wash, and were heading towards a sports park shaped like a futuristic beehive.

'Y'all coming?' Steve shouted defiantly, 'or are you gonna stand there bein' dead all night?' Then he ran, guitar bouncing against his back.

'They want us away from the hotel,' Kurt said.

'And the blood under the rail line,' Alex said.

'We don't need the crowds, the blood or the corpses,' Kurt replied. 'Let's get our daughter.'

The park was wide and green, marked up for rugby and other ball games. It was divided in two by a tree-lined path. Ahead of the vampires, Yuka stopped to beat a tattoo on a power pole with her sticks. A zing of electricity shot from light pole to light pole, the white glow flaring and burning, making the vampires flinch from the fierce light until their eyes adjusted.

When they had, Yuka stood in the path, her arms upraised as she twirled her sticks with feral fervour. She beat them together over her head in a quick heart-beat rhythm – another taunt – before running fleetly over a footbridge that crossed a humming stream of traffic.

The vampires crossed the bridge after her as she ran into the park on the northern bank of the wide Yarra River, beyond the sunken flow of traffic.

Alex could have caught up with Yuka easily. Everyone knew it. He halted under an avenue of trees and put out his arm to stop Kurt from launching himself straight at Yuka where she stood on the path with her bandmates.

Alex smiled at her, letting his fangs show.

Yuka held her sticks over her drum. Steve and Sal held their guitars. On the grass to one side was Laszlo, violin already tucked

under his chin. The new boy with another bass and the girl without
an instrument were nearby, apprehensive and determined.

'Aren't they adorable,' grinned Kurt at the newbies. 'All fierce
and fired up. I remember that.'

'Last chance,' Alex said in a friendly tone. 'Tell us where to find
Gretel and you can all walk away.'

'Ain't happening.' Steve lifted his guitar.

'You don't honestly think we're going to join you under those
trees, do you?' sneered Kurt. 'Do you think we don't remember
Budapest?'

Sal raised his guitar too, and he and Steve began to play. Yuka
flipped her sticks around her fingers, crouched, and began to beat a
tattoo on the concrete path. Laszlo drew the bow across his violin.
The boy with the bass began to strum too. The olive-skinned girl
with the bright hazel eyes breathed deeply, listening.

Kitty and Cadaver. No longer Rome's Burning, because Alex Torni
was dead.

Alex bared his teeth at them. Beside him, Kurt curled his hands
into fists.

All six of the band began to sing, in harmony, the new song:

The dead will not lay down and die
Your soul has fled
Your body now a vessel
For the rage and the hunger
And a twisted memory
Of the one you used to be

The band hadn't only been rehearsing for the hotel gig. They'd been
rehearsing for the confrontation they knew was coming. They knew
they'd need a song Alex and Kurt didn't already know.

This was not the song they'd sung against the vampires in
Budapest.

As we loved you
It is time
To bid you and your love adieu
Time to part our ways

Kitty had written some of the lyrics, making her mark as Steve suggested, separating Kitty and Cadaver from the band that had died in Budapest. The words weren't weapons yet, but singing them prepared the earth and the trees.

The vampires who used to be their friends frowned, puzzled. Alex sneered. But when the next verse began, he knew what was coming. The words and the melody were new, but the purpose was unchanged.

This is where we say goodbye.
This green and growing earth will rise
It will defend
The order of all things

Alex had been the driving, unifying force of Rome's Burning. He wasn't about to be sung to oblivion by a little girl. He'd been a music minstrel when he died. Kurt had been his right hand, his heart, his strength and his solace, and he wasn't going to let these weak and self-righteous bastards who had betrayed them both put an end to them. *Fuck no.*

As the band sang under the trees…

With root and trunk and bough
It will fight to set you free
Of this curse you will not see

…the remnants of Alex's minstrel magic rose up. Corrupted, perhaps, but what remained was his. He let it guide him. He let it borrow from the weapon the others were trying to use against him; let it give him words and notes that would slide into this other song. A shield, at least, if not yet a sword. He sang.

As you loved us and let us die
We are not prepared to say goodbye

Above them, in the otherwise still night, tree branches began to sway, the leaves rustling as though a sharp wind blew through them.

As we fought for you
It is time

'You didn't fight hard enough!' Kurt snarled over the sound of creaking wood and hissing leaves. Alex raised his voice over the growing din, tucking it into the notes of the counter-song he sang.

Our lives cut short
And it's your fault

Yuka's eyes were bright, with tears, with rage, and she beat the ground harder.

To accept your time is throucgh
Time to part our ways

Alex could hear the beating of Yuka's heart as well. He seized onto that rhythm and onto the rage that rose up with the beat. The rage served him as well as it did her. Darkness was where vampires loved it best.

The blood and breath we lost
And yours will repay that cost

The ground was rocking, shifting like giant things burrowed under the surface. Above, a branch stopped swaying and instead it swung. It *jabbed*.

Make a weapon of this branch
Make a sword
Make still the restless dead

Kurt leaped easily aside and began stalking the boy with the bass. The boy kept playing, but moved away, further down the path, away from the others. The girl kept singing at his side, but her expression was troubled.

Steve stepped between Kurt and the youngsters. Alex sensed no rage in Steve, but there was resolve. That was no good to Alex at all.

Sal, though. Sal's heart of doubt and wailing loss was leaking into the song. Plenty of wonderful, dark things lived in there to amplify and spoil the spell. Alex used it to counter the shifting of the trees, those many, moving wooden stakes writhing towards his and Kurt's dead hearts.

You can try to reshape the world
Twisting it to your command

Alex deflected one branch, and another. He tapped Kurt's hand and nodded at Laszlo, Kurt grinned nastily.

A root burst from the soil and tried to lash Kurt's feet, but he leapt high and landed neatly on an unbroken slab of path. With a laugh, he veered towards Laszlo, ducking the stabbing boughs.

With a spear, a dagger blow
My friend is dead, the one I knew
This parasite instead, bid adieu

Nervously, Laszlo played and moved away. Yuka stepped in front of him, a token protection, but Alex lunged at her, and she had to leap out of reach of his grasping hands and bared teeth. She raised one stick in her fist, but hesitated. *Prepared to sing,* Alex thought, *but not to stake me yourself. Coward.*

But the rot under the ground
Has its say
Your weapons will do no harm this day

The tree directly above them began to wilt, shrivel and stiffen, the leaves falling dead from the twigs. Obeying Alex's sung command, the tree swiftly withered from branch tip to root. Then the tree beside it began to die. And the tree next to that.

Kurt snatched at Laszlo's wrist. Steve rounded on him from the right, and Yuka found the courage to approach again. Sal stepped between Kurt and Alex, trying to keep them apart. But Kurt and Alex knew each other well and Kurt had understood Alex's unspoken command. *Get them at their weak point. The violinist. Magic in the instrument, but not in the man. Make him stop and they will lose a sixth of their power.*

The new band sang well together, but Alex had been a Minstrel leader for a decade. His warped magic had power enough to protect him and Kurt for now. Kurt had faith in that.

Kurt twisted Laszlo's wrist and the bow dragged a disharmonious shriek across the strings while the man himself howled at the pain of the joint bent all wrong. Kurt tugged the violinist's arm high and wide, exposing the man's chest and throat.

Laszlo cried out. The cry rose to a sudden, short scream and fell to silence as Kurt bit, hard and deep, into the Hungarian's exposed throat.

Yuka lunged but Kurt, Laszlo locked in his arms, put the violinist between them. Laszlo's eyes were wide and terrified, his grey hair a crazy halo. Kurt laughed around the blood pumping onto his tongue. He nuzzled obscenely into the torn flesh and sucked and suckled.

The song to make the trees a weapon had a frantic note to it. The tree from the other side of the path bent, the green wood of it emitting a high, squeaking cry at the harsh angle of it, and formed into a lance.

Alex raised a hand to ward it with a song, and the two melodies hung in the air, meshed and matched.

Make a weapon of this branch

> *You can try to reshape the world*

Make a sword

> *Twisting it to your command*

Make still the restless dead

> *But the rot under the ground*

With a spear, a dagger blow

> *Has its say*

My friend is dead, the one I knew

> *Your weapons will do no harm this day*

This parasite instead, bid adieu

Stalemate.

Until a voice rose clear above them both, borrowing from both melodies and knitting them together into something new.

> *Grass is green and growing*
> *Under our feet*
> *Leaves are breathing here*
> *Above the street*
> *The pulse of life is pounding*
> *Feel the beat*

Words and notes overlaying and strengthening Steve's song. Steve heard it and played as though refreshed.

Alex felt his hold over the dead things underground waver.

And below the soil
Is decay
That once was life, once knew
the light of day
Life feeds death feeds life
It has always been this way

The tree opposite him stretched and thickened, made robust by the rich soil, made of death and life and death and life. The lance it abruptly made shot into Kurt's torso.

Alex screamed, but not as loudly as Kurt, who pushed Laszlo away and staggered, clutching at the green wood protruding from his belly. He wrapped his hands around the bough, tugging fretfully at it.

'Missed my heart, you stupid bitch,' he wheezed at Kitty, whose eyes shone like a light. Dark blood and scarlet stained the teeth he bared.

Alex seized the branch lodged in his beloved's torso and yanked on it. He didn't dare to sing the wood dead and brittle, and possibly make it more useful as a stake. With a mighty effort, Alex pulled the branch free. He caught Kurt as he stumbled. Blood oozed from the wound, darker and thicker than the glistening sheen of Laszlo's blood on his face and chin.

This green and growing earth will rise, sang Kitty's band, *it will defend the order of all things,* while Kitty sang over them:

Time to say goodbye
To the life you had
Time to let it go
Take your place in the story
Time to die
So that other things may grow

The others joined in; hearing the words once was enough for those with the Minstrel Tongue – especially those who had fought together already and were becoming bound together.

Time to say goodbye
To the life you had

Alex seized Kurt around the chest and dragged him away from them.

Time to let it go
Take your place in the story
Time to die
So that other things may grow

Alex fled, ungainly with his burden but swift, towards the lush botanical gardens, far from the Minstrels and their dying violinist.

CHAPTER TWENTY-SIX

Under the twisted, dead trees of the avenue by the river, instruments were flung aside as the five minstrels dashed to help their fallen comrade.

Kitty pressed her fingers to the tear in Laszlo's throat and tried to summon up a song, but her throat was dry and songless.

Aaron pulled off his shirt as he dropped to his knees and Yuka pressed it to the wound. 'Shh, Laszlo, shh,' she said, her tone more commanding than comforting.

'Steve,' rasped Kitty desperately. 'I can't *think*!'

'Ain't hardly a surprise. It's miracle enough you're still on your feet after the week we've had. Sal, get the van. We need to get him out of here.'

Aaron rose. 'I better go with him, in case those bastards out there doubled back.'

Yuka handed him both her drum sticks. 'If they are, stake them. Hard, through the heart, like we showed you in rehearsal.'

Yuka stayed by Laszlo, pressing the cloth to his throat as Aaron and Sal ran to fetch the van and Steve gathered up the instruments, including the violin, which had landed unscathed on the grass.

Kitty stroked Laszlo's hair and held his hand. His eyes were wide with fear.

'I'm trying,' she whispered roughly. 'Nothing's coming.' He squeezed her hand, attempting to give *her* comfort. She dashed at the tears welling in her eyes. 'Hold on,' she whispered.

Laszlo tried to smile.

Kitty concentrated through exhaustion and a blooming headache to find a single note. She hummed it, and a second. Whether or not it stemmed the flow of blood, Laszlo relaxed slightly.

Ten minutes later, Sal had returned. 'We're near the park. Come on.' He hefted Laszlo into his arms while the others carried the guitars, drum and violin after them. They lifted Laszlo into the back of the van and sat around him while Aaron steered the van into the traffic.

'The hospital...' began Kitty.

Steve shook his head. 'We can't... it ain't that kind of injury, Kitty. This is vampire bite. We need other stuff to fix it.'

'But the bleeding won't stop!' Kitty protested.

'Ain't nothing for it, kid,' he said. 'If we take him to a hospital, they'll be busy with blood transfusions and stitches when what he needs is garlic and silver. Laszlo knows.'

Laszlo was pale and unresponsive and had no opinion to share.

'Where to, then?' Aaron shouted back at them.

'Angus and Taylor are nearest,' Kitty said. 'Unless it's too dangerous.'

'We'll have to risk it,' he said. 'He needs help soon before it's too late.'

'Stop! Let me out!' snapped Yuka. She was clutching the cursed necklace again. 'They mustn't follow me to Gretel. And you must save Laszlo.'

'We can get it off you,' Steve said, attempting to sound confident.

'We have so far failed,' Yuka pointed out. She tugged on the strings again to demonstrate, grating the wires against the raw scrapes in her skin, drawing blood. She hissed at the sting.

The necklace rattled.

Alarmed, Yuka tugged uselessly on it again, drawing more blood. The keys jittered, emitting a faint, off-key note.

Kitty winced then cocked her head. 'Yuka, what can you feel from it?'

'Pain,' snarled Yuka, running her finger between the strings and her bleeding skin.

'I mean what is *it* feeling?' Kitty clarified. 'You said you'd filled it with rage.'

Yuka blinked. 'I filled it with many things.'

'Well, now you're bleeding on it,' Kitty pointed out. 'And it's reacting. How do *you* feel?'

'Afraid,' she said through gritted teeth. 'For Laszlo. For Gretel.'

'That's not just fear then,' Kitty said, young-old in her way. 'That's love.'

Yuka took the necklace and sawed the strings against her bleeding skin. She let her heart pound with her terror for her friend and the little girl she loved with all her heart. She let the fear-and-love flood her body, her bloodstream. She tugged and scraped and bled on the artefact that had held her grief and fury,

The strings snapped. Wire and keys flew into Yuka's hands.

Yuka cracked open the levered side window and stuffed the remnants of the necklace through it onto the road. A sedan swerved slightly; its driver yelled abuse. Yuka tugged the window shut again.

'Hurry,' Yuka shouted to Aaron, her brown eyes clear and determined. 'We must save Laszlo.'

Aaron drove as fast as he dared towards the serviced apartment where Gretel's new parents were keeping her safe.

Steve had phoned ahead, and Taylor, carrying an armful of blankets, met them in the apartment block's low-roofed basement parking lot.

'Hell, Yuka, what happened?' Taylor winced at the inflamed and bleeding lines that Yuka had sawn into her neck trying to remove the necklace.

Yuka impatiently waved away his tentative attempt to inspect the wounds. 'Help us carry Laszlo.'

At the back of the open van, Taylor recoiled from the blood caking Laszlo's neck and chest. 'He should be in a hospital.'

'After we've treated the vampire bite,' snapped Steve.

Sal and Aaron wrapped Laszlo up in the blankets. Taylor helped carry him into the lift. He and Sal held Laszlo upright and shivering at the back. Everyone else crowded at the front and glared daggers at any guests who tried to enter at the foyer. On the third floor, they hustled Laszlo into the apartment and laid him out on the double bed in the main bedroom.

Harper held Gretel – who was waking, fractious, at the noise and sense of panic – close to her chest and Angus chivvied them into the second bedroom. 'Keep her safe,' he said, and closed the door.

'We need garlic and silver. What have you got?' demanded Steve, pulling open cupboards in the unit's small kitchen and flinging aside anything useless, which was almost everything. He banged a pot onto the stove top, sloshed water into it from the kettle and lit the element. 'And I need a piece of cloth for the poultice. Don't suppose you got a handkerchief? Course not. Nobody uses handkerchiefs anymore.' With a curse, he turned to Aaron. 'Go out, get me garlic. If nobody here's got silver, we'll need a pendant or bracelet or something...'

'It's midnight,' Aaron protested. 'Garlic I can find at a 24-hour supermarket, but the market for midnight jewellery shops isn't big, even in Melbourne.'

'I've got this.' Harper emerged from the bedroom while Gretel cried against her shoulder. She held out a necklace in her fist. 'Will I get it back?'

'Nope,' Steve said, taking it from her. 'Aaron – garlic. Fresh if you can, but whatever you can get hold of.'

'How much?'

'As much as you can.'

'I'll go with you,' Kitty volunteered. 'You can keep the engine running while I go in. And you needed a hankie, Steve?'

'A what?'

'Handkerchief.'

'I'll cut a strip out of the sheets. Off you go, quick as you can.'

Aaron and Kitty dashed out as Yuka emerged from the main bedroom.

'It is much worse than we thought,' she said bleakly.

Steve joined Yuka and Sal in the bedroom.

Laszlo was stretched out on the bed, deathly pale and gasping shallowly. His eyes darted wildly from Yuka to Steve, questioning. Yuka had cut away Laszlo's shirt, fully revealing the gory bite in his throat. Splattered around the wound was his own blood, but other, darker stains were mingled with the scarlet.

'When Alex pulled the stake from Kurt, vampire blood sprayed over Laszlo,' Yuka said.

'Wh-what does that mean?' gasped Laszlo.

'If any of it got into the wound, and you've lost enough of your own blood…' Sal trailed off, choked with guilt. 'This is my fault.'

'I c-could become v-vampire?'

'Not necessarily,' Steve said. 'If Kurt's blood is in your bloodstream, you just have to weather the infection.'

'If-f I d-don't?'

'If you die, you might rise. We can't know for sure until it happens. I'll be right back.' With that, Steve dashed from the room.

'I'm so sorry,' Sal said miserably.

'No. I won't. I won't,' Laszlo sobbed. 'You can't let me. You can't. You mustn't let me change.'

Yuka clutched Laszlo's hand and kissed his knuckles.

Steve ran down the emergency exit stairs, which was faster than taking the lift, into the car park just as the van was pulling out. Aaron had to stamp hard on the brake to avoid making Steve a road accident victim for the second time.

'Open up!' Steve banged on the side of the van with his fist. Kitty clambered out of the passenger seat to help.

'What's up?'

Steve was in the back of the van, pushing his way among the instruments. 'Laszlo may be infected. We need wood.'

'What for?'

'In case I have to stake him,' snarled Steve, seizing the violin and bow. He jumped back out onto the concrete, scowling. 'If you find any vervain while you're out, bring it back.'

'Vervain?'

Steve was already striding to the lift. 'Verbena. Check in the herbal teas or health food section. It's in bath salts sometimes, too. But be quick. If we can keep Laszlo from dying, we won't need to stake him.'

Kitty leapt into the van, Aaron floored the accelerator and they tore off for supermarket salvation.

Minutes later, Steve wrenched the hotel room door open again, making Angus jump with fright.

'Angus, you get packing, then you get your family the hell on out of here. I got no idea what's gonna happen next, but it ain't safe.

I'm sorry.' Steve's face crumpled briefly, but he grit his teeth and scowled fiercely, holding onto his resolve. 'It's all gone ass over tit and we might lose Laszlo. You gotta move, maybe keep moving until I call and tell you to stop. And if I can't call, you… you can't stop.'

'Steve–'

'I fucked it up, Angus. I have fucked it all up from start to finish, and I don't know what happens next. I thought we could take Alex and Kurt out of the picture, properly this time, but it wasn't like that. Turns out Minstrels who become vampires can sing a fight, and none of us did much better than hold our ground, till Kurt bit Laszlo. It's all going to hell, Angus my boy, so you take our little girl, your man and your sister and *keep them safe.*'

Angus watched, helpless, as his uncle pushed away from him, disappearing into the bedroom where Laszlo lay in a fever. Then Angus went to tell his family they had to run. Again.

Steve slammed the bedroom door shut behind him. Yuka sat on one side of Laszlo, Sal on the other. Steve lay the violin on top of the small dressing table.

'Hey, Laszlo,' he said softly.

Laszlo, eyes bright with fever and dark with fear, peered at him.

'My violin,' he gasped.

'Yep. Yours,' Steve agreed. 'You earned it.' His voice cracked. 'You earned your place with us. I'm sorry for what it's doing to you.'

'The violin. It's wood. Spruce. Rosewood. Ebony.'

'That's right.'

'You cannot make a good violin from hawthorn.'

'Aw, shit, Laszlo.'

'But spruce and rosewood are good enough for staking vampires, aren't they?'

'I don't want to, man. You know I don't want to. Maybe we won't have to.'

Laszlo's eyes grew brighter; more fierce. He tried to sit up. 'Do not hesitate,' he growled. 'If I am to be lost, do not hesitate to stake me. Do not let me… do not… please. Please. You must not let me betray you.' He sagged back onto the bed. 'Please. Promise me. Do not let me be a traitor again.'

Yuka patted Laszlo's hand. Sal stared at the blankets, lost in memory. *Budapest. Losing Alex.*

'You ain't a traitor, Laszlo,' Steve promised him, leaving the violin on the sideboard and approaching the bed. 'You're a good man and this is not your fault.'

'I *am*. I *was*.' Laszlo gasped for air, and the wound in his throat gaped wetly. The bleeding had slowed, leaving a raw lesion easily visible in the muscle and skin. 'I did not mean to be. I wanted to take care of my family. They promised me. *Threatened me* with promises. They promised my family would be safe, if I did this small thing. Watch. Report. Nothing more. They said it was necessary, so that I could keep my Eva and little Ilka safe.'

Steve frowned. 'Who promised you, Laszlo?'

'The Communists.' Laszlo began to cry. 'The Soviets. The KGB. They did not trust the musicians. I played with the state orchestra, but they did not trust us. They thought someone amongst us was a spy, they said. The orchestra was allowed to travel out of Hungary. Watch them and tell us who they meet, the Soviets said, and your family will be safe while you are gone. Give us reports, and your wife and your daughter will be protected.' Laszlo choked on gulping sobs. 'I only wanted to keep them safe.'

Yuka stroked Laszlo's hand until the worse of the sobs died away. She threaded her shaking fingers through his wild, blood-matted hair.

Laszlo seemed to find strength in her kindness. 'The regime fell,' he said at last. 'The secret police records became known. I meant no harm. I wanted to protect my family. From... from. The KGB. You don't know. What they... you don't know... I meant no harm.'

Crying freely, he looked at Yuka as though expecting her to abandon him. She kissed his hand again and stroked his bloodied hair.

'But harm was done,' he confessed. 'And I lost everything. Wife. Daughter. Music. I was a traitor without knowing how I had become one. I have sworn. I will not. Never again. I will do what is right. I will not be the enemy.'

'You are not the enemy,' Yuka whispered, patting his cheek.

'I may be,' he whispered back.

'You were mistaken. I know what it is to be mistaken. But this is not your fault.'

'No,' he agreed softly. 'But we must choose, now.'

'Yes,' Yuka said.

Laszlo's blue eyes sought out Steve. 'You must not let me become the enemy, Steve. I chose when I joined you in Budapest to be something new. Please. Please. Do not let me betray what I have sworn to protect, not again. Never again.' Laszlo shook, with fever, with grief, with terror.

'I promise,' Steve said gently. 'If it comes to that.'

'Forgive me.'

Yuka made a choked sound, an angry whimper, and squeezed his hand. 'Yes.'

Steve cupped Laszlo's tear-stained cheek in his hand and brushed the skin with his callused thumb. 'You're forgiven, Laszlo. You've fought with us, Budapest, and here. You're a good man. I know you are. You haven't let us down. And we won't let you down. We promise.'

Laszlo nodded stiffly. 'Yes. I know. You are a good man, too, Steve Borman.' He turned his head on the pillow, towards Sal. 'And you, Sal. You are a good man.'

'This is all my fault.'

'If it is, I forgive you. I know you will not fail me.'

'No,' Sal promised, nodding and clenching his jaw against the rising grief. 'I will not fail again.'

'And we ain't giving up on you yet, all right?' Steve said.

'Okay.'

'Right. Vampire bite, that's a bitch, but we can do things. Even if you got vampire blood in that, we can get you back, long as you don't die. So you keep fighting.'

'Yes.'

Yuka squeezed his hand again and nodded encouragement.

'We gotta start by trying to leech the vampire out of you,' Steve explained. 'It's gonna hurt a lot more if it's vampire blood as well as spit in the wound, can't tell you otherwise.'

'Do it.'

'All right. Are you a religious man, Laszlo Kantor?'

Laszlo shook his head. 'No.'

From his pocket, Steve drew the silver necklace Harper had given to him: a bright chain and at the end of it, a small silver cross. 'Then I guess this don't mean that much to you.'

Laszlo stared at the cross, panting. 'Perhaps... a little more... than nothing.'

'It's gonna hurt like nothing you ever felt before.'

'I have lost a family and a life,' Laszlo said hoarsely. 'Mere physical agony I think I can do.'

Steve slipped the cross from the chain and replaced the chain in his pocket. The cross he held in his fingers.

'I'll make a poultice when Kitty and Aaron get back. For now, this is what we've got. Yuka, Sal, hold him down.'

Laszlo submitted himself to the restraint. Steve pressed the silver cross to the bite in Laszlo's throat and held it down with his thumb.

Laszlo began to whimper. He grit his teeth against it, but it grew, a shrill keening, rising to a wailing cry. He thrashed about on the bed while Sal and Yuka held him down.

The vampire waiting inside him for a chance to grow did not want to come out.

Laszlo had other ideas. He moaned and cried and struggled, and he began to chant in Hungarian, a low moan.

Takarodj! Takarodj! Takarodj!

Get out, get out, get out.

Blood bubbled under the silver. Skin reddened and burned. Laszlo's body went rigid and his spine arched in his agony. Steve kept the silver pressed to the wound, with increasing difficulty as his fingers grew slippery with Laszlo's blood and the cross began to shrink, evaporating like ice in heat.

Laszlo collapsed briefly then struggled more violently against the invader in his body, the enemy trying to own him from within. Laszlo bit his tongue, making it bleed, but he kept on chanting.

Takarodj! Takarodj! Takarodj!

The bedroom door opened a crack and Taylor peeked inside. His face was pale.

'Busy,' snarled Steve.

'We've got trouble. Reception called saying friends arrived for us. Then they remembered we have a baby here, and decided a little late that they didn't like the look of our visitors.'

Steve whirled on Taylor, face twisted in fear and fury. His shirt and hands were smeared in Laszlo's blood.

'Then what the hell you doing here, you goddamned *idiot*?' Steve's voice broke. 'You gotta *run*!'

Taylor disappeared, shouting for Angus and Harper.

Laszlo twisted, throwing off Yuka in her horrified distraction, then Sal too. Steve climbed onto Laszlo's body to keep the silver pressed to his throat as he thrashed and cried out *Takarodj*. Blood seeped from the wound, and then flowed freely, getting worse rather than better.

Sal grabbed hold of Laszlo's arm again. Yuka ran to the kitchen to search for a weapon.

The front door slammed open, and Steve dared hope it wasn't too late.

Then Harper screamed, and Yuka swore in Japanese and a creepy, hollow version of a laugh he once knew well made his stomach drop.

Chapter Twenty-Seven

Sal ran to the main room and Steve could no longer hold the thrashing Hungarian to the bed. He was thrown to the floor, losing hold of the evaporated remains of the cross, which fell into the bleeding wound. Laszlo arched, hissed, and clutched at his bleeding throat, and the sliver of cross became more deeply embedded.

Steve struggled to his feet and ran to join the others in the front room.

There he found Alex blocking the exit. Beside him was Kurt, leaning against the wall, his fingers fisted in the cloth around the wound in his chest. Kurt was grinning, bright red blood staining his teeth. Not Laszlo's – that would have been absorbed soon after the attack. Kurt had drunk from someone else, and not long ago. His undead body was already mending and strengthening despite the near-miss with the stake.

Crowded at the entry to the spare room were Taylor, Angus, Harper and Gretel. Gretel was sobbing in the middle of all those adult bodies trying to shield her from the horrors blocking the exit.

Between them and the vampires were Sal and Yuka. Yuka had run out of drum sticks, but she had broken a plate and held the largest shards of it in her hands. Her eyes were hard, her hands unshaking.

Sal was standing tall and fierce, holding a breadknife before him. 'I'm sorry I failed you, Alex, but you will not harm Gretel.'

'I do not plan to *harm* my daughter,' sneered Alex. 'I *love* her. She's my little girl. She's *mine.*'

'*Ours,*' snarled Kurt, straightening from the wall.

Gretel whimpered as Harper backed away. Taylor and Angus moved in front of them to offer what protection they could.

Sal and Yuka advanced towards the vampires and Steve, weaponless, joined them.

Kurt, clearly stronger, bared his teeth and bent his knees, ready to spring.

The main bedroom door banged opened and Laszlo lurched through it. He clung to the frame, chest heaving.

'Hello Laszlo,' Alex's greeted him like an old friend. 'Thank you for guiding us here.'

'I did no such thing.'

'Kurt's blood in you did.'

'No. I will not be that thing again.' He staggered into the room, one blood-smeared hand curled around his violin, the other around the bow. 'Leave,' he said. Blood dribbled from the wound in his throat. 'Go. Away. From. Here.'

'Make me,' grinned Alex, showing his fangs.

Laszlo jammed the violin under his chin, mindless of the pain or the blood. He drew the bow across the strings, throwing a keening, defiant note into the air.

Yuka sprang at Alex, the crockery shards raised for a slashing blow.

The clash was brief and confusing, a blur of limbs and shouts. At the end of it, Yuka had been thrown across the room, colliding with the kitchen bench before collapsing to the floor, too quiet. Sal was pinned to the floor, Kurt kneeling, snarling on his chest. The bread knife was embedded in Kurt's thigh.

Steve stood protectively in front of his Texan family, who held tight to Gretel. Blood stained his lips and pooled in his mouth from where his teeth had cut into the inside of his cheek after Alex had struck him.

And between Steve and Alex stood Laszlo Kantor, his body attenuating and swaying with the motion of the bow across the strings. He bent his knees and played low, stepped sideways, shoulder rising, as the music built up, and then came up onto his toes then down again, sway, sweep, rise and fall, the music flowing through the violin and the bow, through his blood and bone, through the ends of his fingers and the wild, disarrayed ends of even his blood-matted hair. Four hundred years of magic in the instrument; thirty years of regret and the will for redemption in the man.

Laszlo played a wall of sound, the violin a willing collaborator, giving him magic while he gave the music form.

Alex backed away from the violinist, confused. He tried to approach his daughter again, but found himself unable to move forward. Instead, his foot hovered in the air, swung back. Back and down. Onto the floor. He raised his other foot but it too went backward, and down, not forward as intended.

The violin sang: *takarodj, takarodj, takarodj.* Without tongue or lips or teeth, it made that sound: *takarodj, takarodj, takarodj.*

The bow came down hard on the strings *ta*; scraped across and over, spitting out a low *ka*; rolled up and over the bridge again throwing out a pantheresque *ro* and down once more, like a blow, *dj.*

Ta-ka-ro-dj.

Get out.

Laszlo took one step, then another, then another. Despite himself, Alex was edging away from him.

'Kurt!'

Kurt was in the process of pulling the bread knife out of his leg. One hand was clamped to Sal's neck. He was baring his teeth in Sal's face, but then Laszlo shifted and swayed in his direction. The violin cursed *takarodj* at him then swirled into other defiant notes. Kurt rose from Sal's prone body and found himself edging incrementally, involuntarily, towards the door.

Laszlo swayed, staggered, righted himself, played while Sal struggled to his feet and stumbled towards Yuka, who groaned and tried to rise. Fell again.

The violinist and his violin muttered *takarodj, takarodj, takarodj* and the vampires, snarling, scowling, showing fangs, collided at the door, tangled briefly, then burst into the hallway. Kurt was limping. Alex put his arm around his back to keep him from falling.

Laszlo kept playing in the doorway, blood soaking his skin and shirt, his pale blue eyes fierce and unforgiving as arctic ice. Hair plumed wildly about his head. The music crackled off the violin, the bow, out of his fingers and from his skin.

Takarodj.

Alex and Kurt got out. Reluctantly but inexorably they went, unable to defy the command of the human with vampire blood using their magic and that of the violin to defy them.

Takarodj.

The vampires stumbled into the stairwell. Laszlo followed, playing. The fire door slammed closed behind them, and Laszlo kept playing as he sank to his knees. His teeth chattered with stress and exhaustion but his fingers and hands were firm on the violin and bow until he folded, slumped, against the door frame.

At last the violin slid from his hand to the floor, the bow into his lap.

Steve and Sal ran to Laszlo's side in the corridor.

'Laszlo. Hey, man, Laszlo, look at me. Open your eyes. That's it. That's it, man,' Steve coaxed.

'Are they. Gone?'

'Hell yeah,' Steve crowed. 'You were somethin' else, there, man. You were *righteous*!'

Laszlo shook his head wearily. 'I will not be that thing. I will not betray again.'

'You didn't,' Sal said gently. 'You were brilliant.'

'Can you stand?' Steve asked.

Laszlo wobbled, but managed to find his feet with their help. He bent to pick up the violin and nearly fell again. Sal fetched it and the bow for him and slung an arm around his waist.

In the hotel room, Yuka, wincing at her bruised ribs, was on her feet again. Angus, Taylor and Harper were huddled protectively around Gretel.

'Come on,' Steve said. 'We'll get you guys out of here.'

The eight of them progressed cautiously along the corridor to the lift and pressed the button. Waited. Waited. Waited. Looked nervously around. Waited some more.

The lift opened and they all shuffled inside. Gretel was clinging to Angus, sucking on his shirt and her fist at the same time. He cradled her gently, one hand curved around her head to shield her from the world. Taylor stood in front of them both, pale but determined, prepared to slay dragons on their behalf.

In the foyer, the receptionist lay slumped behind the desk, her throat torn open at the jugular. Kurt killed her to mend the wound in his belly before their confrontation. Poor child.

Steve held his hand up as a command for everyone to hold still. He cocked his head. 'I suppose that's *something*.'

'What?' Harper demanded, staring at the dead girl with revulsion and pity.

'Seems like one of them summoned a silence on the place. Nobody's gonna be calling the police yet. The guests'll be sitting in their rooms, staring at the walls with ringing in their ears, not thinking of much.'

'It is a gift among Vladimir's line of vampires,' Yuka explained.

'Gift may not be the word.' Steve opened the glass doors leading to the driveway. He peered outside. 'But it'll do. Gives us time, anyway. Don't know that I want to be wrangling the law at the same time as two Minstrel vampires who can lay down a silence this big.' Nothing stirred outside and Steve waved them urgently through to the footpath under the awning.

Laszlo raked the area with an unhappy glare and held the violin up in shaking hands, intending to be ready.

'What now?' he asked.

'You stay with Yuka and the kids out the front, here. Sal and I'll fetch the hire car. If Kitty gets back with the van, pile in and get the hell out. Don't worry about us.'

'No.'

'*Yes*. Gretel's the priority.'

Laszlo nodded and gripped the violin more firmly.

Then they heard the squealing of tyres and the blare of a horn, blasting out one long, fractious note as the van came tearing *out* of the undercover car park.

Clinging to the roof was Kurt Stefan. Scrabbling at the side door, trying to open it, was Alex Torni.

Through the van's windscreen, Steve could see Kitty hanging onto the dash, her mouth open in either a scream or a note she was trying to hold. Aaron was tugging at the steering wheel, trying to throw the vampires off. He was heading towards the driveway in front of reception, but his eyes widened as he realised who was there and spun the wheel, abruptly changing direction towards the exit instead. The tyres squealed protest and left black marks on the road.

Aaron must have got back damned quick and who do they find in the car lot but those two? thought Steve. *Oh, fuckety piss damnation.*

Alex leapt off the moving car towards the group outside the hotel foyer door. Kurt, lopsided from his injuries, pushed away from the vehicle too. He stumbled into a roll much clumsier than Alex's athletic leap-and-land, and staggered to a crouch. Dark blood dripped from his thigh onto the path. Alex strode single-mindedly towards the baby.

Nobody knew where to run.

The only instrument they had was Laszlo's violin. Yuka and Laszlo were both injured. Between Angus, Taylor, Harper and Gretel there were too many people to protect and not nearly enough Minstrels to do the protecting.

But here came Aaron and Kitty, running towards the vampires. Aaron had one of Yuka's drum sticks in his fist. Yuka held her hand out to him as he neared, and he threw the stick to her. She caught it neatly, spun it in her fingers and held it ready.

Sal stepped in front of Gretel and stalked towards his former bandmates as well.

'Stand aside, Sal,' snarled Alex.

'No. I'm pure now. I won't let you down again. I'll kill you properly this time.'

Instrumentless, Sal raised his hands and sang a single, clear note. Kitty drew alongside him and provided a harmonising note. To the side, Yuka joined in, then Steve. A new song wasn't rising yet. The best song they knew hadn't worked at the river. Sal wasn't sure what would work, and Kitty didn't know many songs anyway. Maybe she would work one out of nothing, as she'd done before.

But a few notes later, what they were singing emerged.

Takarodj!

The song Laszlo had given to his violin, which the violin had sung out to drive off the vampires. The Minstrels were singing it.

Takarodj!

Then Aaron did something unexpected. He began to dance. A foot slapped down heavy on the concrete drive, and another. His shoulders dipped and curved as he bent at the knees and hips, making an arc with his body, another with his raised hands. He sang and stepped forward, a graceful hop and slide, then he brought his body up, attenuating it. His arms curled over his head, then swayed gracefully at their full length in an arc towards the horizon and the setting sun.

And Alex stepped backwards. Puzzled, he tried to step forward again, but Aaron took another foot-slapping pace towards him, every part of his swaying body saying: *This is my place. You can't have it. This ground is mine. Go away. Get out.*

Takarodj!

Steve had heard of dance magic. He'd even seen a few practitioners at work. He'd never been in a band with one. He'd never known a Minstrel who carried the gift.

Well, you learned something new every day.

The Minstrels gathered around Aaron and sang with him, followed him as he took another defiant step towards Alex, forcing Alex further back, with the bend of his knees and the sway of his torso, with the rising of his elbows and the sudden swooping down of his shoulders and back. The sway of Aaron's hips and the elegant flick of his hands and arms reinforced the message.

Go away.

Alex obeyed the command of the music and Aaron's dance, and he went, reluctantly, glaring hungrily over their shoulders at his daughter.

And then Alex grinned.

Oh fucking hell.

'Where's Kurt?' Steve yelled, whirling on his heel. Kurt was lurching at them, limping but still swifter than any human.

Kurt snatched at Gretel in Angus's arms. When Angus crushed the little girl close to his chest, Kurt snatched at Angus's shoulders instead. The momentum dragged both man and child from the midst of the family huddled at the door, propelling them into the open.

Yuka swung at Kurt with the drum stick but she was too far away.

'Missed,' he taunted.

Taylor yelled and pitched after them, arms outstretched, but Kurt was too fast. He threw Angus to the ground, back-first to protect the baby in his arms. Angus landed with an awful gasping noise as the wind was knocked out of him, but before Kurt would swoop again he curled over, shielding Gretel from the vampire with his hands and body.

'Give me my daughter,' snarled Kurt.

'Fuck you.'

'Angus!' Taylor ran to them. Kurt slapped him so hard Taylor was knocked several metres back. He landed hard, blood pouring from a cut lip.

One arm curled around the screaming baby, Angus tried to crawl away as the Minstrels and Alex converged on them.

Alex hauled Angus up by his shoulders. Kicking, cursing, struggling wildly, Angus held close to Gretel and wouldn't let go.

'I'll break every bone in your body,' Alex hissed.

'Break 'em,' Angus yelled back. 'You ain't hurtin' this little girl, Alex. I ain't gonna let you.'

Alex grabbed Angus by the hair and yanked his head back. Gretel, who'd buried her face in Angus's neck, was exposed. Her face was scrunched up, red and wet with tears and terror.

'Hey there, baby girl,' Alex said sweetly, still holding Angus in that contorted position, bent backwards and hyperventilating as he struggled desperately to right himself and protect Gretel. 'Hey honey. It's me. It's Dadda. Look.' Alex gestured at Kurt, on the other side. 'Your daddies are here. Aren't we, *cicci*? Our baby girl's waiting for her daddies.'

Hiccupping, Gretel stared at Alex and then, slowly and cautiously at Kurt, looming behind her.

'Pappa?'

'That's right, Gretel, my little Gretchken, Gremlin-bub,' cooed Kurt. 'Your Pappa and your Dadda are here for you.'

'Dadda?' Gretel said uncertainly.

'That's right, baby girl.' Alex's free hovered over Gretel's puffy, damp cheek.

Gretel opened her mouth and screamed, high and piercing, and dissolved into wracking sobs of fear and distress.

CHAPTER TWENTY-EIGHT

'Please,' Angus said, his head held back hard, leaving the madly beating vein in his throat exposed. 'Please stop it. You're scaring her.'

With a scowl, Alex released his handful of Angus's hair. Angus curled himself around the sobbing child again, then lifted her. He rocked the baby in his arms, unable to do anything but try to shush her between his own sobs. Alex placed his fingers back on the crown of Angus's head, flexing, considering whether or not to crush his skull.

Angus closed his eyes and cuddled Gretel under his chin.

'Shh, s-sweetie,' he murmured to her. 'Shush, now. Shh. You're gonna be all right.'

'Of course she's going to be all right,' snarled Alex. 'She's going to be with her daddies.'

'And what d'you aim to do with her?' asked Steve wearily.

Alex glared balefully at Steve, standing with his exhausted and injured band, with his bereft family. Harper had helped Taylor to his feet, but Taylor had eyes only for his husband and Gretel.

'What any father aims to do,' Alex said. 'Keep his little girl.'

'You gonna turn a baby?'

'Don't be an idiot,' Kurt snapped. 'We're not going to turn Gretel *now*. It would kill her. Later. When she's four or five. They're so cute at that age.'

'Or older. Five is too young to survive the change,' Alex told Kurt sternly. 'Perhaps when she's fifteen; old enough to appreciate what we're doing for her.'

Kurt pursed his lips. 'Teenagers are so bratty, though.'

'Not Gretel,' Alex said. 'She'll be a little angel for her daddies. We'll make sure of it.'

'You wanted her so much you lied to us to have her, and *that* is how you will raise your daughter,' rasped Yuka. 'In chains, to become an obedient monster.'

'You make that sound like a bad thing,' Kurt said. 'We wanted her. We have her. We're keeping her.'

'You want to own her,' Taylor said. 'You don't. You can't.'

'We can do what we like,' sneered Alex. 'I'm her *father*.'

On the ground, Gretel clung to Angus and sobbed into his neck, shivering with fear she couldn't understand. Angus rocked her and tried to soothe her, rubbing his thumb in tiny circles in her hair and between her shoulders. Falteringly and barely audible, he began singing softly against her ear, trying to calm her down.

Heave a sigh, baby girl,
Don't you cry, baby girl

Alex's fingers squeezed against Angus's scalp and growled a warning.

Angus swallowed convulsively. 'It's her lullaby. It helps her to calm down. Please. Please stop. You're scaring her so much.'

Alex crouched beside them.

'Gretel.'

The little girl buried her face in Angus's chest and wouldn't look at him.

'Baby girl, look at your daddy. Look here, sweetheart. **Look at me.**'

Gretel wailed but turned her blotched, snotty face toward him.

'I'm your Dadda,' he said sternly. 'Not him.'

Gretel keened shrilly. Her eyes were fixed on the thing that used to be her Dadda, but she clung to Angus.

Alex reached for her with splayed hands, trying to seem not at all dangerous. Gretel flinched. Alex touched her puffy cheek with the pad of his index finger.

And the pad of his index finger *burned*.

He snatched his hand away and stared unbelievingly at the blister raised on his skin.

Kurt, who had been watching the Minstrels and the civilians, ready for any attempt to rush them, glanced down.

'What's wrong, *sötnos*?'

'She burned me.' Alex's tone was wondering and aggrieved. He showed Kurt the damage. 'See?'

Kurt examined the blister. He glared at Angus.

'What have you done?'

'Nothing. I ain't got magic in me.'

Kurt's eyes narrowed at Gretel. 'Look at your Pappa.'

Reluctantly, Gretel peeked up at her Pappa. Her wide brown eyes filled again with tears. Apart from the blotchiness and the mucus smeared on her skin, she was unmarked. Kurt extended a finger and pressed it to the middle of her forehead.

His skin blistered.

Kitty's brow furrowed, then cleared and she tugged on Sal's sleeve. 'Sing to her,' she said quietly, then remembering that the vampires would certainly hear her anyway, she shouted it out, a command, to everyone. 'Sing to Gretel. Angus, Taylor, you too. Everyone. The lullaby. *Sing it.*'

Angus clutched Gretel close, too tight, and sang to her.

Heave a sigh, baby girl,
Don't you cry, baby girl
Your daddies are guarding the door

With a snarl, Alex tried to snatch Gretel out of Angus's arms, but he recoiled. Where he had touched her, Alex's hands reddened and blistered.

Across the drive, Taylor and Sal were singing. Laszlo joined in. Taylor walked towards the vampires, and to the people he loved who were trapped behind them.

Laugh out loud, baby girl
Be strong and proud, baby girl
Keeping you safe is what your daddies are for

Kurt tried to grab Gretel next and howled as his hands burned. His pinkie finger went grey at the tip and fell away, ashes.

Yuka and Steve joined with the others, Harper singing too.

You are strong, baby girl
Life is long, baby girl
Your daddies will sing you to sleep

Alex lunged at Gretel again. Gretel screamed and clung to Angus, hiding her face against his neck. Eyes closed, face against her flushed skin, nose pressed to Gretel's hair, Angus's broad hands held her and he sang.

You are smart, baby girl
You have heart, baby girl
And the hearts of your daddies to keep

Alex halted before touching her and then finally, slowly, he placed his right hand on Gretel's arm. His hand burned, even after he removed his from her skin. His fingertips blackened. Fell to ash.

Alex looked helplessly at Kurt.

Taylor passed them, unchallenged. He crouched beside Angus and put his arm around his husband's shoulder. 'I'm here, Gusling.' Angus sagged against him. Taylor kissed Gretel's forehead and resumed singing.

'What's going on?' Kurt was bewildered.

'Magic,' explained Kitty, over the volume of the lullaby woven into the air. 'You wrote your daughter a Minstrel song to keep her safe. You sang it to her every day you had her. The whole Minstrel band did, using instruments full of magic. Everyone who loved your daughter, Minstrel or not, sang her Minstrel lullaby to her. The magic's not just in the song anymore. It's in Gretel.'

'How can you know?' Alex demanded.

'Can't you feel all that love in her? All that magic?' Kitty asked. 'You sang that lullaby into her skin, into her cells. You sang her safe from monsters. Your love is still protecting her.'

Alex curled the truncated fingers of his right hand – the tips ashen stumps to the first knuckle – into his palm and rose. Kurt was staring at his own ruined skin, shaking his head.

'If you try to touch her, the love feeds back' said Kitty. 'I think you made a kind of flesh magic. Her daddies are guarding her, like the song says. Even from themselves.'

Kurt frowned. 'But we were going to be a family again, Alex. We were going to keep her and make it so nobody could take her away, ever.'

'You were going to make her a prisoner and then kill her,' Kitty said sternly.

Angus and Taylor held Gretel between them. They crooned at her and held to each other.

'You can't have her,' Alex told them.

'You can't have her, either.' Kitty was closer. Everyone was drawing in on the injured vampires, getting between them and the huddled family. 'You can only hurt yourselves if you try.'

'We can kill her,' snapped Kurt. 'And take her with us.'

Sal faltered mid-line, and around him the lullaby fell into silence.

'Is that what it has come to, Kurt?' asked Sal. 'You would rather murder your daughter than let her have a life apart from you?'

Kurt's gaze shifted uneasily from the little family, to Alex, then away.

'It's over,' Kitty said, not unkindly. 'I'm sorry. People die and it's not fair, but it's the way it is. The world turns and death becomes decay becomes new ground becomes life.'

'What the fuck do you know?' snarled Alex. 'You're just a kid.'

'I know what it's like when someone wants to protect you and they make a cage for you instead,' she said. 'I'm young but I know love isn't meant to be like that. I think love's supposed to help you grow, and that protecting someone should give them that chance. I don't know you, but I think that's how you used to love when you were alive. Your lullaby is all about her growing up strong and going out into the world. Don't you still want that for her?'

'Why should she have it, when we don't?' said Kurt gruffly, but without conviction.

'Because that's selfish and destructive,' Kitty said. 'That's not love.'

'I love my daughter,' growled Alex.

'Then let Gretel go,' Steve said, voice thick with emotion. 'Can you remember how you loved her when you were human? God, I remember when you and Kurt brought her to us. You were both so happy, and she was so beautiful. The things you risked so you could have her. Don't destroy that.'

'You love Gretel,' insisted Sal. 'It's why you've come all this way.'

'Please.' Yuka's habitual rage was extinguished by this one desire, this one goal: for Gretel to live. 'Let her go. Remember who you were before the monsters took you.'

'You're Gretel's fathers.' Taylor said from where he cradled Angus and Gretel. 'You can still protect her.'

Kurt was on Yuka before anyone could react. Yuka tried to adopt a battle stance, despite her injuries. Kurt thrust his face into hers, their noses almost touching. Yuka felt the coolness of his skin, as though coldness and death emanated from his pores. Her brows furrowed in fierce concentration and she clutched her drum stick tightly.

Kurt seized her wrists and twisted them as she struggled. Then he let go, taking her last stick with him.

'Full of magic, are they?' Kurt demanded.

'Yes,' she replied darkly. She threw her shoulders back, preparing to take the coming blow directly and without fear.

Kurt turned his back on her.

'Alex,' he said bleakly. 'I'm her Pappa. It's my job to keep her safe, but I'm not safe. She's not safe from me. I want to keep her in a cage, *sötnos*. I want to eat her all up, one way or another. You can't let me.' He held out the drum stick to Alex. 'A memory inside me is screaming at me to protect her. I don't know how else to shut him up, and I can't stop wanting to bite her.'

Alex stared at Kurt in horror. '*Cicci.*'

'I'll hurt her if you don't,' Kurt said, full of the same horror. 'You know I will.'

'Kurt, baby, no. I can't. I turned so I wouldn't have to watch you die.'

'Do you remember when you brought her to me the first time?'

'She was so tiny, but she had all that potential.'

'All wrapped up in that silly yellow blanket with the balloons on it. She smiled at me. It was probably wind, but you said it was a smile and I wanted to believe it.'

'It was a smile,' insisted Alex.

'Do remember when we wrote her lullaby?'

'We spent hours talking about all the things we wanted her to grow up to be.'

'Strong and brave, happy, funny,' agreed Kurt. 'We imagined watching her sing, learning to play. Do art, maybe. Dance all over Europe and to make every country her own.'

Alex's eyebrows were drawn together in concentration. 'We said, she might grow up to be the greatest Minstrel ever, or a peach farmer, or writer of pirate stories. Anything she wanted, as long as she was happy.'

'Now, I want to keep her small and helpless and mine,' Kurt said. 'I want to drink her blood and never let her change.' He touched Alex's cheek with his injured hand. 'But I remember what I used to want for her.' He thrust the stick at Alex more forcefully. 'Do it, before the memory goes.'

Alex took the stick with one hand, and cradled Kurt's cheek in the palm of his damaged hand. He could see his daughter peeking warily at him over Angus's arms.

'Baby girl. Dadda and Pappa love you. We're sorry we scared you. You be good.'

Gretel blinked at him. 'Dadda?'

'Bye bye, Gretel. My baby girl. Bye bye.' All the unshed tears were in Alex's voice. Kurt couldn't bring himself to speak.

'Bye bye,' she said, confused, but she raised her hand to wave like she used to, little chubby arm held up, her fingers flexing and curling.

'Turn around and sing to her,' he said to Angus. 'She mustn't see this.'

Angus and Taylor made a shield with their bodies and rocked Gretel between them, singing her lullaby.

'I love you, *cicci*.' Alex slipped his hand around Kurt's skull, bringing him close to kiss his brow.

'And I love you, my beautiful boy.' Kurt buried his face in Alex's neck, a cold and sterile place where once he'd sought comfort in the warmth and pulse of Alex's skin. 'Better hurry…eeeaahhhh.' The word became a relieved exhale as Alex stabbed his beloved through the heart.

Alex was strong, the stick had been sung full of magic, and Kurt was sufficiently injured to make this an easy death. The wood pierced Kurt's body effortlessly, through his shirt, through the skin, through the flesh, between the bones and into the shrunken meat of the heart that no longer beat.

Alex knelt on the ground, holding Kurt's body gently as it withered around the stake. He rocked the shrivelling remains, singing softly to the dead man.

And we have no home
But the places we stay
Anchored awhile
And we sleep wherex we may

Kurt's body became more and more desiccated, until Alex was holding a shape made of leather and rags.

Our burdens are heavy
And the light is grey
When the end comes my home
Is wherever you bury my heart.

He kissed the distorted face that had once been the face he adored.

'Finish it,' he said to his former friends. 'And do it properly this time. You used to love us. Don't skimp on the details because of sentiment.'

'We will do it properly,' Yuka assured him, 'because we love you.'

Taylor was watching Alex with horrified compassion.

'Take care of her,' said Alex. 'Don't tell her what we became. Tell her we loved her.'

Taylor nodded.

Kitty was brave enough to put a hand on Alex's shoulder. 'We'll tell her you protected her to the end.'

Alex lowered Kurt's body to the ground and knelt beside it. He pulled the stick out of Kurt's chest. It made a sound like feet through autumn leaves.

Yuka's hand trembled as she took it from him. It was slippery in her sweating palm.

'Give it to me,' Steve said, but Sal took it from her. He wiped her perspiration from it on his shirt.

'I'm sorry I failed you, Alex.' Sal placed his hand on the crown of Alex's head.

'Me too,' Alex said, closing his eyes, 'but it's hard to think straight when you love someone. I remember being glad I saved you in Edinburgh. You were worth it. Now do it right.'

Sal raised the stick, brought it down fast, and plunged it into Alex's dead heart.

Then Sal folded to his knees and, like Alex before him, cradled the already dead monster in his arms until it was reduced to leather and rags.

Chapter Twenty-Nine

The hotel driveway was horribly hushed. Steve broke it with a barrage of urgent instructions.

'Aaron, get their bodies into the van. Angus, Taylor, Harper, take Gretel upstairs and try hush her down. Pack everything then leave as fast as you can. You don't want to be here when the cops arrive.'

'But-' Taylor began.

'Ain't nothing you can do for them that's dead,' Steve said, 'and there ain't no way you can explain this. What'll happen to Gretel if y'all get arrested? So no. You pack your things and light on out of here. Laszlo, you rest till they're ready then go with them.'

'Go where?' Taylor asked.

'Back to my house.' Kitty handed him her keys.

Yuka retrieved one of two bags of groceries from the front seat of the van and shoved it into his hands. 'Garlic, verbena tea. Make a poultice, hold it to the wound. Drink the tea. Eat the garlic.'

'Raw?' Laszlo's skin was waxy, almost grey.

'Yes. It will kill the rest of the vampire infection. You burned most of it out with your song, but we must be sure.'

Laszlo clutched the bag. 'I'll eat all of it.'

'Put some in the poultice to draw the infection,' Yuka corrected him. 'If you have more silver, hold it against the wound, but the garlic and verbena should be enough.'

Laszlo obeyed instructions, following Angus upstairs.

'What about that poor girl at reception?' Kitty asked.

Steve pushed the heels of his hands into his eyes. 'I don't know if Kurt gave her his blood. If he did, she might rise.'

'Oh.'

'I'll see how bad it is while you load the van.'

'I'll come with you,' Kitty said. 'I have to learn these things.'

They went into the foyer while Aaron helped Yuka and Sal load the withered bodies into the back of the van, alongside the instruments.

The bite in the receptionist's neck was ragged but the blood was redly human. Steve gently prised her jaw wide, inspecting her teeth and tongue.

'Can't see any vampire blood,' he said to Kitty. 'Sometimes it gets caught in the crevices of the teeth. Oh, and see, she's wearing silver.' He lifted the fine chain around her neck. Dangling from it was a half heart. Its other half might be worn by a best friend or a lover. Steve pressed the severed silver heart to the girl's mouth, but nothing happened. 'She died clean, at least. Ain't gonna be an atrocity on top of grief for her folks.' He pulled the pendant from her mouth, wiped it with his sleeve and placed it back against her skin.

'The police will be here soon,' Kitty said.

'Nope.'

'Why not?'

''Cos if Melbourne's Finest ain't here yet, they ain't been called. The silence Kurt or Alex sung up over the place must have been damned powerful. Someone'd have broken from it and called the cops before this, otherwise.'

'They sang it?'

'Vampires can summon little silences.' Steve settled the girl's body back onto the carpet. 'I'm guessing with the Minstrel in 'em, our boys sang it stronger. It'll lift soon, now they're proper dead.'

'We'd better hurry then.'

The hire car with the little family and Laszlo pulled away as Steve and Kitty returned to the van. Kitty sat in the front with Aaron. Steve joined Sal and Yuka with the withered bodies in the back.

Aaron drove them back to the warehouse. He parked out the back of the building, overlooking the river, while Sal went inside to retrieve an item from the band's old trunk.

Steve and Yuka laid the two bodies on the ground.

Aaron frowned. 'I'm not sure this is a good idea. What does this do to the land?'

Yuka stood close beside him. 'It gives the dead back to the soil,' she said. 'No evil will remain when we're done.'

Aaron and Kitty helped her to build a funeral pyre away from the building.

Sal returned with a parcel wrapped in an oiled canvas. He folded back the heavy wrapping to reveal a short-bladed sword.

'I can do that.' Steve held out his hand.

'It's all right.' Sal gave him a calm smile. 'I told him I'd do it right this time. I can. I'm helping him keep his word to Gretel.'

Sal placed a kiss on the shrunken brow of the man who'd once saved him; petted the strands of dark hair. He reached across Alex's body to run his thumb over Kurt's desiccated brow, a benediction and farewell.

Then Sal raised the sword high and swung it down, once, twice, neatly beheading both bodies. Yuka and Steve knelt beside him then, with the second shopping bag that Aaron and Kitty had brought. They withdrew a dozen bulbs of garlic.

Aaron and Kitty knelt with them. They had to learn these things, after all. Kitty was used to preparing the dead, anyway. This was another way of helping both the dead and the living to move on.

Between the four of them, they stuffed the mouths of the severed heads with garlic. They pushed garlic cloves into the wounds over the staked hearts of the vampires.

Together, they lowered first Alex's body and head, then Kurt's, into the fire and then stood well back, downwind, to watch the bodies burn. The withered flesh went up quickly, with a flash like magnesium, then died away to embers.

Kitty watched the flames die down and thought of Alex's song.

Our burdens are heavy
And the light is grey
When the end comes my home
Is wherever you bury my heart.

This was her life too, now. Despite everything, she found she didn't mind it. At least it wasn't a cage.

When the fire had burned down to embers, Steve poured water over the ashes. Nothing was left of Kurt and Alex, not even charred bones and teeth.

'We don't need anything else magical for this?' Aaron asked.

'The vampire's burned out of them,' Steve assured him. 'This is only charcoal. Still, bit of water to wash it down won't hurt none. Ashes to ashes, earth to earth. The planet plays her part too, you know. We're here to help keep the balance, remember?'

Aaron uncoiled the green garden hose next to the outdoor tap and hosed down the pyre site while the others repacked the van with all their gear. Aaron thought he could see the roots of the grass shifting, the grass itself accommodating the soil to absorb the ashes, but it was late and it was dark and he couldn't be sure.

Something to learn another time, he thought wearily. With the adrenalin rush over, Aaron wanted only to sleep for days.

When he was satisfied that the ashes were sufficiently sluiced away, Aaron coiled the hose again and trudged back to the van. Sal was loading in the last rucksack.

Steve's phone rang. He heaved a long-suffering sigh and answered the call.

'Yeah, hi, I know we left some of our gear there,' he said before the caller got a chance to say much. 'We had a crisis, had to get our violinist to a hospital.'

Steve listened for a while and then said, 'Well, it was either leave our gear while we took him to emergency or let him have a heart attack so you had a mite more space for the night. I figured I'd rather keep my violinist, if that ain't too difficult a concept for you to grasp. Somebody'll be by for it in the mornin'. Unless you want to stay up there and wait for me to come by tonight? I'll give Laszlo your regards, will I? Yeah, thought so. In the morning. Early. Yeah. Yeah. **Yes**.'

Steve jabbed at the End Call button. 'Asshole.'

'I could ask Mitch to–'

'Hell, no. That dipshit Malone can wait till morning. He doesn't need that space for anything till tomorrow afternoon anyway. He's pushing because he's an asshole. The man don't need any other reason. He can fuckin' well wait.' Steve shoved his fingers through his hair then scrubbed them against his scalp. His shoulders sagged and he was ready to drop. He cast a weary, worried glance at Aaron. 'So, after all this, you still with us, Aussie boy?'

'Is it always like this?'

'Hell, no. Most times it's worse.'

'Great.'

'Well, that ain't quite right. Most times it ain't so personal. Most times the monsters we fight ain't the people we loved.'

'Good. I didn't even know them and that was hard.'

'It's always hard, kid,' Steve said.

'That's okay.' Aaron managed a tired smile. 'My gran always said life's hard, and there always comes a time to put up a fight. She said, if you have to fight anyway, it's best to make it a fight you believe in.'

'Your gran was one hell of a lady.'

'Yep. I'm still in. This is the fight I was made for.'

'I like you, kid. You're going to be a hell of a Minstrel. And you can dance.'

'Mmm.' Aaron studied his feet. 'I don't know what that was. I don't know what side it came from either. Irish or Koori.'

'It came from you,' Steve said. 'Minstrel Tongue and Estampie Feet.'

'Stampy feet?'

'I'll tell you about it later. Let's get back to Kitty's place.'

Yuka, Kitty, Sal and Steve found places in the van. Aaron locked up the warehouse, climbed into the driver's seat and took them all back to Parkville.

Taylor was waiting by the back door to let them in, their return heralded by the squealing of the garage's rusty roller door. He pressed his fingers to his lips in the universal 'shh' sign. 'Everyone's asleep.'

Angus was stretched out on the sofa, his arms around Gretel, who had fallen asleep on his chest. Angus's shirt was scrunched in one of her small fists; she sucked on the other in her sleep. Harper was curled awkwardly in an armchair, head propped on a cushion that had slipped as she slept. Laszlo lay in deep sleep on a camping mattress that had been pulled out of a spare room and placed under the front window. The window was open to offset the strong smell of garlic emanating from a wad of damp cloth bandaged to Laszlo's throat. Laszlo's breathing was a touch laboured, but steady, and healthy colour had returned to his fair skin. An empty coffee mug was on the floor by his head, along with an empty jar of minced garlic and a teaspoon.

Taylor had obviously been sitting on the floor in a nest of cushions to keep an eye on everyone.

Yuka crouched gingerly beside Laszlo to check his pulse and to peer at the poultice. She started to unwrap the bandage and winced at the ache in her ribs.

'Here, let me do that,' Taylor said.

Yuka looked surprised anyone should offer her kindness.

'I've changed it for him twice already. You sit a spell and I'll find you some Tylenol.'

Yuka sat on the floor next to Laszlo and petted his wild hair. Sal sank down at Laszlo's feet and rested a hand on the man's ankle. Aaron was at a loss, but Sal patted the carpet at his side. Aaron folded down beside him, leaned on Sal's arm and closed his eyes. Sal shifted to rest his cheek on the crown of Aaron's head.

'Don't suppose you've got any beer?' Steve asked Kitty.

'Sorry, no. Tea? A proper one. None of that microwaved rubbish. The Tea League would take away my licence to brew.'

Steve huffed a laugh. 'Tea, the Great Restorer, huh? Okay.'

Steve and Kitty followed Taylor into the kitchen, where bulbs and jars of garlic, a packet of tea with verbena and more strips of cotton were laid out. Beside those was a pair of rubber kitchen gloves. To that, Taylor added gauze pads, fresh bandages and the antiseptic cream from the first aid kit. He gathered up his supplies in a bowl that Kitty decided to never again use to mix cake. Kitty found a packet of painkillers in the cupboard and added those to the pile, and gave him a glass of water as well.

'I'll be out to help in a second,' she said.

'Take your time,' Taylor said. 'You look beat.'

Kitty and Steve leaned against the counter as they waited for the kettle to boil, regarding the living room tableau.

Taylor helped Yuka to clean and dress the scabbing raw lines around her neck. Her hands trembled as she took the painkillers, so that the glass rattled against her teeth. That done, she shifted to allow Taylor room to attend his other patient and resumed petting the ends of Laszlo's hair.

Aaron had fallen asleep against Sal's shoulder. Sal moved his feet to give Taylor more space to work in, but was reluctant to let go of Laszlo's ankle. Taylor slotted his slender body into the gap between him and Yuka, and worked on Laszlo's dressing through the clumsy protection of the kitchen gloves. He unwrapped the bandage and removed the soiled, garlic-redolent wad. After rinsing the bite with a damp cloth, he placed a new garlic-and verbena poultice against it and rebound it.

Laszlo muttered in his sleep. Yuka stroked his forehead with her thumb and he subsided.

Taylor returned to the kitchen to dispose of the old bandages. Steve put a hand on his wrist to examine the stains on the dressings before the lot went into the bin.

'Did you find silver to put in that?'

Taylor cast Kitty an embarrassed frown. 'Harper found a box with coins in the bedroom,' he confessed. 'Old Chilean pesos, a couple of silver dollars, some old Australian crowns with some silver in 'em. A bunch of copper and nickel coins too.'

'My grandfather's,' Kitty said. 'He used to collect coins.'

'I hope it's okay. We used one of the silver dollars a on the bite.'

Steve nodded at the wad. 'The dark stuff there, that's vampire blood. The silver helped draw it out. The bright red, that's Laszlo.'

Kitty looked ill. Taylor wrapped the mess up in a plastic bag and put it beside the bin with two similar piles of rubbish. 'Sorry,' he said.

'That's okay,' Kitty replied faintly. 'Laszlo needed it more than I do.' She lifted her gaze to meet Steve's. 'We'll have to burn the bandages, won't we?'

'Yep. Tomorrow'll do, though. It won't go crawling round the house or nothin' while we sleep.'

She glared at him for sharing this unhelpful imagery. 'Steve, you are the worst pep talker I've ever met.'

'I have other charms,' he claimed.

He was surprised when she kissed him on the cheek. 'You do.'

'Does anyone need to keep watch tonight?' Taylor asked.

'Any trouble from the police?'

'Not a peep.'

'Well, if there ain't a car accident victim and the graveyard bones all got laid back down, I guess there's no reason for them make trouble. It's not like we committed an actual crime. We can take it easy tonight and make plans in the morning. Get you guys back home to the States with Gretel.'

'How?'

'With her passport, help from some Minstrels I know and some song magic. Don't you worry, Taylor. It'll all be okay. You go get some shut-eye.'

Taylor washed his hands while wearing the gloves first up, in hot water and bleach retrieved from under the sink. Then he stripped off the gloves and washed his hands for a timed minute.

Taylor returned the living room, which was littered with sleeping bodies. Yuka had curled up by Laszlo's head. At Laszlo's feet, Sal and Aaron were propped up against each other. Everyone was going to be sore and cranky in the morning, but Kitty couldn't find the energy to do anything about it. Taylor simply flopped down and curled into his cushion nest where he could see Angus and Gretel, and drifted off.

Kitty swayed on her feet. Steve steered her gently towards her bedroom, pushed her gently onto the mattress, took off her shoes, then pulled a crocheted blanket over her.

'What about you?' she said sleepily.

'I'll find a patch, don't you worry.'

'There's room next to me.'

Steve considered arguing, then thought what a stupid idea that was. He toed off his shoes, walked around to the other side of the bed and stretched on top of the covers.

'G'nigh', Steve.'

'Night, Kitty.'

But she was already asleep.

CHAPTER THIRTY

Kitty opened her front door and entered the hall. She could hear rattling from the kitchen, someone singing in the shower and the clatter of someone going into the back yard through the rear door.

'I'm home,' she sang out, dropping the keys in a bowl.

'Goulash and potato cakes tonight,' Laszlo announced from the kitchen. Pulped potato and tomato wreckage was spattered on his apron, the worktop and the floor. A good cook, Laszlo, but not a tidy one. 'How was your last day?'

'Good. Trudy and Marcus took me to lunch and wished me *bon voyage*. They're happy with the new guy, too.'

Kitty hadn't wanted to take off on her adventures before the Schumachers could find her replacement. It had only taken a few weeks, plus a week for handover. Ellery Barton was skilled, and Kitty felt relieved she could pass her work on to someone who cared as much as she did about farewelling the dead. He might need some practice to get on as well with the living, but Trudy was confident he'd get there.

Kitty's acceptance to the institute to become a fully qualified mortuary worker was packed away with most of the rest of her personal belongings. It was nice to know she'd met all their requirements, but Kitty knew she had a lot to offer to the living as well as the dead.

She could actively protect the living, not simply try to ease the burden of their losses. She didn't have to live in the shadow of sorrow any more. She could fight for the light.

So she was unemployed; or rather, free to be employed in the poorly paid, mighty erratic and frankly often terrifying role of Lead Minstrel of Kitty and Cadaver.

Kitty couldn't wait.

Yuka passed through from the back door with an armful of dry, clean clothes, nodded a curt greeting, and carried on into the master bedroom to sort the washing into piles for others to iron, fold or jam into backpacks as they saw fit.

Kitty ran her fingers over her keyboard, set up in the living room. They'd retrieved it and the rest of the instruments the day after they'd cremated Alex and Kurt. Malone had attempted to charge them overnight storage, but one look from Yuka made him reconsider.

Laszlo stirred the goulash and clanged a frying pan onto the stovetop, splashing oil into it freely. 'Steve says he has the fares and shipping details to Spain and to Paris, for comparison. He's not sure where we should go next. He said you could make the decision, if you felt a pull to anywhere.'

Kitty mostly felt the pull of away – to finally get into the world and out of this cage of a house – but she supposed Spain might be interesting. She spoke a smattering of Chilean Spanish, probably useless to her, but it was a start. She had a shiny new passport and the urge to make it tattered with use.

'Hey there, Kitty girl!' Steve bounded into the living room from the spare bedroom holding a large, yellow envelope in his hands. 'Bade your farewells and handed in your punch card?'

Kitty rolled her eyes. 'We don't use punch cards in this century, Steve.'

'Ouch, Kitty, that's harsh,' he said, but he was grinning. 'Wanna see what the boys sent in the post?'

From the envelope, he pulled several official photographic portraits of Taylor Griffin and his husband Angus Hensley with their daughter, Gretel Hensley-Griffin, framed in stiff, coloured cardboard. They were clearly ridiculously happy and healthy. One picture showed Gretel laughing and patting Angus's face while Taylor beamed with pride at the pair of them.

A handful of snapshots were included, some showing the little family with Harper. A letter from Angus was clipped to one of them.

> *Dearest Uncle Steve,*
>
> *We know with your job you can't always get online, so we're sending some pictures for your wallets and the trunk. We'll email more later. We're taking hundreds. Taylor says it's too many, but he's the one who keeps taking them.*
>
> *Mom insists on Gretel calling her Grandma Jean, but Gretel can only manage Ji-Ji so far. Mom asked after her little brother too, so I guess she's coming round to you at last, hey? We told her you play a righteous bass and she said you always had done. Good she remembers that, isn't it?*
>
> *I don't know what you did to get the adoption paperwork all squared, but it went like a dream.*
>
> *I don't know your plans, but if you're serious about retirement, we've got room for you. At least come hang with us for a while, tell us all about your crazy life, and Alex and Kurt. I'd like to know more about who they were before everything went wrong for them. We want to be able to tell Gretel about the good men they were as she grows up.*
>
> *More soon,*
>
> *love, Angus, Taylor and Gretel. xxx*

Kitty went through the photos, smiling at how happy everyone was in them.

'How did you square it?' she asked. Getting Gretel back to America hadn't been the problem. The little girl had her EU passport, which Alex organised for her in Italy when she was six months old. She'd been travelling on that with Harper, along with a letter that Alex and Kurt had written, confirming Harper's status as an *au pair*. The letter gave permission for Harper to take Gretel to London, where her fathers would meet her on completion of a business trip.

Steve had simply sung a small shift into the ink so that the letter said Harper was taking Gretel to Los Angeles instead of London.

'Ain't that much to square, really,' Steve said. 'After they got to L.A., I called in some favours – a guy in the State Department who owed us a big banshee-related favour prepped some paperwork, and a couple of Minstrels I know in Chicago got together and bound a sense of truth into the documentation. They'll be accepted as legit by anyone who sees them. So it's as official as it ever needs to get without being actually official. Angus and Taylor are for all purposes her legal dads. They know if anything goes wonky to call me – I'll head right on over and fix it up again.'

'And… will you be going back soon? To retire?'

'I got a lot to teach you and Aaron first. Ain't gonna drop you in it and run. Though I'd be obliged if you can keep me alive until I get to the retiring stage, if you can. I think I'm looking forward to it.'

Yuka spotted the photographs and stared so hungrily that Kitty handed them over. Yuka pored over them, her fingers brushing lightly over the image of Gretel's face in each picture.

'You already hogged those all afternoon,' Steve said, but with indulgent affection. 'Ain't any new ones magically appeared in the meantime.'

Yuka ignored him, except to hold one up. 'I will have this one.' It was of Gretel, laughing while Taylor tickled her. Gretel was wearing the little outfit with the giraffes and a beanie with cute felt cat ears that Yuka had given them at the airport. Yuka handed the rest of the photos back to Steve and went in search of her rucksack.

Sal joined them, damp from his shower, dressed in jeans, but barefoot and bare chested. He had shaved his hair above his ears again. The scars in his scalp had healed well, leaving the lines of the sun behind. As he bent to peer at the top photo of the stack in his hand, Kitty could see the pentagram that had been carved into his back, one evil day in Edinburgh. The lines of it were criss-crossed with smaller scars, not all of them old, though all of them healed. The broken pentagram couldn't hold any power, good or bad, now.

She should have been more surprised to realise he'd cut himself before.

'Read something from your book for me?' Kitty asked.

Sal pulled his notebook from his pocket. 'Three things cannot be long hidden: the sun, the moon, and the truth.'

Steve, passing by, hugged his friend. 'Four things. A good heart, too.'

'Food!' announced Laszlo. 'While it's hot. Come along!' He was shoving plates filled with fat, sizzling Hungarian potato cakes smothered in rich paprika and garlic-infused goulash.

'Why so much garlic?' Yuka asked as she took her place. 'The vampire infection is gone.'

Laszlo grimaced at her. 'This is proper goulash, Yuka. Too much garlic is the right amount.' Yuka wrinkled her nose impishly at him. It took Kitty a second to realise Yuka was flirting with their roadie-violinist.

After dinner, Aaron's arrival was announced by the squealing of the unoiled garage door. 'Man, that smells good,' he said as he came in through the back door. 'Any left?'

Laszlo piled up a plateful, which Aaron shovelled down as he made his report. 'I've got my passport – Mum's been keeping it somewhere safe, which is why it took us a week to find it. Julie says she'd love to house-sit while we're travelling. It's close to uni and she's a gun with the garden. She'll come by tomorrow for the keys, if you like.'

Julie was Aaron's younger sister, studying engineering at Melbourne University. Kitty had met her briefly and instantly liked her. Julie was clever, no-nonsense, and excited about the possibilities of a back yard veggie garden.

Her home would be in safe hands, and the reasonable rent they'd agreed on would keep the band coffers ticking over, along with Kitty's savings and the cash from the gig. Combined with the band's own savings, there was more than enough to take Kitty and Cadaver back to Europe and buy a cheap van for touring once there.

They retired to the cluttered living room, which was full of instruments – Yuka's drums and various guitars on stands as well as

Kitty's keyboard. They'd been rehearsing as often as possible since the night at the Corner.

'When are we leaving?' Aaron asked.

'Soon,' Kitty said.

'Soon as our girl decides where we need to be,' Steve said.

Aaron mouthed The One at her and Kitty shrugged elaborately. Aaron, laughing, picked up his guitar, strummed a few chords, then plugged it into the little amp. He played a more complicated flurry of notes of the counter-melody he'd developed for one of the old band songs. He and Kitty were making their mark with it. Kitty had changed some of the words.

Kitty's fingers dance lightly over her keyboard. A month had done wonders for her confidence.

Laszlo picked up his violin. Yuka sat at her drums and began tapping out a muted three-four time, while Sal and Steve took up their guitars. Kitty launched into the verse.

This is a tapestry
These words spinning out of me
From my mouth and heart
Where they end and start
We'll knit up the threads
And the world will go on

The others came in with harmonies, and Laszlo's violin threaded lightly through the melody, the notes practically dancing out of the strings as Laszlo brought joy to his impeccable bowing.

This is a light in me
This music rising out of me
And when these songs spill
(like I know they will)
The harmony will come
And the world will go on

Laszlo trilled a flutter of notes at Yuka and, with a sparkle in her eye, Yuka skittered a flurry of beats back at him. Steve and Aaron plaited a foundation of bass notes beneath the melody that Kitty and Sal carried with the words.

And sometimes we'll falter
And fall by the way
Sometimes we'll sorrow
For the prices we pay
But the words and the music
Are not locks, they're keys
Uncaged, they escape
To make tapestries

The band continued to play, consolidating their repertoire.

Half way through rehearsals, Steve's phone rang. Laszlo took the call in the kitchen while Steve worked with Aaron on some tricky fingering on a complex bass line.

Laszlo returned with a thoughtful frown lining his brow. 'That was someone called Tristen. She said she's a friend of yours.'

Yuka nodded. 'She is a Minstrel. She stays in London.'

'Apparently Perdita – she said you'd know who that was – caught a train from Brompton Road tube station and as of yesterday she's missing, and something 'very funny' is happening on the Circle Line.'

Sal's eyebrows rose. 'If Perdita caught a train from Brompton, something is definitely up.' At questioning looks from the new band members, he expanded: 'That's a ghost station. Trains haven't stopped there since 1934.'

'Who's Perdita?' asked Kitty.

'Tristen's raven,' Steve said.

'Tristen is Perdita's human,' Yuka corrected him.

'Why was a crow catching a train?' Aaron wanted to know.

'Well,' said Kitty, surprised by how easy the decision turned out to be. 'It looks like Kitty and Cadaver are going to London.

THE END

Narrelle M. Harris writes crime, horror, fantasy, romance and erotica. Her 30+ novels and short stories have been published in Australia, US and UK.

Award nominations include *Fly By Night* (nominated for a Ned Kelly Award), *Witch Honour* and *Witch Faith* (both short-listed for the George Turner Prize), *Walking Shadows* (Chronos Awards; Davitt Awards).

In 2017, her ghost/crime story *Jane* won the Athenaeum Library's Body in the Library prize at the Scarlet Stiletto Awards presented by Sisters in Crime Australia.

Her work includes vampire novels, erotic spy adventures, queer romance, traditional Holmesian mysteries, the Holmes/Watson romances *The Adventure of the Colonial Boy* (2016) *and A Dream to Build a Kiss On* (2018); and the queer paranormal thriller-romance, *Ravenfall* (2017).

Narrelle is releasing her Duo Ex Machina series of gay romance crime stories through her Patreon in partnership with Clan Destine Press.

Find out more: www.narrellemharris.com
Subscribe to her blog, Mortal Words: www.mortalwords.com.au
Support Narrelle M Harris on Patreon:
  www.patreon.com/NarrelleMHarris

Narrelle M. Harris
with Clan Destine Press

RAVENFALL

British soldier, Dr James Sharpe, returned from Afghanistan a changed man. Like most war veterans haunted by deadly choices and the horrors of battle, James struggles against his demons.

Unlike other ex-soldiers, his demons are real. Transformed in the heat of a desert battlefield, James Sharpe is now a vampire.

Struggling London artist, Gabriel Dare, has his own secrets – like who he really is, and why he lived on the streets before lodging with Dr Sharpe; like the ghosts he used to see, that made others question his sanity.

James knows Gabriel is the best thing in his life, but questions his ability to love and fears he's a danger to all. Gabriel knows there's something different about his enigmatic landlord, but can't deny his attraction.

When some of Gabriel's street friends go missing, he discovers that London is full of monsters – real, vicious, otherworldly monsters. The two men join forces with a clairvoyant cop and a Peer of the Realm to uncover the truth, for it seems the vampire who sired James is back in London – with a diabolical agenda that threatens the entire nation.

WALKING SHADOWS

Lissa Wilson's life hasn't been the same since people she cared about started getting themselves killed. By vampires. Lissa learnt that the opposite of life is not always death.

On the plus side, she made a new friend. Gary Hooper may be the worst best-friend a librarian could have – and easily the worst vampire ever – but he has taught Lissa the real meaning of life.

Gary's worldview has also improved remarkably since meeting Lissa, but all that could be lost if she discovers what services he provides Melbourne's undead community.

Meanwhile, as their friendship brings him closer to the humanity he lost, it also puts them both in grave danger.

And there's a big chance that the evil stalking them could them both killed – in Gary's case, for good this time.

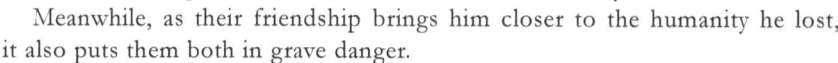

Narrelle M. Harris
with Improbable Press

The Adventure of the Colonial Boy

1893: Dr Watson, still in mourning for the death of his great friend Sherlock Holmes, is now triply bereaved, with his wife Mary's death in childbirth.

Then a telegram from Melbourne, Australia intrudes into his grief. 'Come at once if convenient.' Both suspicious and desperate to believe that Holmes may not, after all, be dead, Watson goes as immediately as the sea voyage will allow.

Soon Holmes and Watson are together again, on an adventure through Bohemian Melbourne and rural Victoria, following a series of murders linked by a repulsive red leech and one of Moriarty's lieutenants. But things are not as they were. Too many words lie unsaid between the Great Detective and his biographer. Too much that they feel is a secret.

Solve the crime, forgive a friend, rediscover trust and admit to love. Surely that is not beyond that legendary duo, Sherlock Holmes and Dr John Watson?

A Dream to Build a Kiss On

John Watson, invalided army doctor and sometimes artist, and Sherlock Holmes, consulting detective, become flatmates and friends in contemporary London.

Love grows too, despite past betrayals and present dangers – for where you have Holmes and Watson, there too are Moriarty and Moran.

A Dream to Build a Kiss On explores love and family, trust and betrayal, brothers and brothers-in-arms, forgiveness and revenge, in an ongoing tale told 221 words at a time.

Other fiction by **Narrelle M Harris**

All but * published by Clan Destine Press as eBooks

SHORT FICTION

* *Sky High, Bone Deep*
Birds of a Feather
Near Miss

COLLECTIONS

Scar Tissue and Other Stories
  paperback & eBook

* *Showtime*

SERIES

Talbot and Burns Mysteries

Homecoming
A Paying Client

Secret Agents, Secret Lives

Double Edged
Expendable
Wilderness

Duo Ex Machina

Fly By Night
Sacrifice
Number One Fan

Coming soon in this series:

Kiss and Cry
Little Star

Narrelle also has short crime, romance, science fiction and fantasy stories in over a dozen anthologies.

See all of Narrelle's novels, shorts stories and anthologies at

www.narrellemharris.com
or
Narrelle M Harris on Amazon Author

www.ingramcontent.com/pod-product-compliance
Lightning Source LLC
Chambersburg PA
CBHW022012010726
47494CB00003B/1010